WILD NIGHT

A LUCAS HALLAM MYSTERY BOOK ONE

L.J. WASHBURN

ROUGH
EDGES
PRESS

Wild Night
Paperback Edition
© Copyright 2022 (As Revised) L.J. Washburn

Rough Edges Press
An Imprint of Wolfpack Publishing
5130 S. Fort Apache Rd. 215-380
Las Vegas, NV 89148

roughedgespress.com

This book is a work of fiction. Any references to historical events, real people or real places are used fictitiously. Other names, characters, places and events are products of the author's imagination, and any resemblance to actual events, places or persons, living or dead, is entirely coincidental.

All rights reserved. No part of this book may be reproduced by any means without the prior written consent of the publisher, other than brief quotes for reviews.

Paperback ISBN 978-1-68549-059-1

This book is dedicated to James M. Reasoner for introducing me to the Gower Gulch Gang, and to my daughters Shayna and Joanna.

WILD NIGHT

ONE

HEAT SLAPPED Lucas Hallam in the face as he stepped from the flivver onto the dusty main street of Chuckwalla, California. He stood with his hands on his hips and watched steam rise from the radiator. Maybe with any luck the place wouldn't be totally deserted—many of the so-called ghost towns weren't—and he could get some water for the car.

Otherwise it was going to be a long walk back to Hollywood.

Hallam left the car there and turned toward the closest of the ramshackle buildings, eager to get into the shade. He had the rolling gait of a man who had spent much of his life on horseback. He could have used a good horse about now. He had ridden all over Texas, New Mexico, and Arizona back in the old days, and not one of the animals he rode had ever had a damn radiator go out!

He stepped up onto a plank sidewalk and into the shade of the wooden awning that overhung it. Pulling a bright handkerchief from his pants pocket, Hallam mopped the sweat from his craggy face and looked around at the place called Chuckwalla.

The name had originated with the miners who had once worked in the mountains overlooking the desert. The town had sprung up here when silver was discovered in the mountains, and every week, on payday, the miners made the trip in for a blowout, twenty-four hours of whiskey and women and whatever else they could lay their hands on before having to return to the holes in the ground. One habit that the miners had picked up from the Indians in the area was a liking for roasted chuckwalla, and attempting to catch the big lizards was a favorite pastime for the drunken mining men. The silver mines had played out a long time ago, and the miners were gone, but the name stayed while the town shrunk.

Now Chuckwalla was maybe a dozen and a half buildings straggling along either side of a wide dirt street. Some of the roofs had fallen in, and quite a few of the walls sagged.

Hallam was standing in front of the boarded-up door of a general mercantile store. It was at one end of a short block of buildings. The next door down the sidewalk had once led into a barber shop—BATHS 15¢, HOT WATER 25¢—and farther down had been a gunsmith and a tack shop. There were three livery stables on the edge of town, two churches, a hardware store, a dress shop, six saloons, and a building that he figured had housed a brothel.

Hallam leaned against one of the posts that held up the awning. He was a big man, tall and wide-shouldered and carrying plenty of meat on him, and the post was old. He was careful not to put too much weight on it.

He looked around Chuckwalla, and he saw it as it was now: old, abandoned, forgotten. A hot wind came off the desert and stirred up the dust, sent tumbleweeds rolling along the street.

But Hallam could see it as it once must have been, too. He had been in a lot of places like Chuckwalla: raw and booming and filled with folks. In those days the street would have been busy with carriages and wagons, men on horseback, and fancy ladies out for a midday stroll with their bright silk gowns and twirling parasols. Miners in rough work clothes would move among the town's regular inhabitants. The town existed for the miners. And the fancy ladies, the gamblers, and the saloon-keepers were all very happy to take the miners' money. Sometimes they took it legally, sometimes not.

Yep, Hallam had seen plenty of places like Chuckwalla in the old days.

He had brought law and order to some of them.

A town marshal had to be damn good in those days, good with his fists, good with a knife, good with a gun. Lucas Hallam had been good, all right. One of the best, people said.

But those days were twenty years and more in the past. Hallam tried not to reminisce too much; a man could get lost in bygone days and not pay enough attention to what was going on around him now.

The way he saw it, he had a lot of living left to do. Daydreaming was a good way not to get around to it. He shook his shaggy gray head and took a deep breath. Hell, a minute ago, he had even imagined that he heard somebody calling him. And as far as he could see, there wasn't a soul in Chuckwalla except him....

"Hey, cowboy!"

Hallam's head snapped around. He wasn't imagining *this*. Instinctively, his big right hand dropped to his hip as his eyes looked for whoever was yelling at him. There was no familiar gun butt there, though; he had brought the Colt Cavalry .45, but it was still in the flivver. He didn't carry it all the time any more, though it was never far from him.

"Over here, cowboy!"

The voice came to him more clearly now, and the tightness of his muscles and nerves eased a little bit. The wind had distorted the voice before, but now he recognized the tones as those of a woman.

What would a woman be doing way out here the hell and gone in the middle of nowhere, though?

He spotted her standing on the sidewalk on the other side of the street, at the far end of town. She had pushed through the batwings that adorned the entrance of the Silver Horseshoe Saloon. Hallam could faintly make out the letters on the big sign that stretched across the second story of the false-fronted building. The paint was flaked off and long gone, but the outlines still remained.

The woman had red hair and wore a bright blue dress with spangles on it. There was laughter in her voice as she called to him, and for a moment Hallam wanted to rub his eyes and see if she disappeared.

He didn't believe in ghosts—even if he *was* in a ghost town.

The woman lifted a bare arm and beckoned him with it.

Hallam stayed where he was, feet planted solidly on the planks of the sidewalk. His eyes narrowed as he looked down the street at the woman. She was no ghost. She was *there,* all right.

Because to admit that she was a ghost would be to admit that he was seeing things.

And there were a lot of people who would tell you that Lucas Hallam was just too damn hard-headed to go around seeing things.

He stepped out into the street and began walking toward her. The wind had gotten up some more, and grit stung Hallam's eyes. The woman stayed where she was, watching him.

She wasn't as young as he had first thought, he saw as he got closer. Her slim figure had fooled him—that and the bright red hair. He imagined she worked hard at both. Now, he figured she was a little younger than him, somewhere between forty-five and fifty.

He lifted his booted right foot, let it rest on the sidewalk. "Howdy," he said, nodding to her.

"Howdy yourself. Welcome to Chuckwalla." She came across the sidewalk and put out a hand. "I'm Elizabeth Fletcher, Liz to my friends. What do I call you besides cowboy?"

"Hallam, Lucas Hallam." He took her hand. "Right pleased to meet you, ma'am."

Her smile was bright and warm. She inclined her head toward the batwings and said, "Come on inside and have a drink, Lucas Hallam. One thing I hate it's drinking alone."

Hallam followed her into the saloon. His eyes adjusted to the dimness after a few seconds. There was a long mahogany bar along the left side of the room, the shelves behind it filled with liquor bottles. A large, gold-framed mirror also took up part of the wall space. Crystal chandeliers hung from the ceiling, overlooking a player piano, a small dance floor, and a cluster of tables. At the back of the room were a roulette wheel and several baize-covered tables for card games. It looked just like a lot of other saloons Hallam had seen... except that everything in it was covered with a fine coating of dust.

Everything except the bottle of whiskey that Liz Fletcher took down from the shelves as she went behind the bar. And the glasses she took from underneath the bar were clean, too. She was a lady who obviously had priorities.

She expertly uncorked the bottle and tipped amber liquid into each of the glasses. "To your health, Lucas Hallam," she said as she picked up one of them.

Hallam picked up the other glass, clinked it against hers, and downed the whiskey. It was raw, and burned going down, but he had tasted worse.

"Hallam," Liz Fletcher said slowly. She leaned her bare arms on the bar and studied him. "Seems I should know the name."

"I've been a few places," Hallam allowed. "Could be we ran into each other before."

"I've been a few places, too." Her smile was rueful. "Could be." Suddenly she looked up at him in recognition. "Lucas Hallam! Now I remember the name. You can't be the same one that shot up the Crowder boys in Santa Fe back in ninety-three, though."

It was Hallam's turn to incline his head and smile ruefully. "Way I recollect it, they got in more shots than

I did." He slapped his right thigh. "I still limp a little on account of Mart Crowder."

"Maybe so, but none of them Crowders did any more walking, not unless they got up out of their graves."

"I didn't go lookin' for that trouble," Hallam said solemnly. "Wasn't going to let 'em shoot me and get away with it, though."

Liz Fletcher shook her head. "Those were wild times, weren't they, Lucas? When I think about how young and sure of myself I was..."

"Reckon we were all a little full of ourselves," Hallam said softly. "Never figured that the world would keep spinnin' and a new crop of youngsters would come along."

She spilled more whiskey into the glasses. "That's what happened, though. Nothing we can do about it, so we might as well drink to it."

"Sounds like a right smart thing to do."

But Hallam wasn't so sure of that. Even as he sipped the fiery whiskey, he wondered if he should be encouraging this woman to drink. He had a feeling these weren't her first of the day. As he glanced along the shelves behind the bar, he saw that most of the bottles were full. Prohibition had gone into effect a couple of years before, but it looked like Liz Fletcher had enough stock on hand to last her quite a while. She might need it.

He set the glass on the bar and looked at the light coating of dust on the hardwood surface. "Live out here by yourself, do you?" he asked. "Not that I'm meaning to cause you any trouble..."

"Hell, I know that. You and me, we're from the old

school, Lucas. You may look like a grizzly bear"—she grinned to show that she meant no offense—" but you're a gentleman underneath. I knew that as soon as I saw you. Not like some of the varmints that come around here."

She reached under the bar again, and Hallam wasn't surprised when she came up with a sawed-off double-barrel. She laid it on the bar with a thump. The smile that creased her face had a touch of savagery in it.

"Yep, I'm by myself except for this little beauty. But let me tell you, Lucas, anybody gives me any grief's going to get himself a hot buckshot kiss."

After a moment, Hallam said. "Why do you stay?"

"Why the hell shouldn't I? It's my town."

"Reckon I understand why you feel that way—"

"Reckon you don't. I meant what I said. This is my town. I own the damn place." She waved a hand at their surroundings. "Just owned the Silver Horseshoe to start. Then, as the other folks gave up and left, I paid the county taxes on their places and took 'em up, too. You're looking at the grand mistress of Chuckwalla, Lucas."

"Guess you're the person I came to see, then," Hallam said.

Liz Fletcher frowned. "You came out here on purpose? I figured you just strayed off the main road and got stuck when your car boiled over. Why would anybody come off out here on purpose?"

"Came to see if you'd want to rent out your town."

A look of apprehension passed over her face. "Rent it? Rent it to who? And what in the world for?"

Hallam grinned. "Fella I work for sometimes, he wants to make movies in it."

"Movies? Lord, I haven't seen a movie in—you mean they still make 'em?"

Hallam nodded. "They sure do. Been in a few myself."

"You're an actor now?" She sounded like she couldn't believe that the same Lucas Hallam who had faced down the Crowder boys in Santa Fe was an actor.

"Just every now and then, when I need a little extra money. My regular line of work sometimes hits dry spells."

"And what might that be?"

"Detective business. Got my own agency." Hallam chuckled. "Course, I sweep out the place, too."

"So you're a detective *and* an actor." Liz Fletcher shook her head, disapproval evident on her face. "Seems like strange work for a man who used to be hell on wheels, no offense, Lucas."

"None taken. Times change, Liz. Nothin' stands still."

But that was just what she was trying to do out here in this ghost town: make time stand still. She had her whiskey and her memories, and Hallam, for one, wasn't going to take it on himself to tell anybody how to live their life.

"Like I said," Hallam went on, "the feller I do some work for sometimes, Mr. Frank Sheldon, he wants to rent this town and shoot some movies here. Seems somebody told him about it and he thought it'd make a good place for that. So he asked me to come out here and look it over, let him know what I thought."

"And what do you think?"

Hallam shrugged. "A little fixin' up here and there, and the place could look about like it used to. It's pretty far out from town, but that's Mr. Sheldon's lookout, not mine. I reckon if you want to rent it to him, I'll tell him to go ahead if he wants to."

"A little fixing up here and there... God, we could all use that."

Hallam thought about the limp in his right leg, the stiffness he sometimes felt in his left shoulder, the bumps and bruises and bullet holes of a hard lifetime that ached when the weather was right. "Yes, ma'am, we surely could," he agreed.

Liz Fletcher was silent for a long moment. Then she said, "I'm sorry, Lucas, but I don't think I can go along with that." She smiled slightly. "Don't think I want a lot of people poking around my town, even if it does get a little bit lonesome hereabouts. I get enough company, what with the drifters and desert rats who sneak around and try to steal my whiskey." She patted the shotgun. "They don't worry us too much, though."

Hallam tossed down the remainder of his drink and shrugged. "All right, Liz, if that's what you want. I'll tell Frank he'll just have to stay in Hollywood."

"You do that, Lucas. Otherwise he might get the seat of his pants dusted with buckshot."

Hallam grinned and nodded a farewell to the woman, then turned to the door of the saloon. He pushed through the batwings and started to step out onto the sidewalk....

The flash of sun on metal, across the street and off to the right—

Hallam threw himself sideways out of the door as a bullet smacked through the right-hand batwing. Splinters stung his face.

TWO

HALLAM LANDED hard on the sidewalk. There was no cover outside, so he did the only thing he could. He rolled back toward the saloon's entrance and went through it in a low dive as another bullet hit the planks of the sidewalk and threw up more splinters.

"What the hell!" Liz Fletcher yelled from behind the bar.

Hallam waved a big hand at her. "Stay back! Get down behind that bar and stay there!"

He got out of the line of fire and crouched below the big window to the left of the door. When he glanced at the bar, he saw that Liz hadn't ducked as he had told her. She was standing behind the bar, the shotgun gripped tightly in her hands, ready to fight.

"Thought I told you to get down," Hallam said.

"Go to hell," she snapped. "I told you this is my town, Lucas. Nobody shoots it up and gets away with it."

Hallam sighed, then hunkered closer to the floor as two more slugs slammed through the walls. From the flat boom of the rifle and the way the bullets went right through thick wood, he knew the gun was a high-powered one.

"Wouldn't happen to have a rifle or a handgun back there, would you?" he asked. "That Greener don't have enough carryin' power."

Liz Fletcher shook her head. "Never needed anything else before to take care of varmints. Where's this one?"

"Other end of town, what used to be a livery barn. Back door?"

She nodded, jerked her head toward the rear. "You bet. What're you planning on doing?"

"Flush that son of a bitch out, pardon my French, ma'am."

Hallam came to his feet and crossed the room in a crouching run. The rifleman couldn't see directly into the saloon from his position, but he was still firing at regular intervals, pouring lead into the old structure. Hallam threw a look at Liz and wished she'd get down and stay down, like he had told her. He thought for a second about asking to take the scatter with him, but he didn't want to leave her here unarmed.

His fingers were itching. He wanted his Colt, wanted it bad. He would have settled for the big Bowie knife, but it was in the flivver with the gun.

A damn fool, that was what he was. Happen he got out of this little scrape alive, he'd keep the Colt and the Bowie even closer to him in the future.

He opened the door to the saloon's back room and saw the other door on the opposite wall. It would lead into the alley. Before he could head that way, though, Liz said, "They after you or me, Lucas?"

He shook his head. "Nobody's got any reason to be gunning for me, not anymore." He chuckled grimly. "Not 'less it's somebody with a damn long memory."

"Then it's another damned skunk who's heard about my whiskey and wants it for himself. Prohibition! Good lord, I never heard the like!"

Hallam might have agreed with her there, but he had other things on his mind. He was sure he could find enough cover to make it to the other end of town, but then he'd have the street to cross before he could get to the man in the barn.

Another slug came screaming into the room, ricocheted off a spittoon, and broke one of the whiskey bottles with a crash of glass and a shower of liquor. "Dammit!" Liz howled. She grabbed a handful of spare shells from under the bar and ran to the door.

Hallam cursed under his breath as the shotgun roared. Liz knew better, she was just too mad to be thinking straight. Hallam raced across the room, looped an arm around her middle as the second barrel of the Greener exploded, and threw them both to the floor.

She was hitting at him now, and Hallam had his hands full just hanging on to her. He grimaced, balled one fist loosely, and clipped her on the chin with it. She sagged in his arms.

He climbed to his feet. Liz's head hung limply as he lifted her and carried her behind the bar. "Should've done this in the first place," he muttered as he gently placed her on the dusty floor. Chances were she would be safer there than anywhere else.

He stood up, broke the shotgun open, and stuffed fresh shells in its barrels. He still had that street to cross, but the scatter might help to even the odds a little bit.

Pausing at the back door, Hallam drew several deep breaths. There was a slight ache in his side, and several other twinges here and there told him he was getting a little old for all this running and jumping around. When the pounding of his heart had slowed slightly, he pushed the back door open, gripped the shotgun tightly in his big fists, and went out into the alley at a run.

The alley led behind the tumbledown buildings lining the street. There was a narrow little creek a few yards away, and some scrubby cottonwood trees threw patches of shade on the dirt. Hallam ran through them. The wind was still rising, and he could taste dust in his mouth as he ran. The sun was shining here, but up in the mountains a storm was boiling up; Hallam knew what that odd, heavy feel to the air meant.

He slowed down as he got closer to the other end of town. The odds of him being spotted got better the closer he approached the gunman. He came to a halt behind what had been the Baptist church years before and caught his breath again. Grit crunched under his boots as he went to the corner of the building and peered cautiously around it, but there was no need to worry about being heard, not with the keening wail of the wind.

From here he could see into the shadows of the livery barn. As he watched, another booming shot, accompanied by a vivid muzzle flash, told him that the would-be killer was still in there.

And Hallam suddenly knew just how old he really was getting. So damn old that he hadn't stopped to think that the man might have somebody else watching the back of the saloon...

He spun, the old instincts warning him. The double

barrels of the Greener came up smoothly as the second man ran out of the trees. All he had was a handgun; that was why he had had to get closer before firing.

Hallam had almost let him get close enough.

He heard the crack of the pistol as his finger squeezed the first trigger. One barrel was enough. The buckshot caught the man full in the stomach, folding him up and throwing him back into the trees. His muscles convulsed, and the pistol in his hand went off again, the slug burrowing into the sand of the alley.

Hallam ran across the alley, ignoring the bloody mess the Greener had made, and snatched up the pistol from where it had fallen. After a quick check to make sure dirt hadn't plugged the barrel, he triggered off three shots into the ground. That left one in the cylinder, which meant that the man had carried it with a live bullet under the hammer. Hallam snorted in contempt, then took up his place against the back wall of the old church.

The man in the livery stable had to have heard the shots, even over the wind. There was no way he could have missed the boom of the shotgun, the whip like cracks of the pistol. He had heard one shot from the pistol, then the blast of the Greener, then four more shots from the pistol. That told a story, a story in which his quarry had sneaked out the back door of the saloon and then been cornered by the man hiding in the trees. That was the way it would have sounded to him...

Hallam stood absolutely still, the pistol tucked into his belt, the Greener ready in his hands.

When his partner didn't come out from behind the church, though, the man in the barn would start to wonder. He might think there were two dead men in the alley, that Hallam had fatally wounded his partner before taking the four shots from the pistol.

If he wanted to find out for sure, he would have to come look for himself.

Hallam wished the wind would die down so that he could hear any approaching footsteps. But it showed no signs of letting up. He would just have to wait and take his chances when the time came.

Wouldn't be the first time, either.

He had been in situations like this before; every manhunter had. You tracked a man down, or, he tracked you down, and then it all came down to two men with guns.

The faster man lived. The slower man died. Simple as that.

The barrel of the rifle was the first thing he saw. Alert for any tricks, he made himself wait until the man stepped around the corner of the church. The man spotted the lifeless body of his partner in the shadows of the trees, started to spin around.

Hallam took one step away from the wall and touched the Greener's second trigger.

He would have liked to capture at least one of the men alive, but work that fine was hard with a shotgun, at least at close range like this. The charge flung the man back and made a rag doll of him. The rifle went spinning off into the dust.

Hallam slowly lowered the shotgun and stood there with the two dead men. He didn't like killing, didn't like it a bit, but these two had called the tune.

"Lucas?"

He whirled, hand going to the pistol, and he had it

out and lined by the time he was around. But his finger stopped before he could pull the trigger.

"Movie actor or not, you're the same Lucas Hallam," Liz Fletcher said as she walked down the alley toward him. The sight of the bloodied bodies didn't appear to disturb her.

"You'd better let me take you back to the saloon," Hallam said.

"Don't you worry about me. I've seen plenty worse, let me tell you." She smiled thinly at the corpses. "Well, there's two more bastards won't try to steal my whiskey."

"Happens pretty often, does it?"

"No, not often. But somehow word gets around that I've got a supply of liquor on hand, and then somebody gets the idea that it'd be easier to steal it than brew their own or run some in from Mexico. Gets annoying sometimes, but I live with it."

Hallam looked at the dead men; they were a pair: coarse-featured, wearing shabby city clothes. There was nothing shabby about the rifle, though, he saw as he picked it up. It was a fine weapon, heavy caliber with a hand-tooled stock. Not the kind of gun a man like that usually carried, which probably meant that it was stolen.

"Got a telephone around that works?"

"What for?"

"I figured one of us ought to call the sheriff."

Liz shook her head. "No telephone. And no need to call the sheriff. Got everything we need back at the saloon."

"What's that?"

"A shovel."

THREE

HALLAM'S APARTMENT was on the third floor of a white stucco building surrounded by brownish grass and stubby palms. There wasn't an elevator, and he could feel the pull of sore muscles as he climbed the outside stairs.

Digging graves was hard work, no two ways about it.

He had been cussing himself all the way back from Chuckwalla. He never should have let Liz Fletcher talk him into burying the two gunmen without notifying the authorities. As a former lawman himself, he knew how important it was to follow the rules... But he had also lost count of the times he had broken those same rules when it seemed like the right thing to do.

He hadn't wanted to bring a bunch of outsiders into Chuckwalla, and Liz didn't want that either. The thought of people poking around in her town and asking a lot of questions scared her. Hallam couldn't blame her for that.

So they had taken the dead men across the creek

and buried them. No markers, just low mounds of earth. Hallam hadn't felt like saying words over men who had tried to shoot him, but he did it anyway. Then he and Liz had shared another drink, she had given him some water from a still-functioning well for the flivver's radiator, and he had driven back to Los Angeles with sore muscles and some nagging doubts.

If anybody ever found out about the two men, he'd lose his license over it, that was for damn sure. Private detectives couldn't go around shooting people, even with good reason, and not report it. The law was peculiar that way.

Hallam didn't want to lose his license. The business was important to him, and not just for the money. He could have made more by working more often in the movies—Bill Hart had told him several times that he was a natural—but acting was just for fun. Hell, he wasn't a real actor anyway; he was just being himself in front of the camera, reliving the old days when he was as wild and woolly as any of the boys.

Manhunting was something else entirely. He had known that from the time he joined the Pinkertons. The old days might be gone, but there were still plenty of owlhoots around. They wore suits and drove cars now, but when Hallam looked at them, he saw the Youngers, the Daltons, and Henry Plummer's gang all over again.

He let himself into the apartment, took a long drink of water to cut some of the dust from his mouth, and went to the window. The sun was low in the western sky. Hallam looked at it for a minute, then shrugged. What was done was done. Chances were the two bodies would never be discovered, and he was sure that

Liz Fletcher wouldn't be doing any talking about what had happened this afternoon. Best thing he could do now was to get on with his business. Maybe he'd take a ride over to Frank Sheldon's and tell him that Chuckwalla just wouldn't do at all as a place to make some movies....

There was a knocking on the door, so quiet that Hallam didn't hear it at first.

He turned from the window when he realized that someone was at the door. His long legs carried him across the room, and he swung the panel open to see a thin, well-dressed man who seemed slightly out of breath from the climb.

"Mr. Hallam?" the man asked.

"That's right. What can I do for you?" Hallam didn't offer to step aside so that the visitor could come in. The man wore rimless glasses and had slicked-down, black hair, and he looked to Hallam like some kind of salesman.

"My name is Elton Forbes." The man reached inside his coat and took out a card. He extended it toward Hallam. "Reverend Elton Forbes. Perhaps you've heard of me?"

There was an anxious note in the man's voice. Hallam didn't care whether or not he hurt his feelings, but it just so happened that he *had* heard of the Reverend Elton Forbes.

"Seen your signs around town," Hallam nodded. His big hand took the card from Forbes, and when he glanced at it he saw fancy gold lettering and an engraved cross. He stepped back, waved a hand to indicate that Forbes should come in.

"Thank you," Forbes said when Hallam had closed

the door behind him. He faced Hallam, clasped his hands behind his back, and came up slightly on his toes. Hallam had seen the pose in newspaper pictures of the famous evangelist. "I've come to talk to you about engaging your services," Forbes went on. "I believe you *are* a private detective?"

"Last time I looked," Hallam grunted. He waited, wondering what in the hell somebody like Elton Forbes needed with a detective.

Hallam was revising his opinion; Forbes didn't look like a salesman. He looked more a professor of some sort, which, come to think of it, he had been before becoming a preacher. Hallam had read several stories about the man, never paid much attention to them, though. Now he tried to coax some of the details out of his memory.

Two years earlier no one had ever heard of Elton Forbes. He labored as an instructor in a small midwestern college, the kind of man who comes and goes and leaves little impression behind him. That had all changed suddenly.

According to Elton Forbes, he had seen a vision, a vision telling him to come to California and spread God's word. Forbes had rented an empty store in Hollywood and started holding services. At first, few came to hear him. He had no religious background, and as a speaker you would think he was still in front of a class of bored students.

But Forbes had learned. He still wasn't flashy, but now his voice could ring out with the best of them, condemning sin and vice... and asking for money to help him continue his crusade.

Somehow, when Hallam looked at Forbes now, he

thought of Professor Thaddeus Morton and his All-Curing Kiowa Tonic.

And the last he had seen of the good professor, the outraged citizens of Amarillo had been escorting him out of town on a rail, tar, feathers, and all.

So maybe there was hope for Forbes yet.

"I was given your name by a parishioner of mine who works in the police department," Forbes was saying. "At first he advised me to go to the Pinkerton agency, but I dislike dealing with a large organization. I was told that you are as honest as any independent private detective."

"Reckon I am."

"Good. I need an honest man. I need a man who is reliable and discreet, as well. I trust you fit the bill, Mr. Hallam?"

"I know when to keep my trap shut," Hallam said. He was liking Elton Forbes less and less.

"Excellent." Forbes reached into his jacket again. This time he removed a thin leather wallet. He took a bill from it and held it out to Hallam. "Consider yourself hired."

Hallam glanced at the bill, then looked again. There were two zeros behind the one. That was five days' work at his normal rates.

He didn't take the hundred. "Hired to do what?"

"It's a very simple job. I want you to accompany me this evening to an appointment I have. When this meeting is concluded, you will return with me to the temple. Then your part of the affair will be over and you can go on your way."

"Bodyguard, huh?" Hallam grimaced. "This a blackmail meeting? Going to buy back some evidence?"

Forbes's eyes widened, and he swayed back on his heels. "Mr. Hallam! Such questions do *not* fall within the scope of your employment. But to set the record straight, this most certainly is not connected with blackmail. The very idea is ludicrous!"

The hundred-dollar bill was still in Forbes's outstretched hand. Hallam took it, shoved it in his shirt pocket. "In that case, I'll take the job."

He didn't put much stock in Forbes's outraged reaction, but now he was curious just what the preacher was up to. And there was only one good way to find out.

"Very well." Forbes frowned. He was obviously not as impressed with Hallam as he had hoped to be, but he was willing to honor the job offer. "Meet me at the temple at eight-thirty." He raised one impeccably plucked eyebrow. "I assume you know where it is?"

"I can find it." In fact, Hallam had passed the Holiness Temple of Faith several times. The abandoned store had changed over the months, going from a rundown building to a showplace with a huge spire and massive stained-glass windows. All financed, of course, by the donations of Forbes's faithful followers. Hallam suppressed a snort of disgust at the thought.

Forbes nodded brusquely and went to the door. Hallam opened it for him, catching a whiff of sweetish toilet water as he did so. That made him think of the professor and his elixir again. Morton had smelled like that... at least until the tar hit him.

Hallam stood on the little balcony outside the doorway and watched Forbes descend the stairs that ran down the outside of the building. There was a long, sleek Marmon 34 parked at the curb, and a man in chauffeur's livery leaned against its fender. He straightened as Forbes came down the stairs, and he had the rear door of the roadster open well before the evangelist got there. Even from the top of the stairs Hallam could see how the muscles in the man's shoulders and back bulged the uniform. The chauffeur looked perfectly capable of fulfilling any bodyguard duties that Forbes might require of him.

Which made Hallam wonder just why he had been hired. Maybe Forbes didn't trust the chauffeur to go with him this evening, wherever it was he was going. Hallam supposed he would find out, sooner or later.

The sedan pulled away from the curb, and Hallam's eyes followed it as it went down the street, turned a corner, and passed out of sight. He leaned on the railing of the balcony, watched the lowering sun again.

He had nothing against preachers. Back in the old days he had known several circuit riders, men who could preach hellfire and damnation with a six-gun on both sides of the pulpit and a Winchester at their feet. Hallam had liked them even though he wasn't sure he believed most of what they had to say. But they helped folks get through the rough times, gave them something to hang on to when things got bad. Hallam could respect them for that.

And some of them could drink a body under the table, too, when they put their minds to it. Hallam remembered a few of those times, too.

Elton Forbes wasn't like that, though. Hallam didn't know the man well enough to speculate on his sincerity, but he didn't like the way Forbes dressed, or the fact that he had a fancy car and a fella to drive it

Maybe that wasn't fair. Maybe Elton Forbes was

the holiest, God-fearingest man on the face of the earth. Or maybe he wasn't.

That didn't change the fact that he had hired Hallam and that Hallam had taken the money. Regardless of the way Hallam felt about him personally, he'd do the job, would let Forbes call the shots.

There was time between now and then, though, to finish up another little chore.

Hallam got back in the flivver and headed for Gower Gulch. He still had to tell Frank Sheldon about what he had found in Chuckwalla.

Most of it, anyway.

FOUR

HALLAM LIKED the area around the intersection of Sunset and Gower. The bigger studios, like Warner Brothers and United Artists, were a little farther west on Sunset, while a few blocks to the east of Gower lay the group of studios known as Poverty Row. The studios of Gower Gulch didn't have the size and fanciness of the major moviemakers, but the people who worked there worked hard and turned out a lot of pictures. Most of them were Westerns, which meant plenty of riding jobs for Hallam and the other old-timers like him.

When the movie companies had come in, they had taken over vacant buildings that were already in the area, so that many of the studios were located in old barns that had been redone to make them suitable for shooting pictures. Frank Sheldon's office was in a tidy bungalow that had started life as a farmhouse a couple of decades earlier. The studio itself was in a barn behind the bungalow. Hallam had filmed plenty of scenes in the old frame building where the sets were almost on top of each other.

Nope, not the fanciest place in the world, but Frank Sheldon had started with not much and was working hard to make it into something.

As Hallam parked the car and got out, he thought again, as he usually did when he drove up here, about the sleepy little pueblo that he had passed through back in the nineties, long before the oil and the orange groves and the movie studios. The City of Angels had been a pretty nice community then. Now it was growing by leaps and bounds, and though Hallam had to admit that it was exciting, he still missed the way it had been.

It would never go back to being that way, though. Not now, not after so much had happened.

Inside, he nodded to a receptionist with bobbed hair and a bright smile. "Frank's expectin' me," he said.

"I know. I'll buzz his secretary."

The girl pressed a button on her big desk, and a minute later another woman appeared from one of the corridors leading off the foyer. This woman was older, in her early thirties, her glasses and severe hairstyle spelling out her position as executive secretary to a studio head. Hallam knew there was more to her than that, though.

"Howdy, Melinda," he said. "Frank busy?"

Melinda Grantham smiled slightly and nodded.

"Of course," she said. "But he told me to bring you in to see him as soon as you got here."

Hallam followed her down a hall. She walked briskly, without all the twitches that some women liked to put on. Hallam liked her for that, and for the way she looked out for Sheldon.

Sheldon's office wasn't big, but it was well-kept. Melinda closed the door behind Hallam.

The walls of the room were lined with photographs of the stars who had worked here. Most of the big names were there—Hoot and Tom, Bill Hart, Art Acord, Neal Hart, Ken and Buck, even Bronco Billy. Hallam counted most of them as friends of his. Some of them were the real thing and some of them were just playactors, but they were all good fellas, always ready to help a man out if need be.

Two windows in the far wall looked out over the back lot and the studio, and mounted on the wall between the windows was a big fish that Sheldon had landed out on the ocean one day. The desk sat under the fish, and behind the desk was Frank Sheldon. He looked up from the papers he had spread in front of him, grinned at Hallam, and said, "I hope you've got good news for me, Lucas."

Without being asked, Hallam took the chair in front of the desk. He leaned forward, hands on his knees, and said, "'Fraid not, Frank. Don't think you'll be doin' any shootin' in Chuckwalla."

Sheldon frowned in surprise. He was well-dressed, well-barbered, a handsome man just starting to run a little to fat. His intense dark eyes were his most striking feature, and they looked sharply at Hallam now. "Why not?" he demanded. "From what I heard, the place would be perfect."

"Then somebody told you wrong," Hallam said. "Half the buildings have fallen down, and the other half are about to. Hell, Frank, you could build you a whole new town for less'n what it'd cost to fix up that one."

Not to mention the fact that two dead gunmen were buried just across the creek, Hallam thought.

Sheldon sighed and nodded slowly. "All right, Lucas. You know I trust your judgment. I have to admit that I am disappointed, though."

"Shoot, Frank, it was too far from town to make a good location, anyway. You'll find a better place."

"I suppose so." Sheldon smiled thinly and opened the middle drawer of his desk. He took out a long, thick checkbook. "I want to pay you for your time and trouble, though."

Hallam waved a hand. "No need for that. I was glad to do you a favor, Frank, you know that."

"Still, you did spend most of a day doing me a favor. Consider it as an investigation you did for me. That's what it was, after all."

Hallam picked up the check Sheldon slid across the desk toward him. "This is for more'n one day's work," he grunted.

"I've paid actors more than that for a minute's work," Sheldon assured him. "Don't worry about it, Lucas. It's worth a lot more than that to me to know that I can count on you."

Hallam folded the piece of paper, put it in his pocket. He nodded at the studio head. "Whatever you say, Frank."

The two men stood up together, and Sheldon extended a hand to Hallam. "Thanks again, Lucas. Say, we've got a new two-reeler starting tomorrow. Feel like taking on a riding job?"

Hallam hesitated. "Don't know, Frank," he said. "Got a new case starting tonight, don't know how long it'll take. Maybe you best line up some of the other fellers."

"Whatever you say, Lucas. Be seeing you."

Hallam said his good-byes and left. The door of the office next to Sheldon's was open, and Melinda Grantham looked up from the desk inside. Hallam smiled and nodded to her, knowing that the intercom between her office and Sheldon's had been open and that she had heard every word of their conversation. That intercom was never turned off except at Sheldon's personal command; as his personal secretary, Melinda had to know what was going on in that big office.

Rumor had it that Melinda kept close to Sheldon in lots of other ways, too. Hallam had never been one for gossip, but a body couldn't help but hear things around a movie studio. And besides, a part of him still remembered the old days when news of any kind was hard to come by and any chuck-line rider with a story to tell was greeted eagerly. A month-old newspaper was a treasure in those days.

As he drove away from the studio, Hallam put Frank Sheldon and Melinda and moviemaking out of his mind. He started thinking instead about Reverend Elton Forbes and the job that was coming up in a few hours. There was still plenty of time for him to get something to eat before he was supposed to meet Forbes at the temple.

Hallam sent the flivver into one of the neighborhoods where the Spanish influence still ran strong, and pulled up in front of an adobe cantina.

Two old men, their faces nut-brown, sat on a bench by the door, and they grinned toothlessly at Hallam as he got out of the car. *"Como 'sta?"* one of them greeted him.

"'Sta bueno," Hallam grunted. He didn't know their names, but they were always sitting there on the bench in the shade of a straggly tree. He also knew that both of them had ridden with Villa and had once been men to stand aside from. He liked them.

The interior of the cantina was dark and cool, all heavy wooden beams and adobe. The floor was hard-pounded dirt. A scarred bar ran along the back of the room. Tables were scattered around haphazardly, and several of them were occupied by Mexican men and women. They glanced at Hallam with little interest; he was known here, and respected.

He went to the bar and smiled at the young man behind it. Jesus Morales's face lit up. *"Señor Lucas!* Long time since you come see us. Where you been?"

"Been workin' most of the time," Hallam said as he rested his palms on the bar. "Had me a little free time today, though, and realized I'd been missin' your mama's cookin'."

"What you want?"

Hallam's grin widened. "Whyn't you just bring me a mess of whatever she's got cooked up back there?"

Jesus nodded his head. "Si." He reached underneath the bar and brought out a frosty mug filled with dark amber liquid. "And I think you could use this as well, señor Lucas."

Hallam inclined his head in appreciation as he took the beer from the boy. *"Gracias,* Jesus." He sipped the icy brew and licked the foam from his drooping mustache. "I reckon them folks back in Washington had the country's best interests in mind when they came up with that Prohibition, but I'd lay odds they never had a mouthful of trail dust needed cuttin', neither."

"*Si.* I get your food."

Jesus disappeared through an arched, curtained doorway behind the bar, and Hallam turned around to lean his elbows on the hardwood and sip his beer as he surveyed the room. This cantina, with its old-style architecture, its good food, and its friendly customers, was one of his favorite places in the city. It reminded him of other cantinas in other border towns. And the law turned a carefully blind eye toward the cold beers that the cantina provided for its thirsty patrons.

An older woman with raven hair tied in a tight bun stuck her head through the curtain and greeted Hallam warmly. Jesus's mother served up the best tamales Hallam had had since the old days in Texas, and she was a handsome woman to boot. Hallam kept his greetings to a smile and a nod, though, since Jesus's papa was still around and was rumored to be a handy man with a knife. Hallam had seen enough Latin jealousy in his time to know when to steer clear.

Nobody in the room paid any attention to him as he wandered over to a vacant table and sat down. Jesus brought two heaping platters of food out to him, and Hallam dug in, savoring the tamales, the beans, and the tender cabrito.

He had the meal about halfway finished when the three youngsters came in.

He heard their laughter and coarse jokes before he saw them. Then they came through the open door, their shadows dark against the early evening sunlight outside. Their clothes were expensive, and heavy rings glittered on their fingers. Hallam knew what they were:

college boys, from USC most likely, and judging by their height and the width of their shoulders, football players. Hallam gave them one look and went back to his food.

Jesus Morales was back behind the bar, and as the three young men walked up, he smiled and said, "How may I serve you, señors?"

One of them held up fingers. "Three beers, Pancho. *Comprendo?*"

"Of course, señor." Jesus didn't lose his smile as he took three mugs from their bed of ice and drew the beers. He carefully placed the full mugs on the bar in front of the college boys.

They scooped the mugs up in big hands and drank noisily. One of them spilled some of the beer down the front of his shirt, and he thumped the mug back down on the bar, a scowl of anger on his face.

"Hey, Pancho, you filled this damn thing too full!" he exclaimed.

"I am sorry, señor," Jesus hastily apologized, and he reached across the bar with a rag to try to dry the young man's shirt.

Hallam's back was to the scene at the bar, but he was listening as he drained the last of his own beer. College boys, with their inflated idea of themselves, didn't belong down here. This was a place for everyday folks to enjoy some good food and a cold drink.

Hallam sighed. Some people just didn't understand things like that.

At the bar, the young man grabbed Jesus's wrist and twisted sharply, bringing a cry of pain from his lips. "Damn it, Pancho, what do you think you're doing? Slinging some boozy bar rag at me isn't going to help!"

He tightened his grip on Jesus. "You're going to have to pay for cleaning my clothes, Pancho."

"*Si.*" Jesus said through clenched teeth. "I will pay."

"Damn right you'll pay," one of the other college boys laughed. "You greasers shouldn't be so careless."

"Please... you will let me go now, señor?" Jesus pleaded. Long, thick fingers squeezed even harder on Jesus's wrist. Bones rubbed together beneath the flesh, and Jesus's face contorted.

"I'll let you go when I'm good and ready," the college boy said.

"You're ready now."

Hallam's voice came low and hard from behind the trio at the bar. They glanced over their shoulders, saw him standing there with feet spread, thumbs hooked in his belt, and then turned back to Jesus. "Go away, old man," one of them snorted, but that was all the concern they spared him.

They weren't afraid of any old man, even one as big as Hallam, and they knew they had nothing to fear from the other customers in the cantina. They weren't through having their fun with the young Mexican behind the bar....

"No, Jesus!" Hallam snapped as Jesus's hand suddenly dipped below the bar and came back up in a move almost too swift for the eye to follow. Hallam's hand shot out and latched onto the shoulder of the one holding Jesus. Muscles bunched in his shoulders, and he tore the boy away from the bar, spinning him off to go crashing over one of the empty tables.

"Get the old coot!" one of the others yelled as he and his companion threw themselves at Hallam, fists bunched.

Neither of them had seen the blade in Jesus's hand, hadn't seen the way it sliced through the air where their friend's throat had been a split second before... before Hallam jerked him out of the way.

All they saw was that one of their own had been attacked, attacked by some crazy old geezer who deserved to be taught a lesson. They swung wildly, expecting Hallam to go down before them.

Hallam let his head go to one side, so that the first punch sailed harmlessly past, then he stepped in close and slammed a right into the boy's stomach. Air gusted out of his lungs and he turned pale. Hallam brought his other elbow up as the boy started to double over, and clipped him on the side of the head. The boy slumped against the bar and grabbed onto it to keep from falling on his face.

Hallam dodged two blows from the only one still on his feet, and this one saw the futility of trying to trade punches. He was the biggest of the lot, a tackle or a guard most likely, and he launched forward, arms spread wide to wrap around Hallam like a tackling dummy. Hallam wasn't quite quick enough to get out of his way.

As the arms locked around him, the top of the boy's head butted into Hallam's face, and for a second he saw stars as bright as any in the Texas sky. He shook his head as the grip tightened. Already his air was cut off and he was starting to feel dizzy. This had been a long day; a lot had happened, and it had taken something out of him. He had to get loose from this bear hug in a hurry....

Hallam slammed his open, callused palms over the boy's ears, then grabbed his hair and yanked his head back as the boy let out a howl. Hallam did a little butting himself then, and blood spurted onto his face as the boy's nose pulped. The grip on Hallam loosened enough for him to loop a punch around and drive it into the boy's side. The choking arms came totally loose then, and the boy staggered back a step.

Hallam hit him on the button, and he folded up on the dirt floor like all the bones had dissolved in his body. Crimson was still leaking from his nose.

"Put the knife up, Jesus," Hallam said hoarsely. "It'll just get you in trouble, no matter how much these hombres deserve it."

Jesus nodded shakily and replaced the long knife below the bar. The other customers had deserted their tables to gather in one corner of the room, and Hallam waved them back to their meals with a grin.

"Show's over, folks," he told them. "Nothing to worry about."

He grabbed the collar of the boy who was leaning against the bar and marched him to the door. A well-placed boot sent him sprawling on the sidewalk. A moment later, his two unconscious companions joined him as Hallam dragged them out of the cantina. An expensive roadster was parked nearby, and Hallam got the three of them loaded inside, the one who was still awake behind the wheel.

Then he put one foot on the running board and leaned in through the open window. "Now listen here, sonny," he said in a low voice, "and you pass it along to your compadres when they wake up. Them folks in there are friends of mine. Now, I know what you're thinkin'. You're thinkin' that you'll get some of your football-playin' friends and come back and bust the place up. Either that, or you'll call your daddies and try to cause my friends some trouble with the law." Hallam shook his head. "Don't do neither one of them things. Sure as you do, you'll see me again." He smiled. "And you won't like it, *sabe?* You won't like it one damn bit." He straightened up and slapped the top of the roadster. "Now git!"

The boy shakily started the car, then looked out at Hallam and said, "You're crazy."

"As a loon, son," Hallam said with a grin. "As a loon. But you mind what I said, anyway."

Hallam stood on the sidewalk and watched the roadster weave its way down the street, then turned and went back into the cantina. If he was lucky, his food wouldn't be too cold.

The two old men still sat in the shade and smiled and nodded at each other.

FIVE

THE SUN HAD DIPPED below the horizon when Hallam parked the flivver down the street from the Holiness Temple of Faith. There were no services going on at the temple tonight, but there were quite a few cars parked in front of it anyway. As Hallam walked toward the entrance, he heard organ music and singing coming from inside, and he wondered if he had read the sign wrong that listed the times of the meetings.

He saw as he went inside, though, that the pews in the big auditorium were empty and that most of the lights were off. There was a big stage up front, with a choir loft behind it, and there were a couple of dozen people standing there with hymn books in their hands. Looked like he was interrupting choir practice.

A tall man with broad shoulders was leading the singing; a young woman played the massive organ that sat to the left of the stage. Her hair was blond and shone prettily in the light from the big chandelier over the stage.

The music drowned out Hallam's footsteps as he

went up a long aisle between two sections of pews, but some instinct must have told the lone man seated in the auditorium that he was there. Elton Forbes stood up and turned around, gave Hallam a curt nod. He didn't smile or offer to shake hands, but then Hallam hadn't expected such, either.

"I assume you're ready to go," Forbes said sharply.

"Whenever you are," Hallam told him. He saw the blond organist glancing in their direction, but she didn't miss a note. The song was building to a big finish, and Forbes let the choir complete it before he gestured to the organist.

In the silence that followed the last crashing notes, the girl said in a low voice, "Mr. Riley," and the choir leader looked over at her. She nodded toward Hallam and Forbes.

The man came down the three steps from the stage with a bouncing stride, hustled down the aisle, and stuck out his hand to Hallam with a grin. "Welcome to the Holiness Temple of Faith, brother," he said.

Hallam returned the handshake, but before he could say anything, Forbes cut in with, "You don't have to try to convert him, Willard. Mr. Hallam and I have some business to attend to. I just wanted to tell you that I'll be gone for a little while." Forbes's voice was brusque and none too friendly.

Hallam wondered just what the man's appeal was as an evangelist. If there was one thing Forbes was in short supply of, it was personal charm. Willard Riley didn't seem offended by the shortness of Forbes's tone, though.

"All right, Elton," he nodded. "We'll carry on." He

hurried back to the stage and called to the organist, "Page one ninety-four in the hymnal, Miss Grey."

Forbes jerked his head toward the church's entrance. "Come along, Hallam."

Hallam didn't like being ordered around, but Forbes *was* his client, after all. And he was paying good money for this job.

As the two of them left the temple, though, Hallam thought that Willard Riley fit the accepted picture of an evangelist better than Forbes did. Riley was big and handsome, with lots of dark hair and white teeth, and he conveyed a great deal of magnetism, even on a first meeting. Compared to him, Forbes seemed flat, pale, and humorless.

Forbes was the one who could sling the hellfire and damnation, though, which proved that you couldn't always judge a person by the way he looked and acted.

"You want to go to this meetin' in your car or mine?" Hallam asked when they were on the sidewalk in front of the temple.

"I would prefer my own," Forbes said. "It's parked right over here."

Hallam recognized the long vehicle parked at the curb. There was no one waiting in it, or nearby, and he asked, "Where's your driver?"

"I've dismissed Claude from his duties this evening," Forbes said, and again Hallam wondered why that was. The big fella in the chauffeur's livery—Hallam assumed that was Claude—had looked like he could hold his own in any kind of scrap. So why wasn't he accompanying Forbes this evening? If Forbes had trusted Claude, he wouldn't have had to hire a private detective to protect himself.

And to protect himself from what?

There were all kinds of questions in Hallam's mind, but he knew the best chance he had to get answers was to go along with Forbes and see what happened. By the time the evening was over, he ought to know considerably more than he did now.

And if he didn't... well, the job would be over, anyway, and he'd be that much richer.

"Like me to drive?" Hallam asked.

"No, thank you. I shall drive. Your job is only to see that no harm comes to me."

So, Forbes was admitting for the first time that this meeting did involve some danger for him. That was further than he had gone before. Hallam leaned back against the plush upholstery of the Marmon and let his left arm rest against the reassuring hardness of the Colt holstered on his hip. The long coat he wore sometimes got a little warm, but it helped hide the Colt in its cross-draw holster. The Bowie rode on his right hip. The trench coat and Panama hat were a far cry from buckskins and a Stetson, but the Bowie and the Colt didn't change. After all these years, they were probably the closest friends Hallam had. After all, he was still alive, wasn't he?

Forbes handled the big car well, cruising through the evening traffic with confidence and skill. Hollywood was full of life, as usual, the restaurants and the movie houses brightly lit and doing a booming business. The speakeasies were busy, too, if you knew where they were, knew where to look. Hallam did. And evidently Elton Forbes did, too, because every time they drove past a speakeasy, the preacher's mouth tightened and a look of dour disapproval came over his face.

Their destination wasn't in Hollywood, though. Forbes pointed the car into the hills, and they climbed steadily until the lights of the city were spread out beneath them. The houses along the road got bigger and farther apart, until they were driving through an area of estates that were owned primarily by the new royalty—the movie stars. Hallam had been in the neighborhood before; Tom Mix lived not far away, and Hallam had been known to sit around and swap a few lies with Tom on occasion.

Forbes wasn't going to Tom Mix's house, though. He turned left, between two huge stone pillars. The wrought-iron gates that would normally be closed were open now. The two of them were expected, obviously.

The house bulked darkly behind a huge lawn. There were no lights on that Hallam could see; the whole place looked deserted. He would have been willing to bet that it wasn't deserted, though; otherwise, they wouldn't have been here. He could tell the house was big from the faint glow of starlight that washed down over the hills.

"Mind tellin' me who lives here?" he asked Forbes.

"Yes, I do mind," Forbes snapped. "That bit of information is not necessary for you to know."

"Just askin'," Hallam said softly, reining in his temper. Wouldn't do to let it flare up at a paying client, even one as rude as Forbes.

There were no other cars parked in the circular drive that led in front of the house, so Forbes was able to bring the Marmon to a stop just feet from the big double doors. He and Hallam got out of the car, and without being told to, Hallam shut his door quietly.

"The door is supposed to be unlocked," Forbes whispered. He had his hand on the knob when Hallam gripped his arm and stopped him.

"Best let me go first," Hallam breathed. He suddenly felt very uneasy about this business. He didn't like secrets; maybe that was one of the reasons he had become a detective.

His right hand dipped under the flap of his coat and came out with the .45. He held the big pistol in an easy, natural grip as he turned the doorknob with his other hand.

Forbes had been telling the truth. The door was unlocked and swung open quietly at Hallam's touch. The inside of the house was darker than outside, which meant Hallam was silhouetted as long as he stayed where he was.

He stepped inside quickly, went to one side, and stood motionless as he let his eyes adjust to the darkness as much as they were going to. Then he hissed to Forbes, "Come on."

Forbes stepped into the foyer, a foyer with some of the deepest carpet Hallam had ever felt, judging by the way his boots sank into it. "Really, there's no need for such dime novel behavior, Mr. Hallam," Forbes said, his voice still low. "We must be careful, but I hardly think we're in danger of our lives—"

The lights came on.

Hallam had been halfway expecting just such a development. His eyes were squinted against the glare. It didn't hit him as strongly as it did Forbes, who gasped and threw his hands over his eyes, but just the same, Hallam was thrown for a loss for a few seconds. He heard a sound to his right and spun in that direction, the Colt coming up—

A big hand clawed at his arm, forcing the gun back down. Hallam twisted, drove his elbow sideways, and was rewarded with a grunt of pain. He was blinking rapidly, trying to get some of his sight back, but so far the man who was attacking him was nothing but a vague blur.

"Damn cowboy!" the man spat. He sent a fist at Hallam's head, and Hallam didn't see it in time. The blow landed solidly. Hallam took a wild step to the side, trying to retain his balance as more punches thudded into his body.

"Get outta here, Forbes!" Hallam shouted as he slashed out with his pistol. It connected with something, but only glancingly. There was another yelp of pain from the attacker.

Hallam was starting to see a little better now. He caught a glimpse of a dark gray uniform as he *ducked* under another punch. His Panama came off, unnoticed. Hallam lowered his head and bulled his way into the other man, unwilling to just start blasting away until he knew what was going on. He had lost track of Forbes now, had no idea where his client was. But the first order of business was to get rid of this big bruiser who was flailing away at him. Hallam had a pretty good idea now of who the man was.

Looked like Forbes had done the right thing by not trusting good ol' Claude....

A fist slammed into Hallam's head and staggered him again. This time, before he could right himself, the other man hooked a foot behind his knee and jerked. Hallam felt himself going down.

He was glad for the thick carpet as his head bounced off the floor. But then a wild kick caught his right wrist and sent the Colt spinning away from him. Another kick sank into his side and set off explosions of pain through his body. Hallam rolled away from the next one, grabbed the foot as it zipped past him, and heaved. Claude—that was who it was, Hallam was sure of that now—Claude came crashing down beside him. A fire of anger was blazing inside Hallam now, and he was tired of roughhousing around like this. His fingers found the hilt of the Bowie. Time to put a stop to this foolishness.

Which same he would have done quickly if somebody else hadn't stepped behind him as he reared up, and hit him in the back of the head with what felt like a railroad tie.

Hallam went down, the Bowie slipping from fingers that couldn't feel a thing anymore.

SIX

THE BRIGHT LIGHTS were gone when Hallam woke up. A shadowy gloom had replaced them.

The next thing that Hallam was aware of were the voices.

"I can't believe you would do something this stupid, Wallace. You must know that I'm going to notify the police."

That was Forbes. Hallam kept his eyes slitted the barest fraction, not wanting to betray the fact that he was again awake. Not that he felt like moving just yet, anyway. His head felt like the wrong end of a buffalo stampede.

"That's just big talk, Forbes. You're not going to call the cops. Not unless you want your flock to desert you. And you know what that would mean: no more of that nice money flowing to you all the time."

This voice was a new one to Hallam, but there was something familiar about it. He was sure he had heard it sometime before, but probably not recently. It was smooth, well-modulated, and very sure of itself.

"I don't take kindly to threats," Forbes said. "And I don't like having my employees beaten by traitors."

"Don't worry about that old hawkshaw. Claude says he didn't hurt him."

Hallam's face rested on a hardwood floor, which meant that he had been hauled out of the foyer into another room. They were still in the big mansion in the hills, he was sure of that. From where he was lying, he could see some bookshelves and the legs of a heavy chair, but that was about all.

"Way the old bastard was acting, he's lucky I didn't bust his head open," a harsh voice put in, and Hallam knew it had to belong to the treacherous chauffeur.

"Shut up, Claude." That was the man called Wallace. "I don't pay you for editorial comments."

"No," Forbes said bitterly, "you just pay him to betray the man who took him out of the gutter."

"And you never let him forget it, did you, Forbes? You make me sick, preacher. You're damn high and mighty—"

There was a sharp crack, and Hallam knew that somebody had just gotten slapped.

"No, Claude!" Wallace rapped. "Let it pass. Reverend Forbes has just dug his own grave. We'll let him say a prayer over it...."

Time to move, Hallam decided. Things were starting to take a deadly turn. He tensed his muscles—

Then Forbes said, "I don't believe you, Wallace. If you had anything on me, you would have revealed it by now."

So this meeting *was* about blackmail, Hallam thought, despite Forbes' earlier denials. Any time you had a man in a high, respected position, especially one who took such a stringent moral stance as Forbes, he was wide open for anybody who could dig up some dirt out of his past. Looked like this Wallace had done just that. Maybe the grave being talked about was just a figure of speech. Wouldn't hurt to find out a little more before he jumped back into this fracas, Hallam mused.

"I'm just enjoying watching you squirm, *Reverend.* You see, I know that even a man of the cloth is only flesh and blood deep down. And pretty soon everybody's going to know that, Forbes. Everybody in this town...! Bring her out here, Claude."

It was the old story, Hallam thought. This Wallace, whoever he was, had come up with some old flame of Forbes', and he was going to use the girl to smear the evangelist's reputation. There might even be a child involved.

He heard heavy footsteps leaving the room, heard a door swing shut. That meant Claude was following orders and had left the room to fetch the girl. If Hallam made his move right now, all he'd have to deal with would be Wallace.

"How about a drink, Forbes?" Wallace asked. "Surely you have more than just the one vice?"

Hallam rolled over, eyes wide open now.

The clink of glasses was his signal to move. As he had hoped, Wallace had his back turned. He was at a bar on the other side of the room, which Hallam now saw was a luxuriously appointed study. Forbes stood in the middle of the room, his narrow face drawn and pale. His eyes widened as Hallam's movement caught his attention. Hallam shook his head as he surged silently to his feet. No need to warn Wallace just yet.

Hallam had been taught how to move by an eighty-year-old Apache named Notayeh. Wallace didn't hear him coming until the last minute.

Wallace spun around, but before he could do anything, Hallam's long fingers were wrapped around his neck. The grip tightened, driving Wallace back against the bar. The man couldn't make a sound, couldn't do anything except start to turn red in the face.

And it was a face that Hallam knew.

He understood now why Wallace's voice had sounded familiar. He had seen Allan Wallace around several of the larger studios. Wallace was too big a name for any of the Poverty Row studios to hire. Hallam had heard him bawling out commands through a megaphone on several sets, putting his actors through their paces as he made another of the pictures for which he was becoming famous. There had been no more promising young director in Hollywood.

Until someone had levied a morals charge against him concerning several of the underage actresses who had worked on his pictures.

The story came back to Hallam as he stood there gripping Wallace's throat. The papers had been full of scandalous allegations for weeks, their columns laced with sex and illicit drugs and bootleg liquor. Wallace had never been brought to trial, had never even been officially charged with anything if Hallam was remembering right, but all the studios had dropped him. There was nothing wrong with a little scandal now and then—best thing in the world to keep folks interested—but this one had been just too sordid.

Allan Wallace had been washed up as a director.

All because one of the actresses involved had gotten

religion and decided that she couldn't hide the guilt she was feeling....

That was Forbes's connection to the scandal, Hallam realized. If Forbes was really behind all the morals charges, that tied the whole thing up like a throwed calf with a piggin' string around its hooves. Wallace had wanted revenge, so he had bought off Claude to help him and had found something—*someone,* more likely—in Forbes's past that would prove an equal embarrassment to the evangelist. And then he had summoned Forbes here tonight to throw it in his face.

But Forbes had been cautious, maybe even a little scared, and had brought somebody along with him.

Hallam tightened his grip on Wallace's throat as the door into the study opened again. He heard Claude exclaim, "Hey!"

"Tell your boy to hold hard there, mister," Hallam hissed at Wallace. "Else you won't tell nobody nothin' else ever again."

Wallace waved weakly at Claude. "Don't... don't do anything!" he croaked as Hallam let off just a little bit on the pressure. "He's crazy!"

"Gettin' tired of bein' called crazy," Hallam grunted. He swung around and brought Wallace with him. Claude was standing motionless in the doorway, anger contorting his face. He wanted to tear into Hallam, that much was obvious, but Wallace's command was holding him back.

There was someone standing behind him, someone hard to make out in the shadows of the corridor.

"Emilie... ?" Forbes said in a husky, unbelieving whisper.

Hallam saw a woman's face float into view next to Claude's massive shoulder. It was a beautiful young face, framed by ringlets of soft brown hair. The kind of a face that could break anybody's heart...

The girl's mouth opened in a circle of surprise. Her deep blue eyes showed the shock she felt at the sight of the tableau in the room. She uttered a soft, stunned "Oh!" and then she was gone.

Forbes took a step toward the door, his arms reaching out, imploring, seemingly unaware of the gesture. He cried out, "Emilie!"

But the girl was gone.

And Wallace picked that moment to grope behind him, get his fingers around the neck of a bootleg gin bottle, and hit Hallam over the head with it.

The bottle didn't break, and neither did Hallam's head, but his fingers came loose from Wallace's throat and he staggered forward a couple of steps. The room was spinning around in front of him, but when he glanced back at Wallace, he saw the former director struggling to get a pistol out from under his coat.

Hallam swung one big paw in a backhand. It smacked into Wallace's face and slewed his head sideways. Wallace slumped against the bar. The pistol slipped from his hand and thumped to the floor.

Then Claude was throwing himself across the room, landing on Hallam's back and wrapping his long arms around him before Hallam could get turned around.

Hallam drove an elbow backward into Claude's stomach, felt it sink into the soft flesh around his middle. Dimly he was aware of Forbes rushing out of the room, running down the hall in the direction in which the girl had disappeared. Hallam didn't have too much time to worry about Forbes, though; he had his hands full keeping Claude from busting up his ribs.

Hallam planted his booted feet, bent his knees, then straightened his legs, driving him and Claude backward into the bar. The shining mahogany bar shuddered under their impact, then tipped over with a crash. Bottles shattered, and strong fumes washed up over Hallam as he and Claude sprawled in the wreckage. Hallam reached behind him, tangled his fingers in Claude's greasy hair, and pulled. The man let out a screech of pain and released his grip.

Hallam rolled over, got his knees on Claude's chest, and hit him twice, once with his right, once with his left. Claude's head thudded into the floor both times, and Hallam felt him go limp.

Chest heaving, Hallam slowly pulled himself to his feet. So far today, he'd been shot at and had had to shoot the two gunmen in Chuckwalla, had taught the college boys a lesson in the cantina, and now he had been knocked out and forced to waltz around with this big bruiser.

Damned if he wasn't getting tired.

Wallace was on his hands and knees, moaning. He was still groggy from being hit. Claude was out cold. Hallam didn't figure either of them to be an immediate threat.

Which meant he needed to get after Forbes and find out what was going on elsewhere in the house.

When he had his breath back, he strode out of the study and stood in the hall, listening for any sounds that might tell him where Forbes and the girl had gone. The rest of the house seemed to be quiet, though.

Then the sound of a car engine came faintly to Hallam's ears.

He loped down the hall toward the sound, feeling the pull of sore muscles and the ache of old wounds as he trotted. His bad leg wouldn't let him go too fast, and he grimaced as he heard the rasp of tires on gravel. Whoever it was in the car was getting away. Maybe Forbes, maybe the girl; either way, Hallam didn't want anybody leaving until he had set all this straight.

The hall led him to a side door that opened onto the lawn. A few yards away was a big garage, a driveway leading from it around to the front of the house. As Hallam pounded out onto the driveway, he saw the rear end of a car disappear around the corner of the house.

He bit back the fiery oaths that sprang to his lips. Cussing wasn't going to do any good. Especially when the patter of running footsteps told him that somebody was still lurking around the house. He spun toward the noise, acutely aware of the fact that his Colt and his Bowie were probably stashed somewhere inside. He didn't have them anymore, that was for sure.

He heard a door slam. Chances were that the girl had been in the car as it roared off into the night. That would mean that Forbes was probably back in the house now, having gone in through a different entrance when he failed to catch up with this Emilie, whoever she was.

Wallace and Claude were still inside, too.

Hallam swung around. He couldn't catch the car, no chance of that; it had been going like a bat out of Hades. But he could get back inside and see that nothing else happened on this wild night.

The shots told him he was too late.

They rang out in a rolling wave, one sharp crack

after another. This time Hallam went ahead and cussed, but he did it while he was running again.

The blasting stopped, and the silence afterward was even worse. Hallam's steps sounded even louder than usual in that ringing silence as he ran down the hall toward the study. The door that he had left open was now closed. He hit it with his shoulder, bursting it open.

The acrid stench of powder smoke stung his nose as he stepped into the room. He stood, heavy-shouldered and tired, and looked at the scene in the study. His craggy face might have been etched out of granite.

Blood was mixed with the spilled liquor now. Wallace and Claude were lying amidst the debris of the wrecked bar, crimson welling from their chests and giving a pink tinge to the puddle of bootleg hooch around them.

And standing over them, Wallace's pistol in his hand, was Hallam's client, the Reverend Elton Forbes.

"Hell," Lucas Hallam said.

SEVEN

FORBES LOOKED UP AT HIM, his face twisted with confusion. "Mr. Hallam!" he exclaimed. "I... I just..."

"Reckon I can see what you just," Hallam said bleakly.

Forbes looked down at the gun in his hand, then back up at Hallam. His grip released spasmodically, and the pistol slipped from his fingers, thudding to the floor. Hallam winced as it hit, but if there were any shells left in it, they didn't discharge.

"Surely you don't think I killed them," Forbes said. He swallowed nervously, his thin throat working.

Hallam stalked across the room and knelt beside the sprawled form of Allan Wallace. He rested his fingers on the director's throat for a moment, then reached across him to check on Claude.

Neither of them had a pulse.

Hallam looked up at Forbes's pale face. "What happened in here?"

"I... I ran back in the house," Forbes said, making a

visible effort to collect himself. "Then I heard the shots and came in here. Wallace and Claude were... well, they were like you see them now."

"Where was the gun?"

"On the floor." Forbes pointed a shaky finger at a spot about ten feet from the outstretched legs of the two dead men. "There."

Hallam glanced back at Wallace and Claude. No powder burns on their clothes. They hadn't been shot from close range.

But he was still a long way from believing what Forbes was trying to tell him.

"What did you do then?"

"I picked up the gun." Forbes passed a hand over his face, then squared his shoulders. When he spoke again, there was a little more firmness in his voice. "I realize that was not an intelligent thing to do. But I didn't know where you had gotten off to, Mr. Hallam. I don't mind admitting that I thought there might be more trouble. The gun seemed like a logical way to protect myself."

Hallam moved around and studied the pistol where it lay on the floor. He didn't touch it.

"Cylinder's empty," he grunted. "Reckon whoever did the shootin' emptied it."

"I promise you, Mr. Hallam, it wasn't me."

"Uh-huh." Hallam paused to listen. Out in the night, there were sirens, and he thought they were coming closer.

The houses were far apart in this neighborhood, but not so far apart that the shots wouldn't have been heard. The residents of the area were well-to-do, too, and paid high taxes, which insured that the police would respond quickly to a report of gunfire around here.

"We'd best get out of here," Hallam said. He started to stoop to pick up the fallen gun. "We'll take this with us."

Forbes stopped him, gripped his arm with more strength than was evident from his thin body.

"No," he said fervently. "I'll not run like a scared dog. No matter how bad this situation makes me look."

"Makes you look like a killer," Hallam told him bluntly. "Not sure I don't think that myself."

"I am a law abiding man. And I am innocent of this crime." Most of his confidence seemed to have come back. "The Lord will see to it that I am not unjustly persecuted."

"Better worry more about being prosecuted," Hallam muttered. He studied Forbes for a moment, considered fetching him a punch to the jaw and hauling him out of here.

It was Forbes's decision to make, though. Hallam's prints weren't on the gun, and he knew it. He was in the clear as far as this shooting went, though the cops might not be too happy with his part in the evening's goings-on.

There was a chance, too, that Forbes was telling the truth, as unlikely as the circumstances made that appear.

"All right," Hallam said abruptly. "The police'll be here soon. There's a couple of things I need to know before they get here."

"I'll answer any questions you have."

"When you were runnin' back in here, did you see or hear anybody else?"

Forbes shook his head, "No. I heard the gunshots, of course, but that was all."

"You ran out that side door, after the girl?"

At the mention of the girl, Forbes's eyes didn't want to meet Hallam's. "That's right," he said. "Then I ran back around to the front of the house. The front door was still unlocked. I started toward this room—I wanted to confront Wallace again— and that's when I heard the shots."

"Back up a minute," Hallam said. "You didn't catch up with the girl?"

"She... she had gotten into a car. She drove off down the driveway. I couldn't catch up to her."

"She was alone in the car?"

"I didn't see anyone else. I'm sure she was alone."

But it was dark outside the mansion, Hallam thought, and evidently Forbes hadn't been that close to the girl as she fled. He was going to keep an open mind on the question of whether or not she was alone.

"Reckon that covers it," Hallam said," 'cept for one thing. Who was that girl?"

Forbes's lips pressed thinly together. "I can't tell you that."

Hallam had been expecting as much. Outside, the sirens were much closer, and he knew they had only minutes now, maybe seconds.

He stepped up to Forbes and glared down at the smaller man. "You ain't asked me to help you, Forbes, but if that's what you've got in mind, you've got to play straight with me. Tell me who the girl is, and I'll do what I can to get you out of this scrape."

Forbes shook his head. "I'm sorry. You're right, I'd like you to help me, but I can't tell you anything else about the girl. It... it wouldn't be fair."

"Fair to her? How about fair to you, mister? Way it

stands now, you're liable to go over for something you didn't do. If you're tellin' the truth, that is."

"I'm telling the truth," Forbes assured him. "But I can't tell you any more."

Both of them heard the sound of car doors slamming outside. The Los Angeles police had arrived in their jitneys.

"I'll tell the police that you had nothing to do with this," Forbes said quickly. "I'm sure after I explain that you came here in my employ, they won't try to cause trouble for you."

"Don't know much about cops, do you?" Hallam said under his breath as he swung around to face the door of the study. The front door of the mansion swung open and footsteps sounded in the hall.

Two uniformed officers appeared in the doorway, drawn by the fact that this was the only lighted room in the house now. They each had service revolvers in their hands, and as they spotted Hallam and Forbes, they threw on the brakes and lifted the guns.

"Easy, boys," Hallam said. "The shooting's all over."

Both of the officers were looking at the corpses. Their eyes were wide with surprise; they had expected to encounter trouble, but they hadn't counted on finding a couple of dead bodies.

"What the hell happened here?" one of them finally demanded.

Hallam stayed where he was, arms in plain sight at his side, and told Forbes with a look to keep still and quiet.

"Why don't one of you fellers call Lieutenant Dunnemore?" he suggested. "I reckon he's the man to sort this out."

Ben Dunnemore had known Hallam for several years, and he had been working the homicide detail last time Hallam heard; if there was one man on the force who would give them a fair shake, it was Dunnemore.

One of the cops glanced at the other. "I'll find a phone," he said.

The other one nodded. He kept his gun trained on the unlikely duo of Hallam and Forbes.

"Tell the lieutenant we got big trouble," he said.

Hallam was ready to second that.

The next twenty minutes were long and uncomfortable. The second cop returned from calling in their discovery, and both of them kept Hallam and Forbes covered. By the time Dunnemore arrived, Hallam was more than ready to see him.

Ben Dunnemore was like Hallam in one way: he remembered the way the city had been before the boom. He was a thick-set man, a little below medium height. His hair and mustache had been sandy at one time but were now almost totally gray. He came into the room with another uniformed officer trailing him, and looked around, his mild blue eyes quickly taking in the scene.

"All right, Lucas," he said after a moment, in a deceptively soft voice, "what happened here?"

"Well, Ben," Hallam said, nodding toward Wallace and Claude, "somebody shot these fellers."

"So they did," Dunnemore agreed. "Do you happen to know who?"

"Can't say as I do."

Dunnemore looked at Forbes. "Who's this?"

Forbes took a step forward, heedless of the fact that he was still being covered by the first two officers on the scene. "I'm Reverend Elton Forbes," he said. "I want to assure you, Lieutenant, that Mr. Hallam is not at fault in this matter."

"Oh?" Dunnemore raised his eyebrows. "Did you blast these two?"

Forbes glanced at the bodies and couldn't repress a shudder of distaste. "I most assuredly did not."

"Did you see who did?"

"No. No, I'm afraid I didn't. There is one thing I should tell you, though."

"And what might that be?"

"When you investigate, you'll find that I handled that gun." Forbes pointed at the pistol on the floor. "I don't deny that I picked it up. But I emphatically deny that I shot those two men."

"Is that so?"

Hallam's wide mouth quirked in a grimace. He knew that when Dunnemore sounded so tolerant and understanding, as he did now, that things didn't look too good.

Dunnemore looked over at him. "Lucas, don't you think your friend should get himself a good lawyer before he says anything else."

"Think that'd be a right smart idea," Hallam said.

"But I have nothing to hide," Forbes insisted.

Hallam put a hand on the evangelist's arm. "Reckon you better keep quiet anyway," he said.

Dunnemore walked over to stand next to Wallace. He looked down at the dead man and said, "This is Allan Wallace, isn't it? Haven't heard much about him since that big to-do a couple of years back. Who's the other one?"

"Feller named Claude," Hallam said. "He drove for the reverend here. Don't know his last name."

"Berlund," Forbes supplied. "Claude Berlund."

Other policemen came trooping in. Dunnemore said, "Why don't you two go stand over there?"

Hallam and Forbes did as he suggested and waited in a corner of the room as photographs were taken and the pistol was bagged as evidence.

"I am in trouble, aren't I?" Forbes asked in a low voice.

"Damn right," Hallam told him. "Reckon maybe you better tell me what it's all about?"

"I... I can't. I wish I could, but... This is going to upset my parishioners terribly."

Hallam studied Forbes's taut features, read the strain and the concern there. The emotions seemed to be genuine. Hallam still didn't much like the reverend, but he didn't care to see anybody in such a mess unless they deserved it.

He wasn't sure Elton Forbes deserved to have a murder charge hanging over his head.

But at the same time, he wasn't convinced that Forbes was innocent. It would have helped a lot if Forbes had opened up when he had the chance and explained who the girl was. Hallam was sure she was someone from Forbes's past, but it might help to know where to find her.

One thing was for sure. The girl hadn't killed Wallace and Claude. She had been driving hell bent for leather away from the house when Hallam heard the shots.

And if Forbes was telling the truth, that could only mean one thing.

Somebody else had been in this house tonight, maybe the whole time.

Proving that was a whole other story, though.

When the bodies had been taken away, Dunnemore came over to Hallam and Forbes. His hands were in his pockets, and he was starting to look sleepy. Hallam knew that wasn't a good sign, either.

"Now, Lucas," Dunnemore began, "I want you to tell me just what you and the reverend were doing here tonight."

"I hired Mr. Hallam to come with me," Forbes answered before Hallam could say anything. "Allan Wallace asked me to meet him here, and I thought it might be wise to bring someone with me."

"There was trouble between you and Wallace?" Dunnemore asked.

"Thought you were going to wait until the reverend had a lawyer," Hallam put in.

"I'm just asking a few preliminary questions, Lucas. Don't get all het up." Dunnemore turned back to Forbes. "How about it, Reverend? What was the beef?"

"I'm not sure I should say any more," Forbes replied slowly. "It might be wise to consult an attorney. The temple has one on retainer..."

"Suit yourself." Dunnemore put his hand on Forbes's arm. "You'll have to call him from downtown, though."

"You takin' us in, Ben?" Hallam asked.

"Got to, Lucas, you know that. There's been a double killing. A lot of questions we need answered." Dunnemore turned and called one of the uniformed officers over. "Take the reverend out to the car, will you?"

Forbes looked over his shoulder at Hallam. Hallam nodded. "You go along with 'em. I'll see you later."

Forbes went, clearly ill at ease at being in this situation. When he was gone, Dunnemore turned to Hallam and said, "Looks to me like your client's in a lot of trouble, Lucas."

"I don't think he shot those two yahoos, Ben."

"Did you see who did?"

Hallam rubbed his jaw ruefully. "Told you I didn't."

"Was the reverend with you all the time you were here?"

"Nope."

Dunnemore shrugged. "He admitted that his prints are on the gun. Now I don't know what led the four of you here, but I do know this: I'll be very surprised if Forbes isn't charged with two counts of murder."

"'Fraid you're right," Hallam said.

That was the bad thing about simple cases, he thought. Sometimes they turned out not so simple after all.

EIGHT

HALLAM AND FORBES were taken to police headquarters in separate cars. Hallam had expected that; the cops didn't want to give them any more time to compare notes and agree on a story.

They were kept apart when they arrived at the new headquarters building on Cahuenga Avenue. Hallam was led into a small room with no windows and meager furnishings. As he sat down in a straight-backed wooden chair at a long, scarred table, he figured that elsewhere in the building Forbes was being seated in similar surroundings.

There wasn't going to be any third degree, he knew that. Forbes might wind up charged with murder, but he was too prominent a citizen to be roughed up like some suspects were.

And he figured Ben Dunnemore wasn't foolish enough to let anybody try to beat something out of *him*.

A thin-faced detective whom Hallam knew by sight but not by name came into the room a few minutes later and said, "All right, cowboy, what's the story?"

"Where's Ben?" Hallam asked right back.

"Lieutenant Dunnemore's whereabouts are none of your concern, Hallam. Just answer my questions, okay? Now tell me what happened at Wallace's house tonight."

Hallam resisted the urge to tell the man to go to Hades. Instead, he said, "I don't know a whole hell of a lot. Reverend Forbes hired me to go with him to a meeting tonight. He didn't tell me where it was or what it was about. When we got to the house, somebody jumped us right after we went inside."

Hallam paused and raised a hand to his head, fingered the sore lump under his shaggy gray hair.

"I got walloped, probably by Wallace. I was in the middle of a fracas with that Claude feller."

"So you admit that you had a fight with Wallace and Berlund?" the detective cut in.

"Never denied it. When I came to, Forbes and Wallace were arguin'. Don't ask me what about, 'cause I never quite got the straight of it."

That was a partial lie, but Hallam had already decided that he was going to let Forbes tell the police about Emilie only if he wanted to. If Forbes *did* tell them about the girl, they might come down harder on him for not being totally honest, but what the hell, Forbes was a client, wasn't he?

Hallam wasn't in the habit of throwing *anybody* to the wolves, much less a client.

The detective took out the makings and started rolling a cigarette. He glanced up at Hallam and said sharply, "Go on."

Hallam shrugged. "Figured it was time to get back in the ruckus. Me and Claude waltzed around a little more. Forbes ran out, I went after him. Before I could catch up to him, I heard the shootin' inside, and when I went back in, I found Forbes in the study with Wallace and Claude."

"They were dead and Forbes had the smoking gun in his hand?"

Hallam nodded grudgingly.

The detective lit the cigarette with a kitchen match and blew smoke toward the low ceiling.

"You're a liar, cowboy," he said.

Hallam took a deep breath. "Folks have been shot for sayin' things like that, boy," he said softly.

"This ain't the wild West." The detective jabbed a finger in Hallam's direction. "This is the damn twentieth century! You and all the other phony badmen can shoot up the movie studios all you like, but you can't take it out in the streets!"

"Didn't shoot nobody... tonight," Hallam said.

"Yeah, well, I ain't sure of that." The detective stopped his pacing on the opposite side of the table and put his palms down on it, leaning forward to stare at Hallam, the cigarette drooping from his lips. "If you didn't shoot those two, who did? Are you asking me to believe that Elton Forbes did? A minister? A well-known public figure?"

"They were dead when I found 'em."

"Sure they were. And I'm supposed to take the *word* of some cheap private peeper?"

Hallam's temper boiled over. He came up fast, the chair overturning behind him. "Mister, if you're tryin' to rile me, you're doin' a damn good job of it! Told you I didn't kill them two. I don't know if Forbes did or not, but you sure as hell ain't goin' to railroad me for the job!

Now why don't you go check and see whose fingerprints are on the gun?"

Hallam's voice had risen without him being really aware of it. The door of the little room swung open, and Ben Dunnemore said dryly, "You're starting to sound like a grizzly bear, Lucas, as well as looking like one."

Hallam picked up the chair, righted it, and sat down again. "Sorry for the commotion, Ben. This fella didn't seem to be payin' any attention to what I had to say, though."

"He usually doesn't." Dunnemore moved into the room and jerked a thumb at the other man. "I want to talk to Hallam. Alone."

"Yeah. Sure, Lieutenant." The detective went to the door, cast one surly glance over his shoulder at Hallam, and left the room.

Dunnemore leaned against the table and stuck his hands in his pockets. "Now, Lucas, I don't know what you told the boy, but I've been talking to Forbes and I think I've got the story. Care to confirm it for me?"

Hallam squinted up at him. "You wouldn't be tryin' to trick me into something, now would you, Ben?"

"Lucas! Have I ever tried to trick you?"

"Can't say as you have. All right, what did Forbes have to say?"

Quickly, Dunnemore went over what Forbes had told him, and the account followed the facts up to the point where the girl made her appearance. There was no mention of her.

Hallam nodded when Dunnemore had finished. "That's the way it happened, all right."

"I'm still not totally satisfied about a few things," the lieutenant said thoughtfully. "I don't understand why

Forbes would run back into the house when the two of you had already escaped. The impression I get is that Wallace intended to kill both of you. He was out for revenge on Forbes, wasn't he?"

"That's the way it looked to me. Reckon he just wasn't thinkin' straight, Ben. Maybe he didn't know that I was behind him. Maybe he thought they still had me and was goin' back to help me."

"Maybe, maybe. But why did Forbes go to meet Wallace in the first place? He had to know that Wallace was holding a grudge against him."

"Reckon I can't answer that one, Ben," Hallam said.

Obviously, Forbes hadn't said anything about the girl, preferring to keep her part in the affair a secret even if that did leave some holes in his story.

"Wallace hated Forbes," Dunnemore mused, "at least according to what you and Forbes have told us. I've got the background on that scandal a few years ago, and I see how Forbes fits in. I'd like to know exactly what Wallace had in mind for getting even with him. You wouldn't know anything about that, either, would you, Lucas?"

" 'Fraid not. I was just a hired hand on this one, Ben."

Dunnemore sighed. "You know, I wish Forbes would just admit that he shot them and get it over with."

"You reckon he's lyin' to you about findin' them the way he claims?"

"I didn't see any evidence to indicate anything except that Forbes shot the two of them. If you didn't do it, and Forbes didn't do it, then somebody else had to have done it, and there's no sign that anyone else had been there."

Hallam had been wondering about that very thing. "Was there any sign that there *wasn't* somebody else in the house?"

Dunnemore inclined his head in acknowledgment of the point. "No, I've got to give you that one. There are three doors, front, back, and side, and all of them were unlocked. The windows were all locked, and there was no sign of a forced entry."

"Somebody could have come in through the back door, though."

"*Could* have. I'm not going to assume that somebody did, though, not when I've got a murder weapon with a suspect's fingerprints on it."

Hallam studied the tired lines of Dunnemore's face for a moment, then asked, "You goin' to charge him?"

"I've got to, Lucas!" Dunnemore snapped. "If he'd just admit that he shot them, he might be able to make a case for self-defense. There's plenty of basis for it, given Wallace's hatred of him and the fact that this Berlund character had sold him out. But he's stubborn, insists he didn't shoot them and doesn't know who did. He's trying to hide something, and in my business, people hide murder more than anything else."

For long seconds Hallam considered telling Dunnemore about the girl, but he wasn't sure himself just what her part in the night's events had been, and anyway, the fact that she had been there didn't really change any of the damning evidence in the case.

Besides, Forbes wanted her kept out of it, regardless of the potential damage to himself.

There was nothing stopping Hallam from trying to find her and getting her to come forward on her own, though.

"Reckon you've got to do what you've got to do, Ben," Hallam said tiredly. "Am I free to go?"

Dunnemore waved a hand in dismissal. "Yeah, go home. Stay where we can find you, though."

"Sure." Hallam stood up. "How about lettin' me see Forbes before I go?"

Dunnemore glanced up at him, eyes narrowing. "You're not thinking about poking around in this case, are you, Lucas? We can handle any investigating that needs to be done."

"Man's got a right to do whatever he can in his own defense, don't he? Like hirin' a detective of his own?"

"All right, all right," Dunnemore agreed grumpily. "Never thought I'd see the day when you tried to drum up some business out of somebody else's problems, Lucas. You're not like most of the other private dicks in this town."

"You just think what you want to, Ben."

Dunnemore's words hurt, but Hallam shrugged them off. If the lieutenant wanted to think that he was trying to take advantage of the situation, there was nothing Hallam could do to change his mind.

Dunnemore took Hallam down the hall to another room like the one he had just left. Forbes was sitting at the table in that room, hands clasped in front of him, face calm and composed. Dunnemore said, "Five minutes," and shut the door behind him as he left Hallam there.

Hallam rested a hip on the table and leaned over close to Forbes. In a low voice, he said, "You're in a whole passel of trouble, Forbes. You want me to help you, you'd better tell me who that girl is and where I can find her. Maybe she knows *something* that'll make the cops change their minds about you."

Forbes looked up at him. "They're going to charge me with murder, then, are they?"

There was no emotion in his voice. It was as tranquil as if he'd been discussing the weather or the orange crop.

"Damn right they're going to charge you."

"Please don't curse, Mr. Hallam."

Hallam bit back the exasperation he felt and went on in urgent tones. "I reckon I believe that you didn't kill those two, Reverend. But the police aren't going to spend much time and energy lookin' for somebody else when they've got you to hang it on. Now, if you'll tell me about the girl, maybe she can give us a line on the real killer."

Forbes shook his head. "Emilie wouldn't know anything about this, Mr. Hallam. And I'm afraid I... I don't know where to find her. I had no idea she was in Los Angeles."

He stared down at the table and fell silent, and nothing Hallam could say would budge him from his stand. He wasn't going to say anything else about the girl, regardless of the effect on his own circumstances.

"All right," Hallam finally said with a sigh. "For a man who needs help so bad, you sure do try to hog-tie your friends, Reverend."

Forbes quirked an eyebrow and said ironically, "I wasn't aware that we were friends, Mr. Hallam. I am your employer, am I not?"

"That you are," Hallam said tightly. "And I'm goin' to earn my fee, mister. Bet on it."

Forbes shook his head. "I don't gamble, Mr. Hallam. It's a sin."

Hallam got out of there in a hurry, before he totally lost control of his temper.

Dunnemore was waiting outside the room, leaning against the wall in a negligent pose. Hallam grunted, "Been listenin' at the keyhole, Ben?"

"I don't have to do things like that, Lucas," Dunnemore replied. "I know what went on in there even without hearing it. You offered to help Forbes, didn't you?"

"I've got a sore head and a client in jail, Ben. I don't take kindly to either one."

"You tried to get him to open up about what really happened, and he wouldn't do it."

"You're doin' the guessin', Ben."

Dunnemore caught at Hallam's arm as the big man started to turn away. "Listen to me, Lucas," he said. "This case is going to get dirty before it's over. It's got all the makings of a real mess. Now, Forbes carries a lot of clout, I know that. I don't care. I'm going to dig, and I'm going to find out what's behind it. By the time I'm through, I'll know everything that happened at Wallace's house tonight. I don't want you getting in my way. Because if you do, some of the dirt's liable to get on you."

"Don't plan on gettin' in your way, Ben. I figure it won't hurt for me to do a little askin' around, too, though."

"This isn't the wild West, Lucas."

Hallam grinned humorlessly. "That slick-haired boy of yours told me the same thing."

"The difference is that I'm not just cracking wise. I mean it."

Hallam turned and started walking down the hallway again, his weariness intensifying the limp in his right leg. Over his shoulder, he said, "I'll be seein' you, Ben."

"That's what I'm afraid of, Lucas," Dunnemore muttered under his breath. "That's what I'm afraid of."

Hallam left headquarters and was glad when he was outside again, away from the smells of stale cigarette smoke and human sweat. The night had cooled off quite nicely, and far to the east there were flickers of lightning in the sky. It was probably raining in the mountains; the storm that he had felt earlier in the day while in Chuckwalla would have arrived by now.

Hallam paused at the curb, drawing the clean night air into his lungs. Forbes's car would have been brought in by the police from Wallace's mansion, but Hallam's car was still parked near the temple, as far as he knew. There wasn't much chance of getting a cab this late at night, either. He could have called one of his friends and asked them to come get him, but he didn't feel like disturbing anyone. Looked like he would have to hoof it back to the temple and retrieve the flivver.

The walk would give him time to think, time to try to sort out the things that had happened. Maybe with any luck he could make some sense of them.

Hallam walked away into the night.

NINE

THE SUNSHINE WAS bright and clear and warm the next morning, which didn't fit Hallam's mood at all. The way he felt, the sky should have been dark with storm clouds.

The storm must have stayed in the mountains, though, instead of drifting farther west. It had probably played itself out with thunder and lightning and slashing sheets of rain. Hallam found himself wondering about Liz Fletcher, about how she had weathered the storm in Chuckwalla. Her saloon home probably had some leaks in the roof....

Hallam hauled himself out of bed. Moping around wasn't going to do anybody any good. Later in the week, maybe, if he had more time, he'd take a run back out to the ghost town and check on Liz. Given her independent nature, she might not like somebody worrying about her, but Hallam couldn't help that.

At the moment, he had bigger problems.

He brewed some bitter coffee and poured it down

his throat, then dressed and headed downtown. Elton Forbes's case wasn't going to wait.

Hallam hadn't slept much the night before, despite the long day and the weariness he had felt. Instead, he had stared up at the dark ceiling of his bedroom, trying to figure out just what had happened at Allan Wallace's house.

There had to have been somebody else in the mansion. Otherwise, except Forbes, no one was left who had the opportunity to kill Wallace and Claude.

Someone who had been there all along, since before he and Forbes arrived, Hallam wondered, or someone who had followed them there?

Hallam had a feeling they had been followed to the mansion. There was no evidence to base that on, but it was a good, solid possibility. He hadn't been watching for a tail as Forbes drove from the temple to Wallace's house; he hadn't had any reason to.

That led to another question. If they had been followed from the temple, had the person who trailed them been waiting for them outside?

Or could it have been someone who was there inside the temple?

It was a place to start, Hallam thought.

The Holiness Temple of Faith had been dark and deserted the night before when he picked up his flivver, but it was bustling with activity this morning. Several cars were parked in front, and the doors of the sanctuary were open. Hallam parked and walked half a block, and just before he reached the doors of the building two men came out rapidly, almost stumbling when their feet hit the sidewalk.

Hallam recognized both of them as reporters. On

their heels came Willard Riley, his face set in angry lines.

"This is a house of God, gentlemen," he said hotly to the reporters, "so I won't allow Satan to take control of my tongue." He put his hands on his hips and glowered at them. "And I'm trying to resist the temptation to do a little smiting of the wicked."

"We're just trying to do our jobs, Reverend Riley," one of the men said. "When a guy like Elton Forbes is hauled up on a murder rap, it's news!"

"There will be an official statement later. Until then, gentlemen, good day!"

Riley started to turn to go back inside, but then he spotted Hallam standing a few feet away. He stepped out with hand extended and said quickly, "Come inside, please, Mr. Hallam."

One of the reporters jerked his head around. "Hallam! Hey, you're the guy who was with Forbes, aren't you? The private dick?"

"Mr. Hallam has nothing to say to you," Riley cut in. He had taken Hallam's hand, shaken it briefly, and now he retained the grip to almost pull him into the church. Hallam let himself be led, ignoring the questions that the reporters called to him.

Riley shut the doors behind them, plunging the foyer of the church into a shadowy dimness. The doors leading into the auditorium were closed as well.

"Scavengers!" Riley exclaimed. "They've been hanging around ever since I got here, maybe all night for all I know. I chase some of them off and five minutes later a new batch takes their place. God save us from the press!"

"I sympathize with you, but like they said, they're just tryin' to do their jobs."

"Like you were doing your job last night?" Riley shot back. Hallam stiffened, but before he could make any reply, Riley sighed and lifted a hand to massage his forehead. "I apologize, Mr. Hallam, I really do. This has been a very difficult morning. Things had been going so well lately; no one expected any trouble...."

An outburst of angry voices came from down a hall that led from the foyer. Hallam looked in that direction.

"The temple's Board of Elders is meeting," Riley explained. "This whole matter has been such an unpleasant surprise, and we're trying to decide what course of action we should follow."

Hallam figured that Forbes had had more unpleasant surprises in the last twenty-four hours than Riley and the Board of Elders, but he didn't make any comment other than to say, "Reckon it has been hard."

"I was so shocked when Elton called me last night and asked me to come down to that... that place."

"Never been in a jail before, huh?" Hallam couldn't resist asking the question.

"I certainly have. A minister's work can take him into many unsavory situations. Like this one." Riley looked earnestly at Hallam. "Could I prevail on you to sit in on the meeting and answer any questions the elders might have about what happened last night?"

Hallam nodded. "Reckon I could do that."

He had been planning on asking some questions of his own, but that could come later. He might wind up with some useful information this way, too.

Riley led the way down the hall and opened the door to a meeting room. Twelve men were grouped around a long table inside. Their voices were raised in loud argument, but they fell silent and stared at the newcomers as Hallam's bulk took up most of the doorway.

Hallam recognized some of them as he scanned their upset faces. Some of Los Angeles's most prominent business and social leaders were in that room. He had known already that Forbes had quite a society following, but he wouldn't have guessed at the extent of it.

"Gentlemen, I think you've already figured out the identity of my companion here," Willard Riley said. "This is Lucas Hallam, the private detective who was with Elton last night."

The stocky, white-haired man at the head of the table, who was evidently in charge of this meeting, said, "I'm not sure it's a good idea to bring an outsider in on temple business, Willard."

"Like it or not, though, Mr. Hallam is already involved," Riley answered. "I don't see any harm in finding out firsthand just what occurred last night."

Hallam glanced over at Riley. "Forbes didn't give you the details?"

Riley shook his head. "Not really. Elton was extremely upset, naturally, though confident that the Lord would see him through this time of trial. He merely told me to pass that on to the flock. I intend to do so at a specially called service tonight." He stepped over to the table and pulled out a vacant chair. "Won't you sit down, Mr. Hallam? I'm sure the elders have many questions that they would like to ask."

Hallam sat.

The leader of the elders fired the first question at

him. "Just what connection is there between Reverend Forbes and a man like this Wallace? I understand he had quite a reputation as a roué."

"He was a ladies' man, all right, if that's what you mean," Hallam said. "Reckon he did plenty of things he shouldn't. It caught up with him a couple of years ago, and he figured your Reverend Forbes had something to do with it."

"That's what I don't understand," one of the other men said. "I never heard Elton mention Wallace."

"Do you remember a young lady, a movie actress, who saw the light and left her wicked ways behind by joining our little congregation?" Riley asked. "Her real name was Judy Miller. I don't remember what name she was using in the picture business."

There were nods from several of the elders. The leader said, "Of course. She went back home to Iowa after a few months, didn't she?"

"I believe so. She was one of Wallace's... ah... protégées. She appeared in several pictures that he made and then decided that she didn't want to live the kind of sinful life into which he had led her. Elton was instrumental in helping her see the error of her ways."

"Which led to a heap of trouble for Wallace," Hallam put in.

"I remember that scandal," one of the men said. "A dreadful business, perfectly dreadful."

They all seemed a bit embarrassed by the whole discussion. Hallam went on, "Wallace got Reverend Forbes to come see him last night, and I went along as a bodyguard. Didn't do too good a job, as it turned out."

"Nothing happened to Elton," Riley pointed out.

"He didn't get shot or roughed up, if that's what you

mean. I should've headed off the trouble, though, so he wouldn't be in the fix he is now."

"Don't blame yourself, Mr. Hallam. I'm sure you did the best you could under difficult circumstances. Now, tell us what happened after you got to Wallace's house."

Hallam ran through the story again, for what seemed like the hundredth time in the last twelve hours. The elders listened attentively. Again, he left out any mention of the girl Emilie, not knowing whether Forbes had told Riley about her.

He could imagine the reaction of these stuffy old men if he told them that their preacher was mixed up somehow with a beautiful young mystery woman. Despite the seriousness of the situation, the corner of his mouth quirked as he suppressed a grin.

When the story was done, he turned to Riley and said, "I haven't talked to the reverend yet this morning. Do you know if they've charged him yet?"

Riley pulled a turnip watch from his vest pocket and looked at it. "The arraignment was set for half an hour ago. I should have been there. I'll go down to the courthouse right now." He pushed his chair back and stood up, but didn't leave the table just yet. "Before I go, I think there should be a vote on the question that we discussed earlier."

"I'm still not sure about hiring a detective, Willard," the leader said.

Hallam put his palms on the table and pushed himself up out of his chair. "Hold up there," he said. "If you're talkin' about hirin' me, I've already got a client. Reverend Forbes said he wanted me to poke into this thing, and that's what I intend to do."

Riley nodded. "Of course. Elton told me last night

after the police released you that he intended to continue your services. But there's nothing to stop you from working for the church, too, is there? It's the same thing."

"Not hardly."

There was a moment of tense, almost angry silence, then one of the elders broke it by saying, "Do you think we could arrange somehow to at least get Elton out of jail?"

"I've already spoken to Mark about that," Riley said. "He says it's not possible if they charge Elton with first-degree murder like they intend. He was at the proceedings this morning, though, so I'm sure he did all he could." Riley turned to Hallam and explained, "Mark Etchison is the temple's attorney, and naturally he's handling Elton's case."

"Might be wise to find somebody who's handled murder cases before," Hallam advised. "Current can get a mite swift for somebody who ain't used to it."

"I'm sure Mark knows what he's doing." Riley glanced at his watch again. "Well, if we can't talk Mr. Hallam into changing his mind about our offer, I have to run. I'm sure Elton is wondering where I am this morning. Can I walk you out, Mr. Hallam, and keep those reporters off your back?"

"Reckon I can handle a few reporters," Hallam said. "Thought I'd ask a few questions around here before I go see the reverend."

"Very well." Riley smiled wearily at him, nodded to the elders, and left the meeting room.

He hadn't looked too happy at the idea of leaving Hallam there, however. Hallam wondered what the reason might be for that.

When Riley was gone, one of the elders said, "Really, Mr. Hallam, whether or not you're working for us, I know we'd appreciate it if you'd let us know what you find out. We're all very worried about Elton."

"Happen I run across anything interestin', I'll try to let you know," Hallam said. "My first responsibility is to Reverend Forbes, though."

"Of course, of course. You mustn't mind Willard. He's just worried about Elton, like the rest of us. He has a lot on his mind these days."

Hallam turned the chair around and straddled it as he sat down again. "Reckon you could tell me a little about your operation here?"

"What do you want to know?" the leader asked.

"Has there been any trouble lately?"

"Trouble? What kind of trouble?"

"Fussin' and fightin' amongst the members, for one thing. Anybody left the church holdin' a grudge?"

The man smiled at Hallam. "Every church has its little arguments among the members. They don't mean anything, though, when everyone is united in the Lord's cause."

"The reverend have any particularly enemies?"

"Only among the ungodly."

"Them's the worst kind to have," Hallam said. "You got anybody special in mind?"

One of the elders, a mild-looking man who hadn't spoken up so far, now leaned forward and said to the leader, "What about Jeremiah?"

The leader shook his head. "Jeremiah's a harmless, crazy old man. He wouldn't hurt anybody."

"He hates Elton, you know that."

"Maybe so, but—"

"Who's this Jeremiah feller?" Hallam cut in.

The leader sighed. "He's a street-corner preacher with his own rather warped sense of religion. He's tried to disrupt our services before, and Elton called the police to deal with him. I hardly think he could be involved with this, though."

"Might be worth checkin' out," Hallam said. "The way I see it, one possibility is that somebody with a grudge against Reverend Forbes shot those two knowing that the reverend would be blamed for it."

"Isn't it just as likely, though, that someone totally unconnected with Elton killed them? You and Elton may have simply been in the wrong place at the wrong time, Mr. Hallam. Lord knows, a man like this Wallace might have had many enemies."

Hallam nodded his head. "You could be on the right trail there. Only one way to find out, though, and that's to lay everything out in the open." He looked around the table at the solemn faces. "Might not be too pretty by the time it's over."

"That doesn't matter," the leader said firmly. "We're going to stand by Elton. I'm sure he'll be proven innocent, either by you or by the police."

"Wouldn't count too much on the cops," Hallam told him. "I'll do what I can."

A few more minutes of conversation with the elders revealed only that Elton Forbes was a sterling individual with no enemies, at least not any that would frame him for murder. Hallam was going to reserve judgment on the street preacher called Jeremiah until he had located the man and talked to him.

"I'll be talkin' to you," he said as he stood up once again.

The elders said their good-byes, and as Hallam left the meeting room, he had the distinct feeling that they were glad to see him go. He made them nervous, he supposed. They were the pillars of the community, and they didn't know how to deal with the fact that their minister was in jail for murder.

They also didn't know how to deal with an old cowboy who asked indelicate questions.

As he walked down the hall toward the entrance foyer, Hallam hadn't decided what his next stop would be. He could go down to the jail and talk to Forbes again, but he didn't see what good that would do right now. He might run into Willard Riley there, too, and he wasn't sure he wanted to see Riley again so soon.

A sound interrupted Hallam's musing. It came from behind a closed door near the foyer. Hallam's sun-bronzed forehead wrinkled in a frown.

It was the sound of someone weeping.

He stood in front of the door for a moment just to be sure that the sound was coming from behind it, then he reached down and tried the knob. It turned, and he pushed the door open a few inches.

The room was small and dark and evidently some sort of storage area. He saw several crates sitting around in the gloom; one of them was open, and inside were hymnals. Hallam only had time for a glance, though. He was more interested in the girl who was leaning on one of the crates and crying.

Her blond head jerked around at his entrance, and her wet eyes widened as she saw him standing there. He must have startled her, because she gasped and suddenly rushed toward him.

Hallam stood aside without thinking, and the girl

scurried past him. She ran to the double doors leading into the auditorium and banged through them.

Hallam followed her to the doors and paused there, watching her hurry down the center aisle. She turned to the left in front of the altar and went past the massive organ, vanishing through a small door at the rear of the sanctuary.

Now that was interesting, he thought. The last time he had seen the girl she had been playing that organ during choir rehearsal the night before. Her name was Alice Grey, if he was remembering right.

And from the looks of things, Alice Grey was one upset young lady.

TEN

HALLAM PULLED A handkerchief from his pocket and wiped beads of sweat off his forehead as he walked down Hollywood Boulevard. The palm trees that lined the road cast some shade, but not enough. The temperature was rising, even though it wasn't noon yet, and it looked like it was going to be another scorcher, just like the day before.

Hallam just hoped it wasn't quite as violent.

He had come down here from the temple to look for the man called Jeremiah. Street-corner preachers were easy to find in this part of town; in fact, finding a corner *without* a preacher was harder, especially at certain times of day. He wasn't sure how many would be out and about before noon, though.

At least one.

"Repent, brother, repent! Cast aside your evil ways and embrace the true path, the path of the light!"

The words were shouted in a hoarse voice by a man standing on the sidewalk up ahead. He wore a woolen robe that had to be sweltering. His face was bathed in sweat, and his head, bald except for tufts of gray hair over the ears, was glistening. The people on the sidewalk hurried past him for the most part; only occasionally did someone pause to look at him and listen for a moment.

The preacher broke into song as Hallam approached him, his voice wavering as he chanted the tuneless words. He seemed to be having a hard time catching his breath, and Hallam wondered why he didn't at least move into a patch of shade.

Hallam stopped in front of him and waited for the song to wind down. The preacher broke it off rather abruptly, faced Hallam with a wide-eyed stare, and asked, "Have you come for the word, brother?"

Hallam nodded. "Reckon I have."

The preacher cast a quick glance up and down the street, then said in a low voice that was almost a whisper, "Randado in the fifth."

Hallam just looked at him.

"It's a can't miss, I tell you," the preacher went on. "He's ready, and the odds are eight to one."

Hallam nodded solemnly.

The preacher jerked his head to the side, fastened his burning gaze on another passerby, and intoned, "Many are the paths of Satan, but only one road leads to the truth."

Hallam stayed where he was.

When there was another lull in the foot traffic, the preacher glanced at Hallam and snapped, "What is it with you, bud? You deaf or something?"

Hallam grinned at him. "Don't reckon I can use that little bit of gospel you just passed on, preacher, but I'd be grateful if you could tell me where to find a feller called Jeremiah."

The man stared at him for a second, then took a sudden step backward. "You a cop?" he demanded.

"Nope. Just lookin' for Jeremiah."

"Don't know him. My name's Ezekiel. I'm God's chosen messenger on Earth."

Hallam slipped a big hand in his pants pocket and took out a bill. He held it so that just a corner showed. "Always like to support good causes," he said slowly.

Ezekial shook his head. "Sorry, mister. I still don't know any Jeremiah. This is my spot. Most of the other guys know to stay away from it. Why don't you try a few blocks up the street?"

Hallam glanced in the direction Ezekial indicated and saw several more men standing on the sidewalk and talking in loud voices. He nodded to Ezekial and said, "Reckon I'll just take a pasear up there. Thanks, friend."

With practiced ease, Ezekial's hand darted out and snatched the bill from Hallam's hand. He clapped his other hand down on Hallam's shoulder and shouted, "Praise the Lord, brother! God has shown you the light and put your feet on the true path!"

Hallam shrugged off the hand and leveled an angry glare at the preacher. There were quite a few people walking past on the sidewalk, though, so he resisted the impulse to put a little real fear of God into Ezekial.

"Call it a donation," he said in a soft voice. "But I wouldn't try that again, brother."

"Go with God, my son," the preacher said smugly.

You never knew what you'd see in this town, Hallam thought as he moved off down the sidewalk. When he looked back over his shoulder, he saw someone else slipping a bill to Ezekial, no doubt for the tip on the horse this time. Well, a street preacher could be a tout as well as anyone else, he supposed.

He approached two more men in ragged clothes who were exhorting pedestrians in strident voices. Neither of them knew Jeremiah, and it took Hallam a while just to get that out of them. His patience was running thin when a man stepped out from the doorway of a closed shop.

"Are you looking for me?" he asked. "I heard you mention my name."

Hallam looked him over carefully. This could be just a bum out to put the touch on him. The man was tall and thin, wore work pants and a shirt that had once been white. His clothes were unkempt but not too dirty, and his dark hair was neatly brushed back away from a high forehead. The most unusual note about him was the pair of bare feet that protruded from his pants legs.

"I'm lookin' for a man called Jeremiah," Hallam said.

The man nodded. "I am Jeremiah. Once I was not, but now I am."

"Meanin' what?"

"When I was called to spread the Gospel, my name was changed. I am no longer the sinful man that I once was, so I took a new name to go along with my newfound salvation."

He spoke quietly, sincerely. His eyes were bright and clear.

"You know a man named Elton Forbes?" Hallam asked.

The pale skin of Jeremiah's forehead wrinkled in a frown. "I know the man," he admitted. "A false prophet. Why do you ask about him?"

"Heard tell you had a little run-in with him not long ago." Hallam spoke casually, not wanting to alarm the man.

Jeremiah just smiled at him for several seconds, then said, "You're a policeman, aren't you?"

Hallam grimaced. "Don't know why people keep thinkin' that. Do I look like a cop?"

"No." Jeremiah shook his head. "You look like a cowboy. But you ask questions like a policeman."

"I'm a private detective."

"Ah. That explains it. You're working for Forbes and trying to clear him of the murder charges against him."

"You seem to know something about it."

"There's a newsstand down the street. I read the paper, though I usually lack the funds to purchase it. Forbes is in a lot of trouble, isn't he?"

"Wouldn't know anything about it, would you?"

Jeremiah smiled tightly. "I don't like what you're implying, my friend. If you're thinking that I might be involved in those murders, let me remind you that the Lord said, Thou shalt not kill. I follow all of the commandments."

"You did have some trouble with Forbes, though, didn't you?" Hallam prodded.

Jeremiah shrugged and said, "We have had our differences. I'm a servant of the Lord. Forbes serves only himself."

"How do you figure that?"

"Have you seen the car he drives? A gaudy symbol of his devotion to things of the flesh." Jeremiah snorted in contempt. "He spends as much time begging for money as he does spreading the word of God. More time. He pleads for money to build a temple, then asks for more money to expand it." He waved his arms at their surroundings. "The world is my temple, the clear blue sky the vaulted arch of my cathedral!"

Maybe Jeremiah meant what he said, maybe he didn't. But Hallam could come closer to understanding this man than he ever could someone like Elton Forbes. He'd never considered himself a particularly religious person, but he'd long since discovered that any feelings he had in that direction surfaced when he was out by himself, in the desert or the high mountains or the forests.... Not in some church with stained-glass windows and hard wooden pews that'd get a man down in his back.

"That why you disrupted services at Forbes' temple?" Hallam asked.

"I merely tried to show the hypocrites and the sinners the error of their ways. Our Lord cleansed another temple of money changers and thieves," Jeremiah pointed out with a touch of pride in his voice.

"But you got hauled off to the *juzgado* for what you did," Hallam said.

"Our Lord suffered much more. Besides, the police just told me to stay away from Forbes's services. I was not jailed."

"Must've made you a little mad, though."

Jeremiah smiled beatifically. "I forgave the ones who transgressed against me." He glanced up at the sun, then went on. "Excuse me, my friend, but it's nearing the noon hour. I must get to my regular station. I have a message to tell the many poor souls who wander the streets."

Which meant that traffic was heavier around

lunchtime and he stood a better chance of panhandling. Hallam said, "I'll see you around."

"I'm sure you will."

Hallam watched him walk away with a firm, confident stride. He wasn't quite sure what to make of Jeremiah, but he had a feeling that the man would bear further watching.

He started back to where his flivver was parked, a few blocks away. Now that he had checked out Jeremiah, it was as good a time as any to try to change angles for a while.

Something one of the elders back at the temple had said was nagging at him. A man like Allan Wallace, who had been in a position of power and who hadn't had the highest moral code in the world, was bound to have made a few enemies. Maybe the real killer *didn't* have any connection with Forbes and Emilie. That idea could use some looking into.

Hallam headed for Gower Gulch.

MELINDA GRANTHAM WAS LEAVING Frank Sheldon's office just as Hallam appeared in the hall leading to it. She greeted him with a smile and said, "Hello, Lucas. Did you want to see Frank?"

"Reckon he could spare me a few minutes? Something I want to talk over with him."

"I'm sure he'd be glad to talk to you. He's at his desk, working through lunch. Again." She sighed. "I wish he'd take it a little easier, but you know how obsessed Frank can be. I'm just on my way out to get some lunch. Can I bring you something?"

Hallam shook his head. "No, thanks. Figured I'd meet some o' my ridin' pards. I won't keep Frank from his work for long."

He reached out for the doorknob but stopped when Melinda suddenly said, "Oh!" Hallam looked over at her and saw that she had lifted her hand to her mouth. Her usual cool competence had been shaken.

"I just realized," she went on, "this is about those murders last night, isn't it? I saw your name in the paper this morning and thought then how awful it must be for you to be involved in such a mess. But then we got busy around here this morning and the whole affair completely slipped my mind."

"Don't you worry about it," Hallam told her. "I just thought I'd ask Frank a few questions about Allan Wallace. He did a few pictures here, didn't he?"

"I think so. That was before I came to work for Frank, though. I don't think I ever saw Wallace except at a few parties, back before his... his troubles."

Hallam nodded. "I'll see what Frank can tell me," he said, and he went on into the office while Melinda hurried off down the hall.

Frank Sheldon looked up from the paper-cluttered desk with an expression of annoyance on his face. His features eased into a smile when he saw who his visitor was,

"Hello, Lucas," he said. The smile became a look of concern. "I heard about what happened last night. Sounds like a real mess."

"You heard right," Hallam said, turning a chair around and straddling it. "Mind me askin' you a few questions, Frank?"

Sheldon shrugged, waved a hand at the mass of

papers on the desk. "I'm kind of busy, but—for you, sure, Lucas."

"How well did you know Allan Wallace?"

"Not very well. He did a couple of two-reelers here about five years ago, right after I started the studio. He was a good director, and his pictures made money. That was all I was worried about at the time."

"Know anything about the trouble he got into?"

Sheldon's mouth quirked in a grimace of distaste. "I read the same things everybody else did in the papers. I knew Wallace had an eye for the ladies—even executives hear some of the gossip that goes around a studio—but I didn't know just how young he liked them. We had a girl in the company then who was fifteen, I think. I've wondered since then if Wallace had anything going with her."

"Was she in any of his pictures?"

"Both of them." Sheldon shook his head. "I don't mind telling you, Lucas, I worried about her after the stories came out about some of the parties Wallace had at his house."

"Is the girl still with the company?"

"She left after a couple of years, went back home to her folks, I think. They lived out in Glendale, so she didn't have far to go."

Hallam felt a stirring of interest. He hadn't counted on finding the trail of one of the girls with whom Wallace had supposedly had his scandalous involvements. "Mind telling me her name?"

Sheldon studied him for a long moment before replying. "Her name was Nola McGuire. Don't tell me you're thinking she might be hooked up with what happened to Wallace last night!"

"Just considerin' all the possibilities, Frank. Like you said, Glendale's not far."

"You're on the wrong track, Lucas," Sheldon said firmly. "Nola was no Virginia Rappe. She was a sweet kid. Even if she was... involved... with Wallace, she wouldn't try to hurt him to get even. Anyway, why would she wait so long? If getting back at Wallace was what she had in mind, she had plenty of chances a couple of years ago when the press was having a field day with him."

"Maybe she didn't want any public connection with him," Hallam pointed out. "Maybe she wanted a little private revenge."

"Not a chance. It's just not like her."

"You said she had a father. Maybe he wanted to get even."

"Yeah, but still, I think you're wrong to even be considering her, Lucas." Sheldon snorted in disgust. "I know he's your client, but a religious fanatic like that Forbes strikes me as a much more likely suspect."

"Like you said, though, he's my client. Anyway, I'm just pokin' around about Wallace, Frank. Chances are I could talk to the heads of the other studios where he worked and find other actresses who might've been mixed up with him. Right now I'm just lookin' for something solid to grab hold of."

"Okay. I'd just hate for Nola's name to get dragged into this."

"You know me, Frank. I can keep my mouth shut."

"Sure, I know. What else can I tell you?"

Hallam leaned forward and crossed his arms on the back of the chair. "Did Wallace have any run-ins with anybody while he was workin' here?"

Sheldon shook his head. "Not that I know of. He was a hard worker and expected everybody else to be, too, but he wasn't a tyrant like DeMille. We got along all right while he was here, but he had loftier goals than we could accommodate at the time. He moved on to the bigger studios, and I was sorry to see him go."

Hallam nodded, then pushed to his feet. "'Preciate your time, Frank. Reckon that's all you can tell me about the feller, though."

Sheldon stood up as well. "I don't feel like I helped you much. You're really convinced that that preacher didn't kill him?"

"He says he didn't."

"Look, Lucas, I've got to tell you... a lot of people didn't like Wallace. The last few years have been tough on this town, what with the Arbuckle thing and Wally Reid and Bill Taylor's murder. The last thing the industry needed was another scandal. So if you're looking for suspects"—Sheldon waved his hand at the window behind him— "you've got your pick of Hollywood."

Hallam reached up and rubbed his craggy jaw. "Thanks for them encouragin' words, Frank. You happen to think of anything more definite, you let me know, will you?"

"Of course." Sheldon came out from behind the desk and put a hand on Hallam's shoulder. "I'm sorry you had to get mixed up with this, Lucas. It's like I've always said about the movies, though: no matter how fancy they get, they're a lot simpler than real life."

"Reckon that's true enough," Hallam agreed. "Be seein' you, Frank."

As he drove away from the studio, Hallam thought

about what Frank Sheldon had told him. Sheldon hadn't been much help, though Hallam made a mental note of Nola McGuire's name. If nothing else turned up, the young actress might be worth a few questions. As he had told Sheldon, though, based on the allegations about Wallace's behavior, there might be dozens of young women in the city with reason to despise him. And any one of them might have hated him enough to go to his house and pull the trigger of a convenient gun.

As for Sheldon's other contention, that the industry in general bore a grudge against Wallace, Hallam didn't doubt it. Depending on the goodwill of the public as the movie business did, it couldn't afford to outrage too many people. A lot of livelihoods were at stake.

But a general anger at Wallace for creating yet another scandal seemed a mighty poor excuse for murder. Wallace had been unable to find work after the floodtide of innuendo; Hallam felt sure that in the minds of most, that was punishment enough. There hadn't even been an official ban of his films, as there had been of Fatty Arbuckle's work.

Hallam considered the morning's activities. He had been busy, all right, visiting the temple, talking to Jeremiah, seeing Frank Sheldon. He had a number of things to think about, including Nola McGuire and the weeping Alice Grey. This was a case with a lot of threads.

But unfortunately he didn't feel like he was one damn inch closer to clearing Elton Forbes.

ELEVEN

ON A SIDE STREET a few blocks from Gower Gulch was a large frame building with a plain exterior that gave no hint of what was inside.

Hallam and his friends called it the Waterhole.

He walked into the speakeasy not long after his talk with Frank Sheldon, and the immediate change from the hot brassy midday outside was welcome. The Waterhole was cool and shadowy, and for the cowboys who had found in the movies a slice of the life they had once known, it was a second home. It was handy to the studios, and the beer was always cold.

The place was busy at this time of day, since you could also get a pretty good chunk of steak cooked up the way you liked it. Hallam paused just inside the door to let his eyes adjust to the dimness, then scanned the crowd of men in Stetsons, jeans, and boots. He spotted Art Acord, Neal Hart, and the youngster known only as Pecos sitting at a table in the back corner.

The three of them nodded a greeting to Hallam as he made his way across the room to join them. All three were in costume, and Hallam knew they must have come here after a morning's shooting.

Art Acord wore a huge black hat pushed back on his head, and he grinned up at Hallam. "Howdy, Lucas," he said. "Rest that ol' carcass o' yourn."

"B'lieve I will," Hallam replied, taking one of the empty chairs and swinging it around so that its back rested against the wall. "You boys been picture-makin'?"

"Doin' some interiors over at Vitagraph," Neal Hart told him. "When we took our lunch break, Art got a hankerin' for some beef steak."

Art Acord and Neal Hart were stars, Art a solid, chunky man wearing a white shirt, a calfskin vest, and chaps over his jeans, Neal a little taller and looking a little more like a matinee idol in a wine-colored shirt and a white hat with a concha studded band. Despite the fact that both of them had played leads in features, they were sitting with Pecos who had never been more than a riding extra. The boy had sand in his craw, though, and would do any kind of stunt gag the director asked for. None of them knew where he came from or what his real name was, but he was rumored to be the son of a very wealthy man who had forsaken his father's lifestyle. If he did come from a rich family, none of his friends held that against him. Men like Acord and Hart didn't put on airs, knowing that their own success was largely a matter of luck.

Now Pecos leaned forward eagerly and said, "Heard about that fracas you was mixed up in last night, Lucas."

Hallam grimaced. "Reckon the whole town's heard about it. Almost wish I never had."

"What happened?"

Art Acord put in, "Could be Lucas don't feel like talkin' about it, boy."

Hallam shook his head. "Reckon I don't mind." Once again, he told the story of what had occurred at Allan Wallace's house. Pecos listened intently, and Hallam could tell that Art and Neal were interested, too, though they continued to attack their steaks with a pretended casualness.

When he was done, Pecos asked, "Who do you think actually killed them fellers, Lucas?"

"Wish I knew, son. That's what I've been tryin' to get a line on all morning."

"You're sure Forbes didn't do it himself?" Neal asked.

Hallam shrugged. "He's my client. Reckon I got to believe him until I find something that proves different."

Art Acord picked up his big mug of beer and swallowed nearly half of it. "You know, I made a picture for Wallace a few years back."

Hallam had been hoping that someone here at the Waterhole might be able to tell him more about the murdered director. He said, "Have any trouble with him?"

Art shook his head. "Not me. 'Course, he was stuck on himself pretty good, and not everybody liked him. He didn't have much trouble rubbin' some people the wrong way."

"Anybody in particular?"

"He rode herd pretty hard on the young feller that was the assistant director, was always on his back about something. That A.D. worked hard, too. Just couldn't seem to please Wallace. The real trouble came when Wallace got interested in a gal who was workin' in the picture. The A.D. had a crush on her, too, but he couldn't compete with Wallace." Art jabbed a massive bite of steak with his fork and stuck it in his mouth. "Thought they was goin' to come to blows over her," he said around the meat.

"You happen to remember the A.D.'s name?" Hallam asked.

Acord squinted in concentration. "Culhane? Collins? Cowling, that was it. Marty Cowling. Nice young feller."

"He still in the business?" The name was unfamiliar to Hallam.

"I think so. Couldn't say for sure, though. That was the only picture we worked together on."

"I remember Cowling," Neal Hart added. "He was the A.D. on a picture of mine last year. Would you like me to hunt him up for you, Lucas?"

" 'Preciate that, Neal. I wouldn't mind talkin' to him."

"Sounds like you think he might be a suspect in this case o' yourn," Art Acord said. "I think you might be barkin' up the wrong tree. Marty wouldn'ta shot nobody."

"Won't hurt to talk to him," Hallam replied. A grin creased his leathery face. "Seems I've spent my day bein' told I'm on the wrong trail."

"Well, I think you are this time. Marty just got mad over that young actress. That's been a long time ago; reckon he's got over Nola by now."

Hallam leaned forward, trying not to look too surprised or interested. "What'd you say, Art?"

"I said Marty's probably got over that girl by now. You losin' your hearin' in your old age, Lucas?"

"What was her name again, the girl's?"

"Nola. Nola McGuire. Sweet little lady, and not a bad actress. Think she decided the picture-makin' life wasn't for her, though."

"Why are you interested in this girl, Lucas?" Pecos asked.

"Her name came up when I was talkin' to somebody else," Hallam said. "Seems Wallace may have had a little fling with her."

"Wouldn't know about that," Art grunted. "I don't snoop in other people's business."

Hallam sensed some disapproval in the other man's tone. "Happens that's what I get paid for," he said.

"Oh, hell, I know that. You got a job to do, just like ever'body else."

A waiter had finally made his way through the press of people in the dimly lit room, and Hallam broke off his conversation with the other three men long enough to order a beer and steak with trimmings, like the others. The beer arrived quickly, and he took a long drink from the mug, the cold flow of it washing away some of the frustration he was feeling.

"Hard pinnin' anything down when Wallace had so many enemies," he mused. "But at the same time, the people I've talked to all got along with him all right themselves. It's always other folks who had it in for Wallace."

"You'll find the killer, Lucas," Pecos assured him. "Ain't no better detective than you."

"Much obliged for the kind words, son," Hallam chuckled. "Wished I was as sure as you seem to be."

"I'll let you know if I turn up Marty Cowling," Neal Hart promised. "Though I agree with Art, Marty's sure not the type to shoot somebody, even somebody he didn't like."

The waiter reappeared, setting a massive plate on the table. The big steak was in the center of it, juices still sizzling, surrounded by potatoes and peas and thick slices of bread. A bowl with a more than generous helping of deep-dish apple pie joined the plate on the scarred wooden surface of the table.

Hallam dug in.

The food was good, as usual, and he was enjoying himself listening to the other three shooting the breeze after finishing their meals. There was a loud mutter of conversation filling the air along with the blue smoke that drifted up from innumerable quirlies. The first hint Hallam had that something was wrong came when the talking and laughter started to die down.

He looked up from his plate. A man was walking toward him, his stride just erratic enough to tell Hallam that he had had too much bootleg booze.

The man was big, topping six feet, with shoulders to match and ham- like hands that hung at the end of the long arms. His boots were old and broken-down, and he wore range clothes that had seen better days. His black hat was a shapeless mass of felt. His blocky face flushed, he stopped by the table and cuffed back his hat, then glowered down at Hallam.

"You that dee-tective?" he asked in a thick voice.

"Reckon I am," Hallam replied quietly. He laid his fork down beside the mostly empty plate.

"Heard you was hell on wheels. Look like a broke-down ol' cowboy to me."

"Look, mister," Pecos said, "nobody asked you to

come over here and bother us. Why don't you go sleep it off?"

The big man didn't even spare him a glance. He spat on the floor and said, "Shut up, younker."

Pecos started to his feet, his face tight and angry. The slim young man was inches shorter and many pounds lighter than the big man, but Hallam knew he wouldn't hesitate to tear into him. He reached out and put a hand on Pecos's arm. "Think this feller's quarrel is with me," he said. "Don't have no idea what it's about, though."

"I've heard a lot about you since I blew into this town," the man said. He leaned over and placed his hands flat on the tabletop. It was an aggressive stance, but it also enabled him to bring his drunken swaying a little more under control. "Figger it was all a pack o' lies," he went on with a contemptuous grin.

Art Acord said quickly, "Friend, anything you heard 'bout Lucas Hallam ain't but a shadow of the truth. You run along now."

The man shook his head slowly, ponderously. "I want to see this he-coon for hisself. Unless you got yeller in your old age, Hallam."

Hallam had seen dramas just like this played out dozens of times in his life. Here lately they had only been make-believe scenes in front of movie cameras, but there had been plenty of occasions when they were all too real, when the blood that flowed wasn't fake.

He didn't feel like rasslin' around with this drunk. But it didn't appear that the man was giving him much choice.

"Don't 'preciate talk like that, mister," he said. "I'll thank you to take it back."

"Why'n hell should I?"

Hallam's hand dipped down below the level of the table and came back up almost faster than the eye could follow. The tip of the Bowie knife gripped casually in his callused palm rested against the man's shirt just below the breastbone.

"'Cause if you don't I aim to let a little air into your gullet," Hallam said. "Simple as that."

The man was suddenly very still, and the blood drained from his face. Hallam's voice had been quiet and calm, but there was no mistaking the menace in it.

"All right, all right," the man muttered. "Lemme just stand up, okay?"

"Sure," Hallam agreed. "Just do it slow. And keep your hands where I can see 'em."

The man straightened up. He took a deep breath to calm his obviously shaken nerves and said, "I was just funnin', Hallam. No call to get so touchy."

"I was born touchy, mister. Don't you forget it. Now, skedaddle."

The man turned with a surly glare and moved away from the table. The room was utterly quiet as he made his way to the door and let himself out. A brilliant shaft of sunlight lanced into the dark room as the door opened, then was chopped off as the panel slammed behind the would-be troublemaker.

"Whooo-eee!" Pecos exclaimed as Hallam slid his Bowie back into its sheath on his left hip. "I reckon you really told him, Lucas!"

"Any of you happen to know that peckerwood?" Hallam asked.

All of them shook their heads. The pleasant buzz of

laughter and talking was beginning to start up again. "Never saw him before," Neal Hart said.

"Me neither," Art Acord echoed.

"You surely put the run on him," Pecos said happily. "Nothin' like a Bowie ticklin' your ribs to sober a man up, is there?"

"Nope," Hallam agreed. "You want to watch that hooch, son. 'Less you want to wind up makin' trouble in saloons and maybe gettin' your gizzard cut out and handed to you."

Pecos nodded. "I'll remember, Pa."

Hallam swiped at him in response to the gibe, knocking his hat down over his eyes. The four of them laughed, and the incident seemed quickly forgotten. Just another drunk on the prod, anxious, maybe, to make a name for himself. Hallam had seen it all before....

But he didn't forget about it. His mind was worrying at it like a hound with a bone, all because of one simple thing.

Despite Pecos's comment about the Bowie sobering up the troublemaker, he hadn't been drunk to start with. When the man had leaned over the table, Hallam had been able to smell his breath.

There was no liquor on it.

Which same meant that the man had been putting on an act, trying to draw him into a fight, a fight that could have turned dangerously ugly when a man who was supposed to be drunk suddenly turned out not to be.

And all Hallam could do at the moment was wonder why.

TWELVE

GLENDALE CALLED itself the Fastest Growing City in America, and Hallam thought there might be some validity to the claim. The place had been a sleepy little suburb only a few years before; but now, following the great land boom in the region, it was starting to sprawl. Housing developments sprang up seemingly overnight, and a flock of potential settlers were crowding into the area.

But the town was still small enough that finding one particular family didn't pose that much of a problem.

Hallam's first stop was the office of the local telephone exchange. The woman who was in charge there supervised two switchboard operators and served as an operator herself. She frowned up at him and pushed the headset off her ears when he asked her where he could find the McGuire family.

"Got several McGuires around here," she told him tersely. "Which one? And why do you want to know?"

"The family I'm lookin' for would have a daughter named Nola, ma'am," Hallam said. "She may not be livin' with her folks anymore, though. I figure she's about twenty now."

"You didn't answer my question about why you're looking for them." She studied him with narrowed eyes. "We watch after our neighbors here, mister. I don't want to cause anybody any trouble."

"No, ma'am, neither do I. But I've got to talk to them, y'see, about some personal business."

The woman's intent gaze suddenly changed to a look of recognition. "I know you!" she exclaimed. "I've seen you in moving pictures, haven't I?"

"Could be, ma'am. I've made a few."

"I knew it. I just knew it." She was excited now, her initial suspicions vanished. "You were in *The Lone Star Ranger* with Tom Mix, weren't you? I just saw it last week."

Hallam grinned, further disarming her. "That was a good 'un, all right."

"Are you and Tom Mix friends?"

"I reckon you could say that."

"I think he's so... so manly. And that horse Tony is so smart! Why, I've never seen the like. Oh, excuse me. I didn't even ask your name."

"Hallam, ma'am. Lucas Hallam."

She waved a finger at him in a mock reprimand. "You were a very bad man in that picture, Mr. Hallam. You shouldn't have given Tom Mix so much trouble."

"Reckon you're right. Ol' Tom, he gave me what was comin' to me, though."

"He certainly did. Now, Mr. Hallam, what was it you wanted to know?"

As he left the telephone office a few minutes later armed with an address for a family named McGuire with a daughter named Nola, Hallam reflected that sometimes being involved with the moviemaking business had its advantages, despite all the hoopla you had to put up with.

He had intended on saving Nola McGuire for later, but he took Art Acord's mention of her as an omen. If her name was going to keep popping up in this investigation, he might as well go talk to her and get it out of the way. Especially since he had the added knowledge now that a young assistant director had clashed with Allan Wallace over her attentions.

Maybe it was grasping at straws, but so far this case hadn't taken on any kind of shape. He had to admit that Elton Forbes was really the strongest suspect; proving him innocent might just turn out to be impossible, especially when the victim had had so many possible enemies. Even if Forbes wasn't guilty—and Hallam told himself he still believed that—pinning down the real killer wasn't going to be easy.

All his life, though, he had faced chores that weren't very easy, and he had come out on top more times than he had failed. He still had lots of plugging away to do on this one.

The McGuires lived on a tree-shaded street of small houses behind neat lawns. Hallam parked the flivver at the curb and went up a sidewalk bordered with narrow flowerbeds. Honeysuckle climbed the porch railing and filled the air with perfume. Bees zipped busily around the blossoms.

Hallam climbed the two shallow steps to the porch and rapped on the doorframe with bony knuckles. There was no response. He waited a minute, then knocked again.

This time the inner door opened. A woman stood there in the opening, looked at him curiously, and said, "Yes?" She didn't offer to open the screen door.

Hallam nodded and kept a carefully neutral expression on his face. "Howdy, ma'am," he said quietly. He didn't want to throw any kind of a scare into the woman. She had to be surprised enough just to find a big cowboy-looking fellow on her front porch.

"My name's Lucas Hallam," he went on, "and I'm lookin' for a young lady by the name of Nola McGuire."

"She's my daughter," the woman answered forthrightly. "She's not here right now, though. Could I ask what your business is with her?"

"Yes, ma'am, you surely can. I'm a detective, and I'd like to ask her a few questions."

"A detective?" Surprise and curiosity were clearly evident on the woman's thin, middle-aged face.

"Yes, ma'am, from Hollywood." That was true enough. He just hadn't mentioned the fact that he was a *private* detective. Maybe this woman hadn't read in the paper about Wallace's murder, and maybe even if she had, she wouldn't remember the name of the man who had been there acting as Forbes' bodyguard.

Mrs. McGuire pushed the screen open and stepped aside to let him in. "Well, if the police want to ask questions, we certainly want to cooperate," she said, a hint of fear in her voice.

"Your daughter's not in any trouble," he said quickly as he stepped into the house, wanting to reassure the woman and not spook her.

"Of course not. Nola's a good girl." Even surprised and a little overawed, Mrs. McGuire wasn't going to believe anything bad about her daughter. And from the tone of her voice, she didn't want anyone saying anything bad about Nola.

"We're just conductin' an investigation and tryin' to establish the whereabouts of a few folks last night," Hallam said.

"What kind of investigation?"

"Well, ma'am... it's a murder case." Hallam hadn't wanted to spring that on her yet, but he wasn't going to out-and-out lie, either.

Mrs. McGuire lifted a hand to her mouth and took a step backward in involuntary reaction.

That was normal enough, Hallam told himself. Best not to leap to any conclusions. Anybody would be a little shocked if they were going about their daily routine and somebody came in and started talking about murder.

He had glanced around the room as soon as he came in. It looked nice enough, with a sofa on one wall and a couple of overstuffed armchairs arranged in opposite corners. A thin woven rug lay on the hardwood floor in the center of the room, and a gas lamp stood on a pole next to one of the armchairs. On the wall above the sofa was a large framed piece of cloth with words embroidered on it. Now Hallam looked closer and read them:

> *But as for me and my house,*
> *we will serve the Lord.*
> *Joshua 24:15.*

"A murder case?" Mrs. McGuire asked in a hushed voice. "There must be some mistake. Nola would never be involved in... in something like that."

"No, ma'am, I'm sure she wouldn't. But she might have some information that could help out."

The woman didn't say anything in reply to that, just stood there catching at her underlip with her teeth. She held her body tense and rigid, and after a long moment, heaved a sigh and lifted a hand to brush back her short gray hair.

"All right," she said. "If you insist on bothering Nola, she works in Mr. Bentley's insurance office as a secretary. I really wish you wouldn't go down there and disturb her, though. Isn't there anything I can do? Perhaps I can answer your questions."

"You might be able to at that, ma'am," Hallam said. "The main thing I need to know is where your daughter was last night."

Relief broke over the woman's face. "Now, you see, I know you've got the wrong girl. Nola was at home last night with her father and myself."

"All night?"

"All night. So she couldn't know anything about any murder last night, now could she?"

"Didn't say the murder took place last night," Hallam pointed out.

An uneasy look flickered through Mrs. McGuire's eyes as she realized that he was right. But then she said, "That doesn't matter. I've told you that Nola was here last night. What else do you want to know?"

Hallam rubbed his jaw. He felt a little uneasy here in this house, as big and rough as he was. And he just didn't feel like browbeating a woman who was only sticking up for her daughter. "Reckon that's about all," he said.

"Are you going down to the insurance office and bother Nola?"

"Don't think that'll be necessary, least not today."

"Very well. I... I appreciate that."

Hallam gestured at the embroidered Bible verse in its frame. "Good words to live by," he commented.

Mrs. McGuire's attitude softened somewhat. "We think so. My husband and I are God-fearing people."

"I'm sure you are. What about Nola?"

"Of course. I told you she was a nice girl. She loves the Lord."

"Actress for a while, wasn't she?"

The suspicion immediately reappeared on the woman's face. "I thought you were through asking questions, Mr.—Hallam, was it?"

"Yes, ma'am. Just makin' conversation."

"Well, I don't think I care for your conversation, Mr. Hallam," she said firmly. "That part of Nola's life is behind her, and I intend to see that it stays that way. She has a good job and a nice young man who calls on her, if it's any of your business, and I think it's time you were leaving now."

"Yes, ma'am." Hallam started toward the door, but he paused to say, "This nice young man courtin' Nola... his name wouldn't be Marty Cowling, would it?"

"Definitely not!" Mrs. McGuire looked like she had bitten into something that had gone bad. "Martin Cowling knows very well that he is *not* welcome in this house!"

"Why's that?"

"Nola... thought she loved him. But he threw her over just because of what happened. He acted like it was her fault because that evil man—"

She broke off and stared at Hallam, horrified.

"It's Wallace, isn't it?" she asked after a moment. "Is he the one that's dead?"

So she hadn't heard yet.

Hallam nodded. "Yes, ma'am. Him and another man who was workin' for him."

"Lord forgive me, but good riddance!" She spat the words out, her face twisted with emotion. "I'm a good Christian, but I've cursed that man many times. I'm glad he's dead!"

"Why do you say that, ma'am?"

She looked up at him, eyes damp now as tears started. "You don't give up, do you? You say you're through asking questions, but you keep dredging up things you've no right to bother us about. We've been bothered enough. Now get out! Just get out!"

Her voice rose, broke, fell to a whisper. "Please just get out."

Hallam stood there for a moment in the heavy silence, then said, "Yes, ma'am. I'm sorry."

He let himself out the front door and went back down the flower-bordered walk to his car.

This detective business sometimes made you feel lower than a snake, he thought as he drove away down the quiet street. You had questions that needed answers, but to get the answers you had to dig around in people's feelings and stir up things that would just hurt them.

He had found someone who had a definite hatred for Allan Wallace, though. It looked like the rumors about Wallace and Nola McGuire were true. At least there had been something there, enough to cause Marty

Cowling to break off any relationship he might have had with Nola.

And it had sounded like Mrs. McGuire didn't like Cowling much more than she liked Wallace. Hallam wondered exactly what *had* happened between the three of them.

He was a long way from any proof, though, that Nola or her parents or Cowling had had anything to do with shooting Wallace and Claude. Maybe when he had talked with Cowling...

Damned if it hadn't been simpler in the old days.

THIRTEEN

HALLAM HAD NEVER PARTICULARLY LIKED the county jail, but he had put off talking to Forbes for about as long as he felt comfortable. He stopped by police headquarters first and cleared the visit with Ben Dunnemore, then went to see his client.

Forbes looked to be in good spirits as he was ushered into a visiting room and took his place across a scarred wooden table from Hallam. He wore the standard jail issue outfit of khaki pants and shirt, but he invested them with a certain dignity. From the way he carried himself, you would have almost thought that he was in his pulpit addressing the faithful.

"Well, Mr. Hallam," he said briskly as he sat down, "I trust you're making progress in your investigation."

Hallam clasped his rawboned hands on the table in front of him. "Not as much as I'd like," he said. "I've done some askin' around, found out that lots of folks 'sides yourself were carryin' a grudge against Wallace, but I'd be lyin' if I said I had any good suspects just yet."

"You mean any good suspects besides myself." A thin, humorless smile tugged at Forbes's wide mouth.

"Reckon things don't look too good," Hallam admitted. "You might could do something that would help us both out, though."

"And what would that be?"

"You could tell me who that gal was and how she ties in with this."

Forbes shook his head. "I told you last night, Mr. Hallam, Emilie has no part in this."

"Beggin' your pardon, Reverend, but she sure as blazes does! She was there, and Wallace had her there for a reason. I figger I can come a lot closer to helpin' you if I know what that reason was."

Hallam's voice was urgent as he spoke, but he could tell that the words were having no effect on Forbes. The evangelist just stared stonily at him and said, "That matter has no bearing on this case, Mr. Hallam. My theory is that someone else who felt animosity toward Wallace took advantage of an opportunity and killed him. Our being there was simply an unfortunate coincidence."

"That thought crossed my mind, too," Hallam said. "In fact, that's the trail I've been on today. Does the name Nola McGuire mean anything to you?"

Forbes looked at him blankly for a moment, then said, "Nola McGuire... I seem to have heard the name. Yes. Yes, I remember now. She was one of the actresses that Wallace was rumored to have corrupted."

"How about Marty Cowling?"

"No, I don't think I know that name. I'm sure I don't."

"Jeremiah?"

Forbes gave that thin smile again. "A very misguided soul."

"He says the same about you."

"You talked to him, then?"

Hallam nodded.

"I didn't want to call the police and report him," Forbes went on. "But when he disrupted our services and refused to leave, I had no other choice. I think that the man means well, but he has deluded himself as to the true nature of God. I suppose Willard told you about the incident."

"One of the elders at the temple brought it up," Hallam said. "I went down to Jeremiah's street corner and talked to him."

"Surely you don't think *he* might have killed Wallace?"

Hallam rubbed a hand along his jaw and then said, "Don't rightly see how he could have. He would have had to follow us from the temple out to Wallace's house, and he don't seem the type to have a car."

"I doubt he has much more than the shirt on his back," Forbes agreed.

"He couldn't have been waitin' at Wallace's house unless he was tied in with Wallace some way, otherwise he wouldn't have known that we were goin' to be there. I guess maybe he *could* have known Wallace, but it don't seem likely."

"Nor to me. Actually, Jeremiah strikes me as harmless, at least physically. There is no calculating the spiritual damage he could do to anyone foolish enough to follow him, though."

"Reckon I'll leave the spiritual end o' things to you,

Reverend." Hallam changed tack abruptly. "How do you and Riley get along?"

"Willard?" Forbes frowned. "Why do you ask?"

"Like to get to know as much about the people involved in a case as I can."

Forbes looked at him for a long moment, suspicion in his eyes. "You can't possibly think that Willard might have something to do with the murders," he finally said. "We're brothers in the Lord, Mr. Hallam, fighters in the same cause. I know that may sound a bit melodramatic, but that's the way it is."

"He come down to see you today?"

"Indeed he did. He and Mark and I had a long discussion about the best ways to keep the temple running smoothly and on course during this unpleasantness."

"This fella Mark would be your lawyer, that right?"

"That's right. Mark Etchison is a member of the temple and also handles all of our legal matters."

Hallam leaned forward. "He ever try a murder case before?"

"Well... not that I know of."

"Well, let me tell you, Reverend, when he gets up in front of that jury, he ain't goin' to be talkin' about 'legal matters.' He's goin' to be talkin' about your *life,* which same the district attorney's gonna try to take away from you. Both of you best remember that."

Forbes swallowed, slightly shaken perhaps by the intensity of Hallam's words. "Are you suggesting that I retain another attorney to handle my defense?"

"I ain't suggestin' nothing. I don't know Etchison; he might be just what you need. But you think on what I said."

Forbes brightened a bit. "Perhaps the case won't even come to trial. I'm sure you'll have found the real murderer by then."

"Hope you're right."

"Do you have anything else to report to me, Mr. Hallam?"

"No, but I've got another question. How close are you to Alice Grey?"

"The girl who plays the organ at the temple?"

"That's the one I mean."

Forbes spread his hands in puzzlement and said, "She is one of my flock. And she is an excellent musician. That's all I really know about her, though."

"Have any idea why she was cryin' when I saw her at the temple this morning?"

"None at all." Forbes smiled. "You see suspicious behavior in everything, don't you, Mr. Hallam? Did it ever occur to you that she was upset because her spiritual leader has been unjustly imprisoned?"

"It occurred to me," Hallam nodded. "But bein' a mite curious is what you're payin' me for, Reverend."

"Quite."

"And I'm still curious about that Emilie." Hallam's voice hardened.

Forbes's reply matched the question in tone. "I suppose you'll have to remain curious, then."

Hallam stood up abruptly. "I've seen mules less stubborn! I'm tryin' to help you, Forbes, but you make it damned hard!"

Forbes was on his feet by the time Hallam was finished, and he was glaring across the table with just as much anger on his face. "I'll thank you not to use profanity in my presence, Mr. Hallam," he snapped. "I thought that you might be able to help right the wrong that has been done here, but perhaps I was wrong. I'm sure there are other private detectives that I could hire to assist in my defense!"

"Damn right there are! You can have your lawyer find one, for all I care."

Hallam swung away from the table and stalked to the door of the visiting room. He stopped with his hand on the doorknob and looked back over his shoulder. Forbes still stood by the table, face set in grim, angry lines. He wasn't going to bend an inch. Hallam could tell that by looking at him.

"Ah, hell," Hallam muttered under his breath. Then he said in a louder voice, "Look, Reverend, I'm already on the case. Anyway, I was there when it happened. Reckon I take the whole thing kinda personal-like. So I'll keep diggin', happen it's all right with you."

"You'll do what you must," Forbes said. "Just as I will."

"Fair enough," Hallam nodded. Then he went out before his anger got the best of him again.

The visit hadn't really accomplished anything, he reflected as he walked down the corridor toward the lobby of the building, accompanied by the guard who had brought him to see Forbes. His weapons, which had been taken before he was escorted to the visiting room, were waiting for him at the reception desk. It would feel good to get them back. Hallam didn't like being unarmed anywhere, and damn sure not when he was in a jail.

All he had learned for sure was that Forbes knew who Nola McGuire was, and that could have come from reading the newspapers at the time of the Wallace scandal. He wasn't a bit closer to the mysterious Emilie.

When he stepped out into the bright afternoon sunlight a few minutes later, he found Ben Dunnemore waiting for him.

"Have a good visit with your client, Lucas?" Dunnemore asked as he fell into step beside Hallam.

"He ain't the most endearing cuss in the world, if that's what you mean," Hallam answered with a grin.

"That's true enough. How's the investigation going?"

"Don't reckon that's any of your business just yet, Ben. No offense."

Dunnemore shook his head. "None taken. I just wanted to let you know that we haven't closed our eyes to other possibilities."

"Meanin' what?"

"Meaning that I'm still poking into this case, too, Lucas. Forbes was arraigned on murder charges this morning, and the D.A. might not like it if he knew I was doing something other than trying to find more evidence to convict him, but damn it, I'm out for the truth, just like you are."

Hallam shot a glance at the police detective. "You ain't convinced that Forbes is guilty?"

"I didn't say that. I think from the evidence I've seen that he probably *is* guilty. But I'm not so muleheaded that I won't give him a fair shake."

A grin creased Hallam's leathery face. "Might be hope for you yet, Ben."

Dunnemore stopped on the sidewalk; they had almost reached Hallam's flivver. "I'm just telling you this so that if you turn up anything you won't be so leery of the cops that you won't bring it to me. I give you my word, Lucas, you find any evidence that might create a doubt and I'll do everything I can with it."

Hallam nodded. "I'll remember that, Ben. And thanks."

"Sure. So long, cowboy."

Hallam waved a hand, climbed into the flivver, and pulled away from the curb, leaving Dunnemore's rumpled figure behind.

The trip to Glendale and the visit to the jail had taken up a sizable chunk of the afternoon, and it was too late now to drive out to Chuckwalla and check on Liz Fletcher. Willard Riley had mentioned that morning that there would be a special service at the temple that evening. He was going to pass on Forbes's reassurances to the flock, as he had put it.

Hallam had decided to attend that meeting.

FOURTEEN

THE LAST TIME he had seen such a fandango was at one of DeMille's premieres. All that was lacking were the spotlights lancing into the night sky.

There wasn't a parking space to be found for blocks around the temple. All of them were taken up, and well over half the vehicles occupying them were long and expensive. There were a few older models scattered along the crowded streets, but by and large the cars were a telling indicator of the standing enjoyed by most of the congregation.

Hallam had to walk more than a quarter of a mile from where he had parked his own car, and by the time he reached the temple his bad leg was starting to ache. He had called the temple earlier and asked the girl who answered when the special service was scheduled to start. She had told him 7:30, and he had timed his arrival so that he would get there just as the meeting was beginning. He had hoped that he could slip in less obtrusively that way.

He hadn't counted on the fact that some of the flock

were used to making late entrances. High society did that to you, he supposed. At any rate, there were several couples just going in as he reached the big front doors of the sanctuary.

The men wore dark, sober suits, the women conservative frocks and hats. There was a lot of expensive jewelry in evidence, though—diamond rings, pearl necklaces, stickpins and brooches and chokers.

He looked out of place in a crowd like that, and he felt their stares on him as he joined them and went into the temple. He was wearing his best suit, but it was old-fashioned and fit him a little tight through the shoulders. His boots were polished. There was no disguising his tall, brawny build, though, or the bearlike gait, the shaggy mane of grey hair, the rugged, weather-hardened features.

The sun was lowering in the western sky and its rays struck directly against the stained-glass windows on that side of the building, creating brilliant patterns of light that fell like shards of colored glass on the thick carpet inside.

Hallam had been to the temple twice before, but he had never seen it like this. He paused in the foyer to look through the open auditorium doors and take in the spectacle.

The massive electric chandeliers were on and blazing in competition with the sunlight. They glittered high above the heads of the crowd, and their glow illuminated the burnished arch of the vaulted ceiling.

The wooden pews were polished to a high sheen, and they were crowded. Almost every seat was occupied, but by craning his neck, Hallam could see that there were some empty pews down front. As he watched, the latecomers made their way up the aisles and took their seats there, and Hallam knew that they were the temple's upper crust, their seats saved and in a position where the rest of the worshipers couldn't fail to notice them. He recognized some of the elders who had talked to him that morning; the others were no doubt already in their places.

There were four carpeted aisles, one running up each side of the auditorium and two more that divided the pews into three separate sections. An usher stood at the back of each aisle, and the four of them stared hard at Hallam as he waited in the foyer, just outside the sanctuary itself but perfectly visible from there. He moved aside to let two more couples go past him and into the temple, and they gave him stern looks as well.

He didn't feel overly welcome.

Far down front and to the side, he could barely make out the blond head of Alice Grey as she played the organ and filled the air with rich, melodious tones. There was an ineffable sadness about the hymn she was playing, and it seemed to Hallam that it would have been more appropriate at a funeral.

Maybe, considering the fix Elton Forbes was in, the song was all too appropriate, Hallam mused.

Blue-robed choir members filled the huge loft that curved around behind the altar. Row after row of them rose up, until the ones on top were a good twenty feet higher than the altar, Hallam estimated. The altar itself was raised at least ten feet from floor level, so taking a tumble from the top row of the choir would mean a pretty good fall, about like rolling down some of the foothills he had seen in his time.

On the back wall of the temple, above the heads of

the choir, was the largest cross he had ever seen. Higher still, above the top of the cross, wooden letters spelling out JESUS SAVES were fastened to the wall. Hallam lowered his eyes from the giant message to the flowers that made the floor area directly in front of the altar look almost like a garden. There were plants of all shapes and sizes and colors, and they all appeared to be fresh. Even in sunny California, that many flowers didn't come cheap.

Flowers also festooned the huge pulpit that stood in the middle of the altar. Hallam saw two big microphones rising from the pulpit, their stands topped with the concentric metal frames that enclosed the actual microphones. Newfangled equipment like that wasn't cheap, either.

In fact, Hallam thought, he had seen whole towns in the old days that might have been able to live for a year on what it had cost to outfit this place.

On either side of the pulpit were rows of chairs. These weren't benches, like the pews down below, but individual chairs with thick cushions covered in rich purple fabric. There were four people on the platform, two on each side of the pulpit, and one of the four was Willard Riley, looking handsome but suitably dignified and sober. As Hallam watched, Riley nodded to the man sitting beside him.

The man got to his feet and walked slowly to the pulpit as the notes of the organ music faded away and down. One of the ushers left his appointed spot and came over to the double doors to close them. Hallam slipped inside just before the usher shut him out. In a whisper that wasn't very friendly, the man asked, "Could I help you find a seat, sir?"

"'This here's fine, son,'" Hallam told him, toning down his natural rumble as much as he could. "I don't mind standin'."

The usher went back to his place with a glare for Hallam, and the man on the pulpit said in a deep, solemn voice, "Let us pray."

He lowered his head and closed his eyes, and the congregation followed suit. Hallam bowed his head but left his eyes slitted.

"Lord, we come to You tonight heavy-hearted," the man intoned, the microphones catching his words and amplifying them with only a little distortion. "We ask that You help us through the trials and tribulations that have been placed on us and on our beloved pastor and Your devoted servant. Let Your presence be a comfort to him, even though he is surrounded by wickedness and set upon by servants of Satan. We know that Thou will sustain him, and us, and will let Your loving hand guide us out of the wilderness. We thank Thee for all Thy blessings and praise Your holy name. Amen."

"Amen," echoed back from the congregation.

The man who had led the prayer went back to his seat, and his place was taken by one of the other men. This one asked the congregation to turn to page 137 in their hymnals and join in the singing of praise. He turned, faced the choir, and motioned them to stand. There had to be at least three hundred of them, but they rose as one. Alice Grey played the prelude on the organ, and then close to a thousand voices launched into song.

The whole shebang was impressive, Hallam had to give them that.

Willard Riley stayed seated where he was, though

he sang along with the hymn. Hallam had been under the impression that he usually led the singing, because he had been rehearsing the choir the night before when he had met Forbes here. Now, though, with Forbes in jail, Riley had evidently moved up a notch for the time being, and somebody else got to direct the choir.

Two more hymns followed the first one, and they were all slow and sonorous. Hallam's suit itched, and he wanted to run a finger around inside his collar. He resisted the urge, though, and reflected that now he remembered why he had never particularly cared to do his worshiping in church. The high country was a hell of a lot more comfortable, and a lot less boring besides.

When the singing was done, the third man took his turn at the pulpit. It was time for the most important part of the service, Hallam realized.

They were going to take up the collection.

The third man announced the offering, and the ushers were joined by several other men to help with the passing of the plates. Hallam watched as the brightly polished silver trays were passed back and forth along the pews. It was a smart touch using metal plates, he thought. That way it would be immediately obvious —and embarrassing for the giver—if anybody dropped change into the collection.

Folding money, on the other hand, didn't make any noise at all.

When the offering was complete, the man at the pulpit offered up another prayer, then a heavy-set woman came down out of the choir, her billowing robe resembling a blue silk tent. As Alice began to play again, the woman took her place in the pulpit and sang a solo that reminded Hallam vaguely of two catamounts on the prod. He was glad when it was over.

Finally, when the soloist had resumed her seat in the choir, Willard Riley got up to speak.

He walked slowly to the pulpit and rested his hands on the sides, leaning forward slightly and letting his solemn gaze play out over the packed auditorium. He drew the pause out dramatically, then took a deep breath and spoke.

"Dear brothers and sisters," he said, "I come to you bearing bad tidings, as most of you no doubt already know. A great trouble has beset our little church. Our brother, our leader, the beloved Reverend Elton Forbes, stands accused of the most heinous sin that a man can commit—the murder of a fellow human being! When Moses was on the mountain, the Lord God told him *'Thou shalt not kill'!*"

He raised his right fist and thundered it down on the pulpit to punctuate the shouted commandment, then leaned forward and grasped the sides of the pulpit once more.

"But the Lord also said unto Moses *'Thou shalt not bear false witness'*! Those who accuse our brother of this crime are but mouthing the lies of Satan! The Devil has brought this tragedy upon us, and it is up to us to fight that devil and his evil minions!"

Hallam wondered if the evil minions Riley was referring to were the district attorney and the police. The D.A. maybe, but Ben Dunnemore damn sure didn't fit into that category.

"The psalmist says that God is our refuge and our strength, a help in our troubles, that we should be not afraid. The Lord shall rest His hand upon us and show us the way!"

Riley paused again and looked out over the congregation, his face stern. When he spoke again, his voice was lower, more intimate, though it still carried to every corner of the temple.

"I have spoken with Brother Elton. He gave me reassurances of something that I already knew quite well. He told me that he is innocent of the crimes of which he has been accused. He asked that I pass along to you, his dear brothers and sisters in the Lord, his promise that he will soon be with us again, leading us in our holy crusade with his goodness and wisdom."

Riley came out from behind the pulpit then, pacing first to one side, then to the other, as he continued, "We went down on our knees together in that jail, my friends, and asked for God's help in this battle! Brother Elton prayed that the Lord would shed His light on the blind eyes of those who are persecuting him. He asked that the Lord give him the strength and the will to endure the lies and the vilifications that are being said about him."

His voice dropped even lower.

"And the Lord will give him that strength. No matter how dark things appear, no matter how evil the accusations, no matter how long it takes to restore Brother Elton's good name, we will persevere together with the help of the Lord."

It was an interesting performance, Hallam thought from the back of the huge room. He was too far away to read all the subtleties of expression in Riley's face, but he could hear them in that powerful, commanding voice. While on the surface he was being reassuring, as

Forbes had requested, his voice took on an added emphasis whenever he mentioned the accusations against his fellow evangelist. Words like *evil* and *sin* cut through the emotion-charged air and brought home to everyone in the place just how serious the whole affair really was.

There was a good chance, in fact, that Elton Forbes wouldn't be coming back to his church.

Which, Hallam supposed, would leave Willard Riley in charge indefinitely.

Might be interesting to see just how much money there was in an average collection....

That was stretching, and Hallam knew it. Still, he didn't see that it would do any harm to talk to Riley and find out just how he had spent his evening between the time Hallam and Forbes left the temple and the time Forbes called him to come down to the jail.

On the platform, Riley had raised his arms to the congregation and now said in a loud voice, "Let us pray, brothers and sisters, pray for Elton Forbes in his hour of need!"

The prayer droned on for several minutes, and Riley managed to work in several more references to the long, hard fight that was in store for Forbes. He was trying to prepare the congregation, Hallam knew, getting them used to the idea that *he* was in charge now and for the foreseeable future.

Riley might be innocent of any complicity in the murders of Wallace and Claude, but the man knew how to make the most of an opportunity, Hallam thought.

About the only thing that could foul him up now

would be if somebody actually solved the murders and cleared Forbes of the charges.

And if he had needed any more reasons to do just that, Hallam thought, the idea of upsetting Riley's apple cart was a mighty appealing motive.

Riley closed the prayer with a thunderous "Amen!" and then an unobtrusive signal to Alice Grey started the music again. The congregation stood and started to flow out into the aisles. One of the ushers started toward the doors, but Hallam was right there and beat him to the job of opening them. He slipped into the foyer before the crowd got there, and moved on outside, leaving the doors open behind him.

The sun had gone down during the service, and Hallam could see a faint glow in the western sky as he walked quickly to the corner of the building. He glanced back as the first of the worshipers came out through the doors. They seemed subdued, and there was none of the chattering and laughter that usually accompanied a departing church crowd.

Hallam turned into the narrow alley that ran down the side of the temple. When he had walked up earlier, he had spotted a side entrance around here, and he was hoping it would be unlocked. He wanted to get Willard Riley alone for a few minutes and ask him a couple of questions, and he had figured that making his way up the aisles against the flow inside would be too slow.

As he strode down the alley, he looked up at the sky and saw the stars beginning to emerge as the last glow of sunlight faded. The massive steeple that had been erected on top of the temple cut off some of the sky, thrusting sharply into the soft, black velvet like a giant dagger.

The door of the side entrance was heavy and wooden, but the knob turned under Hallam's grasp and the panel swung open on well-oiled hinges. He stepped inside and shut the door behind him.

He was in a corridor that seemed to run the width of the building at the rear. On the wall to his right, two widely spaced doors opened into the auditorium, if he had his bearings right. Organ music came strongly from behind the nearest door, which meant it was close to Alice Grey's position and that she hadn't finished playing as the congregation left.

There were more doors on the left-hand wall, but these were smaller and closer together. Hallam tried the first one he came to and found that it led into a small, sparsely furnished office. There was a desk, a chair, a typewriter, and a metal filing cabinet, no doubt where some of the temple's records were kept. A look through these files, and any others he might find in these rear offices, might turn up something interesting or important, but he didn't have the time for snooping. As he stood there, the organ music stopped.

He had taken a step back toward the hall door, which he had left open about a foot, when he heard another door open and close. The sound of voices followed as soon as the other door had been shut.

"You're upset, sister. The strain of seeing Reverend Forbes in such a predicament has unnerved you."

That was Riley's voice, his tones low and persuasive.

"I am not unnerved, as you put it, Reverend Riley. I'm angry!" a woman's voice shot the reply back at him.

"Now, Alice," Riley said, "you don't want to be like that. Anger is an ugly emotion, my dear."

"So is ambition."

Hallam stayed right where he was. He hadn't heard Alice Grey's voice until now, but he was sure that was her talking to Riley out in the hall. The last time he had seen her she had been weeping and upset, but she sounded downright feisty tonight.

"I'll forgive you for that," Riley said, but there was an edge of something else in his own voice now. "You're upset, and you don't know what you're saying."

"Father forgive them, for they know not what they do? Is that it, Reverend?" The words were tinged with bitterness, and they drew a sharp intake of breath from Riley.

"There's no need to be blasphemous," he said. "I won't listen to you when you're like this, Alice. You come and see me when you've calmed down. Perhaps then I can explain to you that these suspicions of yours are groundless. Satan is toying with your mind."

"You'd know. Now leave me alone."

"I hate to see you like this. Here, if you would only *let* me comfort you—"

There was a sharp little cry, then Alice Grey exclaimed, "Get away from me! I heard the stories about you, but I never really believed them until now."

Hallam heard the patter of rapid footsteps down the hall toward the office where he waited, then they stopped suddenly. Riley barked, "Wait a minute! I won't have you going around spreading evil rumors. The temple has enough trouble right now."

"Let go of me," Alice said, a tremor in her voice now.

"I'm just trying to reason with you—"

"Let me go!"

Inside the little office, Hallam grimaced. Under his breath, he said, "Ah, hell..."

Then he stepped out into the hall and said harshly, "Reason with me, Riley."

A few feet away, Willard Riley and Alice Grey stood frozen in poses that were definitely hostile. Riley's hand was on her upper arm, and Hallam could tell that the grip was tight enough to hurt. Alice's back was to Hallam, but she turned her head enough to see him. Riley stared over her shoulder at the big detective. His face was flushed, the features drawn.

"Mr. Hallam!" he exclaimed after a couple of seconds. "What are you doing here?"

"Came to see you," Hallam said.

With a visible effort, Riley calmed himself and put a strained smile on his face. "What can I do for you?"

"You can start by lettin' the lady go, like she asked," Hallam told him.

Riley said, "I don't think you understand," but he released Alice's arm and stepped past her to face Hallam.

"I understand that you're botherin' Miss Grey," Hallam rumbled. He felt a familiar tension in his shoulders. Riley was a big man, but Hallam didn't particularly care at that moment whether the preacher backed down or not.

"I was just trying to comfort Alice—" Riley began, but he broke off when the girl moved smoothly between them.

"It's all right, Mr. Hallam," she said. "We haven't been introduced, but I'm Alice Grey."

"Yes, ma'am," Hallam nodded. "You play that organ real nice; I enjoyed listenin' to you."

"Thank you, Mr. Hallam." She cast a nervous glance over her shoulder at Riley, then went on. "I appreciate what you're trying to do, but I'm all right, really. I... I don't want to cause any trouble."

"No trouble, ma'am," Hallam said, speaking to her but looking at Riley. "If you don't mind me interruptin', I'd sort of like to talk to the reverend here."

"Of course." She moved past him, walking quickly down the hall toward the side entrance of the temple. Hallam stayed where he was, his presence making sure that Riley didn't get any ideas about following her.

When she had gone outside and the door was shut behind her, Riley glared at Hallam and said with barely controlled anger, "That wasn't necessary, Hallam."

"Looked necessary to me," Hallam replied coolly. "Looked like the young lady didn't want any comfortin', leastways not from you."

"She's a little fool. All she can see is the great Elton Forbes—"

He stopped abruptly, aware that he was giving away too much of his real feelings. Hallam thought he had Riley pretty well sized up now, and he didn't like the man. Not one bit.

That didn't make him guilty of murder, though.

"Reckon you mean your brother in the Lord, your beloved leader," Hallam said, his voice cold.

Riley's mouth tightened. "What do you want, Hallam?"

"Main thing I want is to know what you were doin' last night after Forbes and I left here."

Riley stared at him, then a sudden laugh ripped from him. "You can't think that I had anything to do with the murders!" He shook his head. "Oh, no, Hallam. Elton has to face up to that himself."

"A little while ago you were convinced that he was innocent... or was that just a show for the congregation?"

Riley started to turn away. "I don't have to talk to you," he said contemptuously.

Hallam's hand came down hard on Riley's shoulder, stopping him in his tracks. Hallam wasn't too careful about holding back.

"I asked you a question, mister," he grated. "Don't recall you answerin' it."

Riley looked down at the thick fingers digging into his shoulder, then up at the cold blue eyes boring into his. He swallowed. "I could call for help," he said.

"Do that. And I'll tell the elders about you tryin' to molest Miss Grey."

"They'd never take your word over mine!"

"Try me."

Riley swallowed again. "All right, all right," he said. He twisted his shoulder out of Hallam's grasp. Hallam let him go. "This is ridiculous, but if it's an alibi you're looking for, I was right here last night after the two of you left. Choir practice went on for at least another forty-five minutes, probably an hour. After that I went home. But I have plenty of witnesses to prove that I couldn't have followed you and Elton to Wallace's house."

"Forbes tell you where he was goin' before we left?"

"No. No, he didn't. But I can't prove that. Surely you see, though, that I couldn't have been involved!"

Hallam had to admit that if Riley had been at the temple for at least forty-five minutes after he and

Forbes left, it was really stretching it to think that the assistant minister could have gotten to Wallace's house in time to commit murder. It was damn near impossible, in fact.

Which was a shame. Considering the fact that Riley was an ambitious hypocrite who lusted after Forbes's position—and after Alice Grey as well—it wouldn't have bothered Hallam at all to prove that he was a killer, too.

But facts were facts.

"I'll be talkin' to people and checkin' on your story," Hallam growled.

"You do that," Riley snapped. Now that the potential for violence seemed to have eased, he was getting some of his self-confidence back. "Just stay out of my way."

"Long as you stay outta mine."

Riley glared at him for a moment, then squared his shoulders and stalked away. Hallam watched him disappear into one of the offices and made a mental note of which one it was.

There didn't seem to be any more to be accomplished here at the moment. He went to the side entrance and opened it, glad that none of the other church officials had come along during the altercation with Riley. If they had witnessed it, they might have become more difficult for him to deal with, and he wasn't through asking questions around the temple just yet.

He didn't think Riley would be telling anybody about what had happened in the rear hall. The incident would be more damaging to him than it would to Hallam, if the true facts of it came out.

Hallam started down the alley toward the street. He hadn't gone ten feet when a soft voice stopped him.

"Mr. Hallam," Alice Grey said, "can I talk to you?"

She came out of the shadows of the alley, blond hair shining in the starlight.

Hallam had already decided that he was going to have to have a talk with Alice, and this was as good a time as any. He said, "Sure. What can I do for you?"

"Thank you for what you did... in there. I'm sure Reverend Riley meant well, but he was... well, bothering me. Of course, I was upset to start with; he may not have meant anything."

"Wouldn't count on that," Hallam told her. "I reckon you've got him figured about right."

"You didn't have to... strike him, did you?"

"Nope. Reckon he's got a little sense."

Alice's hands were clasped together in front of her, and she was looking off down the alley, having trouble meeting Hallam's gaze. It was clear that the situation was embarrassing for her. Finally she said, "You're trying to help Elton, aren't you, Mr. Hallam?"

"He's my client. Anyway, I don't figure he's a killer. He don't strike me as the type."

"Oh, he's not! He's the nicest man you could imagine—"

Hallam waited a moment for her to go on, then when she didn't he said quietly, "Reckon you think pretty highly of him."

"Yes. Yes, very highly."

"When I saw you this mornin', cryin' in that storeroom... had you just found out that he was in jail?"

"Reverend Riley had told me just a little while earlier. I... I couldn't believe it, I just couldn't believe that Elton was in jail, that he was accused of murdering two men. I'm afraid I... I broke down for a while."

"You seem to be bearin' up well tonight."

Now she looked at him, eyes bright in the gloom. "Elton would want me to carry on with my duties. I have a responsibility to the temple."

She sounded sincere, and Hallam believed her. He asked, "How did Riley sound when he broke the news to you this morning?"

"He was properly upset and solemn." A grim little laugh came from her. "I think he wanted to comfort me then, too."

"You don't like Riley much, do you?"

"Oh..." Again her hands twisted together. "It's very unchristian of me, but... no, I don't. I don't trust him. He's too friendly with the young ladies in the temple."

"Is he married?"

"No."

"Could be he's lookin' for a wife."

Alice laughed again. "I don't think marriage is what Reverend Riley has in mind."

Hallam looked at her and said, "I come from a time when we believed in plain talk, ma'am. Willard Riley looks to me like a scoundrel and a woman-chaser."

"In plain talk, Mr. Hallam—that's what he is."

"I don't reckon he's too unhappy 'bout Forbes bein' in jail, neither. That leaves him in charge here. Seems he might like for things to stay that way."

"I'd say that's an accurate assumption, Mr. Hallam."

"Riley claims he was here at the temple at least forty-five minutes after Forbes and I left last night. Is that right?"

Alice Grey sighed heavily. "I know what you're

getting at. You want to know if it's possible he could have followed you and been the actual killer of those men. I'm sorry, Mr. Hallam. Choir practice went on for closer to an hour after you and Elton left. I don't think Reverend Riley is a killer, either. If I could put him in Elton's place, though, and clear Elton's name..."

"Wouldn't do no good to lie," Hallam told her. "Not with as many other witnesses Riley could come up with. 'Sides, you wouldn't want to send an innocent man to jail, not even one as downright unpleasant as Riley." He paused a moment, not totally willing to give up his suspicions, then asked, "Did Riley and Forbes have any trouble between them in the past? A problem over runnin' the temple or anything like that?"

"I don't think they always agreed on things, but there was no real trouble. Elton is so forceful. He didn't have a problem getting other people to see things his way."

Hallam didn't really think of Forbes as forceful, but he supposed under the right circumstances, it was possible. The whole temple operation bore his stamp, and he was responsible for making it grow into what it had become. That had taken a lot of leadership ability.

"No ruckus over money, or anything like that?"

Alice shook her head. "Reverend Riley, despite his ambition and his other faults, is an honest man, I believe. He wouldn't steal from the temple. Even if he had, Elton would have found out about it, and he would not have tolerated it, no matter what explanations Reverend Riley might have had."

This was turning into a dead end all the way around. Just as he had thought, Riley had all the makings of a no-account bastard, but that didn't make him a killer.

Hallam inclined his head toward the side entrance through which both of them had come. "Not many folks use that door, do they?"

"Not many. The congregation always leaves through the front doors. Some of the staff might come out this way from time to time."

"We'd best move along. Don't reckon it'd do much for your reputation to be caught talkin' to a cowboy in an alley."

The stars overhead cast enough light that he could see her smile shyly. "I doubt that being seen with a gentleman like you would damage anyone's reputation, Mr. Hallam."

"Don't be too sure of that, gal," he said as he took her arm and started to walk with her toward the street. "Time was, I was considered a mite wild and woolly."

"Yes, but that was a long time—I mean—"

Hallam grinned. "I reckon I know what you mean. And don't you worry about it for a second. Shoot, you're right; it was a long time ago."

Most of the congregation seemed to have left Hallam had seen quite a few of the big expensive cars go past on the street as they had stood talking in the alley. The curbs weren't nearly as crowded now as when he had arrived. As he and Alice reached the sidewalk, he reached up with his free hand and yanked loose the string tie that was around his neck.

He turned his head as he loosened the collar and said, "There. That's a whole heap better..."

Behind them, someone opened the side entrance of the temple, and light spilled out into the alley. From the corner of his eye, Hallam caught a flicker of movement against that light.

He shoved Alice hard to the side and went the other way in a dive.

A gun roared, echoing hollowly in the alley, and the muzzle flash split the shadows.

Even as he landed on the hard sidewalk, Hallam saw Alice Grey sprawled several feet away. She gave a startled cry and started to stand up. Hallam yelled, "Stay down!"

She was almost out of the line of fire where she was. It was up to him to distract the gunman and keep his fire away from her.

He figured it was him the bushwhacker was after, anyway.

Hallam surged to his feet. He was unarmed, and the lights of the street were at his back, making him a good target.

He didn't have time to worry about that. He started down the alley at a shambling run.

The gun cracked again, and he could tell from the sound of it that it was a heavy caliber pistol. The roar of its blast drowned out any sound of a passing bullet, but he felt the old familiar breeze of passing lead close by his cheek.

From the side entrance of the temple, someone shouted, "Hey! What's going on out there?"

Hallam saw the shadowy shape of the ambusher as the man turned and began to run. Like most backshooters, he didn't have the grit to stand up and face off with his target. If the first couple of shots didn't do the trick, he was ready to turn tail and try again later.

The pounding of running feet came to Hallam's

ears, and he put on more speed as he saw the gunman brush past whoever it was who had come from the temple. As Hallam passed the side entrance, the man cried out, "Mr. Hallam, what—" Then Hallam was by him, having taken only a split-second to glance at the man and see that he was one of the elders.

The far end of the alley opened into another street, this one more dimly lit than the one that ran in front of the temple. There was enough of a glow from a distant streetlight to show Hallam the fleeing form of the gunman as he emerged from the alley and turned left.

If he had a car waiting...

Hallam heard an engine cranking for long seconds, then sputtering to life. Just as he reached the end of the alley, he saw a Model T pull away from the curb and start to gather speed. If he had been twenty-five years younger, he could have run after it and caught up, he was sure.

But there had been too many years, too many wounds. His leg was throbbing already. If he had had his Colt, he could have blown the Ford's tires right off their wheels, but that was useless speculation, too. The Colt was blocks away, in his own flivver.

Hallam watched the Ford squeal around a corner and disappear. His face might have been carved out of solid rock.

The temple elder met him as he limped back up the alley. "What's wrong, Mr. Hallam?" he demanded. "What happened out here?"

"Reckon somebody just tried to ventilate this ol' carcass," Hallam replied. The elder hurried along beside him, trying to match his long strides, but Hallam paid little attention to him. He was more worried about Alice Grey.

To his relief, she was on her feet as he reached the sidewalk, and seemed to be all right. She ran to him and caught his hands.

"Someone was shooting at us, Mr. Hallam!" she exclaimed. Her hands were trembling in his. "You saved my life!"

"Sorry about havin' to sling you around like that," he rumbled. "Didn't have much time to think about it after I spotted that yahoo with the gun."

"Are you all right? When I realized what was going on, and when I saw you go charging down the alley after him, I was so frightened—"

"You get a look at him when he ran past you?" Hallam asked the elder.

"I didn't get a good look at anything!" the man answered, exasperated. "I'm still not sure what's going on."

Hallam looked off into the night, a thoughtful expression on his craggy face. "Reckon I'm gettin' too close to something," he muttered. "Or some-*body*."

FIFTEEN

HALLAM HAD a few extra aches and pains when he hauled himself out of bed the next morning. Diving onto concrete sidewalks wasn't the easiest thing in the world on old bones.

Maybe the impact had jarred something loose in his brain, though.

As on the previous night, he had spent some long, sleepless hours trying to come up with a handle on this case. He had found out quite a bit in his poking around the day before, and he didn't doubt that there were quite a few folks with a motive for wanting Allan Wallace dead. And there were at least as many who wouldn't mind seeing Elton Forbes framed for a double murder.

Despite that, he wouldn't have felt like he was making any real progress if it hadn't been for a couple of things.

First was the incident at the Waterhole. If he had let that supposedly drunk cowboy push him into a fight, he might well have wound up dead. The man had looked like the type that someone could hire for just that sort of dirty work. And in the confusion, the fellow could've slipped away from the speakeasy.

Then, of course, there was the attempt on his life at the temple. Hallam didn't believe for a second that the shots had been meant for Alice Grey or anyone else.

Nope, he was the bull's-eye on somebody's target, and he didn't like the feeling one damn bit. The way he figured it, he had seen or heard something important, something he wasn't even aware that he knew yet.

Now he was going to have to keep digging, in self-preservation if nothing else.

Alice had been mighty upset the night before, which was easy to understand. She wasn't used to guns going off, especially in her direction. Hallam had calmed her down the best he could and sent her home, assuring her that nobody else would bother her. To make certain of that, he had followed her in the flivver and watched until she was safely inside her little bungalow a few miles from the temple. Then he had gone home to try—mostly unsuccessfully—to get some sleep himself.

Staring up at the ceiling of his darkened bedroom, he had kept seeing a face that was by now familiar to him, though he had seen it in the flesh for only a few seconds.

Emilie.

Dark hair, soft, shining, parted in the middle to fall in gentle waves around her face. Wide blue eyes... the mirror of an innocent soul? She was young, no more than twenty, Hallam would guess.

About the same age as Nola McGuire.

And about the same age as that other actress, the

one that Forbes had converted to help start all of Wallace's troubles. What was her name? Miller? Judy Miller?

Three young women, Hallam thought. Young and pretty. Were there any other links between them? Nola McGuire and Judy Miller had both been exploited by Wallace, who had taken advantage of their ambition to star in the movies.

Could the same thing have happened to the mysterious Emilie?

Forbes's reaction on seeing her in Wallace's house had been too strong for that, Hallam thought. From the look of stunned surprise on his face, the note of disbelief and panic in his voice as he first whispered, then cried out her name, she was something more to him than an actress to whom he had shown the light.

Like a daughter, maybe?

Hallam had considered the idea that perhaps she and Forbes had been lovers, then discarded it. Forbes was too old to have had any kind of romantic entanglement with a teenage girl. Hallam had known plenty of men who lost their heads over a young filly, but he would have bet the ranch that Forbes wasn't the type.

Now, as he stood leaning in the open door of his apartment, sipping a cup of coffee and watching the early morning sunlight washing over the palm trees and flower beds that lined the road, Hallam knew that the answers he needed were in the past, buried there along with Elton Forbes' beginnings as an evangelist. It was time to take up that trail. For that, he would need help.

THEY KNEW him at the morgue of the *Citizen*. A newspaper morgue was one of the best sources of free information that a detective had; Hallam's stint as a Pinkerton had taught him that, among other things. He had made an effort to become friends with the folks down at the *Citizen,* and it had paid off several times in the past.

Gladys Wilks was on duty at the morgue when Hallam clattered down the iron steps to the big musty basement room. Her daughter was a secretary at one of the studios, and Hallam had become Gladys's friend for life by promising to keep an eye on the girl. Actually, the daughter was quite sensible and level-headed and didn't need anyone watching over her, but Hallam didn't tell her mama that.

"Howdy, Gladys," Hallam greeted her, his voice booming hollowly against the low ceiling. "Reckon you could do me a favor?"

She smiled up at him, her position behind a big desk making her seem even more diminutive than she really was. She was a widow lady and not hard on the eyes, and Hallam had suspected more than once that she had designs on him.

"I think I can manage a favor for you, Lucas," she said sweetly. "But when are you going to come over and have Sunday dinner with us?"

"Soon's I clear up this whole mess o' problems I already got on my plate," he told her with a grin.

She sighed. "I guess that'll have to do. I swear, Lucas Hallam, you're a hard man to pin down for something as simple as a dinner invitation."

Somehow, Hallam doubted it was all that simple. He changed the subject by saying, "I need all the information you can give me on Elton Forbes and his church."

Gladys nodded briskly and stood up. "I've been reading about the case in the paper. I wondered how long it would be before you came to see me." She waved a hand at the tables in the front of the room. "You sit down, and I'll bring the items to you."

With that, she disappeared into the rows upon rows of tall filing cabinets that filled most of the room. Hallam sat down at one of the tables, took out a pad of paper and the stub of a pencil.

Gladys came back a few minutes later carrying a thick wad of clippings. She placed them on the table in front of Hallam and said, "This is just the start of it. The man's good copy."

"Can see that," Hallam grunted. He picked up the first clipping as Gladys went back for more.

It was a story about the dedication of the newly remodeled temple, and included was a list of some of the dignitaries in attendance. As Hallam scanned the list he recognized many of the names. He had already known that Forbes' flock had some well-known and influential members; he had met some of them on the Board of Elders and seen others at the service the night before. But he was still surprised at some of the names he saw now. The old rich, the new rich, and every kind of rich in between.

Forbes had a real knack for attracting sinners with plenty of money.

Couldn't hold that against the man, though, Hallam thought. If folks wanted to give you honest money, only a fool turned it down. Elton Forbes was no fool. He just had some stubborn, unexpected blind spots.

Like Emilie.

Hallam went to the next clipping, which was a short article announcing a week-long revival at the temple. Others in the same vein followed, detailing various happenings at the church. The dates on the stories were going backward, Hallam noted. None of them contained much specific information on Forbes. The stories referred to Forbes as the "fiery evangelist from the Midwest" and other similar phrases, and some compared him to Billy Sunday, but there was nothing there that Hallam didn't already know.

Willard Riley was also mentioned in a few places, the article writers calling him Forbes's "dynamic young assistant minister." There was nothing else about his background.

Gladys returned with more clippings and asked, "Finding what you're looking for?"

Hallam shook his shaggy head. "Not yet. Never know when you'll run across something important, though, so keep 'em comin'."

"Sure. One more trip ought to do it."

Hallam began rummaging through the new batch of clippings. The first ones were more of the same, but he noticed as he glanced over the stories that a trend was developing. Forbes's success as an evangelist was more of a new thing the farther back the stories went. Hallam found one clipping that mentioned Riley becoming associated with the temple, indicating that its growth now warranted an assistant for Forbes.

It was like turning back the clock, Hallam thought, and being able to watch time flow in reverse. The stories were starting to give him a picture of Forbes, first as the powerful, successful man that he had been until two nights before, then as an up-and-coming force in the city's religious circles, then finally as an intriguing newcomer to Los Angeles. For all its burgeoning growth, the town still had some of the community feeling left, and a new preacher was still a newsworthy item.

Especially one who had just conducted a spectacularly successful revival, packing the worshipers in at an old storefront that would one day become a glorious temple.

Hallam found what he was looking for in this last story. He remembered reading it at the time it first appeared, but he had forgotten most of the background details on Forbes that it included. Now, with the clipping spread out in front of him, he used the stub of pencil to start making notes in a scrawling hand.

Elton Forbes, according to the newspaper story, came to Los Angeles from a small town in Kansas called Holloway, where he had been a professor of English and philosophy at Holloway Teachers College. He gave up the academic life in order to answer a call from God and spend the rest of his life spreading the Gospel. If he had any formal religious education or training, the paper didn't mention it. Nor did it mention if he had ever been formally ordained by any recognized church. Hallam doubted that he had.

There was no explanation of how Forbes had gotten from Kansas to California. Maybe he had just followed the sinners, Hallam thought.

He checked the date on the clipping again. Forbes had been in Los Angeles about six months at the time the story was written. Hallam wondered what those first six months had been like.

"That's all I could dig up," Gladys said as she handed him a third sheaf of clippings. This one was smaller than the first two groups.

Hallam thumbed through the stories and saw that they detailed the period of time he had just been wondering about. He plucked the bottom one from the pile, glanced at the date, and knew that this was probably the first mention of Elton Forbes in the *Citizen*.

It was a small item, only a few lines long, announcing that a religious service would be held the next Sunday morning and that Forbes would be bringing the message. It gave the time of the meeting and the address of the storefront, and that was all.

Hallam kept working from the bottom of this pile, reading the stories in chronological order this time instead of going backward as he had with the others. The next two clippings were not news stories at all, but rather small advertisements that had run in the religious section of the paper. Forbes had already begun calling his church the Holiness Temple of Faith by the time of the second service. The first ad mentioned only that Forbes would be preaching, but the other one made Hallam's eyebrows quirk in interest.

In very small print at the bottom of the ad, Alice Grey was listed as the organist.

So, Alice had been with Forbes almost from the first. When asked about her, though, Forbes had responded very casually, almost as if he had trouble remembering who Hallam was talking about.

Either he had been putting on an act, or he was actually so self-centered that he just didn't think much about the people around him. Hallam hated to admit it about a client, but he wasn't sure which was true.

The other clippings told a story of slow but steady growth for several months. The rate of growth picked up dramatically when Forbes began to attract wealthy members of society to his services. What had first drawn those people to the temple was still a mystery to Hallam, but there was no denying the effect they had on Forbes and his newly formed church. They had given it a base, and the present influential makeup of the congregation was built on that base.

A thought occurred to Hallam as he flipped through the clippings, and he turned back to the first two bunches to make sure of his idea. Sure enough, many of the stories were bylined J. Emerson Drake. His name turned up more than any other. Hallam didn't know the man, but he assumed that Drake was the reporter who got assigned to most of the religious stories.

He wondered for a second which reporter had been given the murders and the follow-up, then decided he didn't want to know. Reading in the paper about a case you were working on was usually a bad thing. You could get things all fouled up if you paid too much attention to the reporters.

Still, it might be worth his time to have a little talk with J. Emerson Drake.

He gathered up the clippings into one pile and shoved back his chair. Gladys came hurrying over to him as he stood up. "Did you find everything you needed, Lucas?" she asked.

"Maybe," Hallam replied as he handed the clippings back to her for refiling. "If I didn't, reckon you'll let me come back and look some more?"

"Any time, Lucas, any time."

"One more thing..."

"Yes?" The eagerness was evident in her voice.

"You got any idea where I could find a feller name of J. Emerson Drake?"

Her smile lost some of its brightness, but it didn't desert her entirely. "Drake? He's usually somewhere around the city room," she said.

"Thank you kindly." Hallam nodded to her. "Be seein' ya, Gladys."

"Good-bye, Lucas."

Hallam took note of the wistful tone in her voice as she bid him farewell, and his steps up the iron staircase got a little faster. There was something about widow women that could spook a man a mite....

The city room of the *Citizen* was on the second floor, and it was filled with the clatter of typewriters and the pounding thump of the press downstairs. Hallam stopped at the first desk he came to and asked the man working there where he could find J. Emerson Drake.

The man didn't look up, just jerked a thumb over his shoulder and grunted, "Back in that corner."

Hallam looked in the direction indicated and saw a white-haired man hunched over a typewriter, slowly and laboriously pecking at the keys. "Much obliged," Hallam said to the man he had questioned. He got no response, so he shrugged and began making his way across the crowded room.

"Mr. Drake?" Hallam asked when he stood in front of the white-haired man's desk.

The man lifted his head and peered up at him through thick glasses. "Yes? Can I help you?"

"Name's Lucas Hallam. Reckon I could talk to you for a few minutes?"

Drake stared, clearly puzzled by what this big cowboy might want with him. "Well, I do have a deadline to meet," he said slowly. Then he appeared to make up his mind and let his curiosity get the better of him. "But I suppose I can spare a few minutes. Have a seat, won't you?"

Hallam sank down on a wooden chair that he didn't totally trust with his weight. Balanced there, he said, "Been down in the morgue lookin' over some stories you wrote about Elton Forbes. Reckon you could tell me some more about him?"

Drake looked at him with growing interest. "Hallam... ," he mused. "You wouldn't be that private detective who's mixed up with Forbes, now would you?"

Hallam leaned forward and regarded Drake intently. "Happen I am, would that make a difference?" he asked.

"Oh, yes, indeed, Mr. Hallam." Drake's eyes were sparkling now behind the glasses. "You see, I've been a reporter for a long time. I've covered a great many different types of stories. But in the last few years, as I've grown older, the editors have decided that I couldn't handle certain stories anymore. They give the best ones to the young go-getters. That's how I got stuck writing the religious news." He sighed and shook his head. "I'd love to show those youngsters that I can still handle a hot story."

"No point in beatin' around the bush," Hallam said when the reporter paused. "What do you want in exchange?"

"You're conducting your own investigation into the Wallace murder, aren't you?"

Hallam nodded.

"I want the story," Drake said bluntly. "Whatever you come up with, I want it. Exclusively." He grinned. "A nice hot murder story would show some of the people around here a thing or two."

Hallam had to grin back at him. "Reckon I know how you feel. A few folks have tried to put *me* out to pasture, too."

"Then we have a deal?"

Hallam extended a big hand across the desk and said, "Deal."

Drake shook with him, then said rather sheepishly, "I'm afraid I may have struck this deal under false pretenses, Mr. Hallam. I'm not sure I know anything about Forbes that you haven't already found out."

"Did you ever talk to him much when you were writin' stories about him?"

"I interviewed him a couple of times, primarily for background."

"That's what I'm interested in," Hallam said. "He tell you much about his life 'fore he came out here?"

"Not a great deal. I know he was a professor at some small teachers' college in Kansas..."

"Holloway, Kansas," Hallam supplied.

"That's right, Holloway. He taught English and philosophy, there, I believe. They speak English in Kansas, I suppose, but I'm not sure what sort of philosophy they have."

Drake smiled at his little joke. Hallam didn't bother telling him that in the Kansas he had known, philosophical discussions usually centered around who was quicker on the draw with a hogleg.

"Anything unusual about Forbes' life there?" he asked.

Drake shook his head. "If there was, it was well-concealed."

"Was he married?"

"Not that I know of. He said nothing about a wife, but he did mention having a room in a boardinghouse not far from the campus. So I doubt that he was married."

"Did he ever say why he left teachin' and decided to preach?"

Drake picked up a pencil, leaned back in his chair, and tapped on his teeth reflectively. "You know, I asked him that very question," he said after a moment. "Never did get a good answer out of him. Never did get any kind of answer from him. And I approached the question from several different angles. It was very frustrating."

Hallam, remembering his own futile questioning of Forbes, could sympathize with the reporter. He clasped his hands together in front of him and said, "Seems to me folks don't just up 'n' move halfway across the country without a mighty good reason. Reckon something happened to Forbes to make him change?"

Drake nodded thoughtfully. "You may have something there. He was certainly evasive when I tried to ask him what led him to California. Something dramatic may have occurred that caused him to change his life completely."

"That's what I was thinkin'."

"But what could that have to do with Wallace's murder? The way I understand it, there was bad blood between Wallace and Forbes because Wallace blamed him for that scandal a few years back."

Hallam inclined his head in agreement. "There is

that," he admitted. "I'm workin' on the assumption that Forbes is innocent, though."

"Then who killed Wallace? Somebody else with a grudge against him?"

"Or somebody who had it in for Forbes and knew he'd be blamed for the killin'. That'd make mighty good revenge for somebody with a score to settle," Hallam pointed out.

"I suppose that's possible. What else can I help you with, Mr. Hallam?"

"Know anybody out here who might've known Forbes in Kansas?"

Drake thought for a moment, then shook his head. "Can't think of a soul."

"Ever hear Forbes mention somebody called Emilie?"

"No... no, I can't say as I did." Drake pulled a pad around and poised his pencil over it. "Now it's my turn. What have you found out so far in your investigation?"

"Not a whole hell of a lot. Wallace wasn't a well-liked feller."

"That's not news," Drake grunted.

"Reckon not, but it's about all I know that ain't just guesswork."

"I don't mind a little guesswork."

"I do." Hallam stood up. "Soon's I know something for sure, you'll be the first newspaperman to hear it."

Drake didn't look too happy with this turn of events, but there was nothing he could do about it. "I was hoping for some kind of story *now*," he muttered. "I played straight with you, Hallam."

"Know that. Appreciate it. And you'll get your story." He nodded his head. "You got my word on that."

SIXTEEN

HALLAM WAS thirsty when he left the *Citizen;* poring over old newspaper clippings was dry work. It wasn't noon yet, but the Waterhole would be open.

Not only was the speakeasy open, it was doing a brisk business as Hallam walked in a few minutes later. More than just a place to get a drink and shoot the breeze with friends, the Waterhole was also where the casting directors came when they needed riding extras and stunt doubles. You never knew when somebody from the studios might show up with a handful of jobs to fill.

That made the Waterhole just about the most popular spot in Gower Gulch, as cowboys waited there for possible work, and today was no exception. Hallam nodded greetings to several of the boys as he went across the room to the long mahogany bar that ran along one wall.

He found a spot next to a leathery, rail-thin old-timer named Bill Gillis. Ol' Bill had been around Hollywood longer than anyone could remember, and he worked steadily as a riding extra despite his advanced age. He glanced over at Hallam and said in his cracked voice, "Howdy-do, Lucas. How you doin', boy?"

Hallam grinned. Bill Gillis was probably the only man in the place who'd refer to him as a boy. "Fair to middlin', Bill," he replied.

"Lookin' for work? 'Fraid most o' the ridin' jobs're filled fer the day."

"Just thought I'd stop in and wet my whistle," Hallam told him. "I'm not doin' any picture work right now. Got a case I'm messin' with instead."

Gillis shook his head in disgust. "Don't know how a smart boy like you got mixed up with that there dee-tective business, Lucas. Cain't do much of it from a saddle, now can you?"

"No, sir, sure can't." Hallam turned to the bartender and ordered a beer. The man drew it into an icy mug and set it in front of Hallam. Hallam picked up the mug, nodded to Bill Gillis, and downed a long, healthy swallow.

Gillis sipped his own beer and said, "Neal Hart come by a little bit ago lookin' fer you, Lucas. Said he'd done that favor you asked of him yestiddy."

That meant Neal had located Marty Cowling, Hallam realized. Neal had offered to do that. "He say where I could find him?" he asked.

"He's workin' over to Vitagraph on one o' them chapter-plays. Reckon you could rustle him up over there."

"Thanks, Bill," Hallam said. "'Preciate you passin' on the message."

"This somethin' to do with that case you're workin' on?"

"Could be," Hallam nodded.

Gillis sent a dark stream of tobacco juice clanging into the spittoon at his feet. "Shoulda kept my mouth shut," he said. "Then maybe you'd go back to honest work, boy."

Hallam drank more of his beer to hide the grin that split his face. "Maybe I'll reform someday, Bill."

Gillis snorted. "Doubt it."

Hallam spun a coin onto the bar to pay for the drink, said, "So long, Bill," and left the Waterhole, wincing slightly as he left the comfortable dimness of the building as well.

It was close to lunchtime now. Chances were he could catch Neal Hart on a break if he drove over to the studio.

As Hallam piloted the flivver through the Hollywood streets, he thought about Marty Cowling. The young assistant director had plenty of reason to hate Allan Wallace. There was Wallace's ill treatment of him on the picture Art Acord had spoken of, plus their rivalry for the affections of Nola McGuire. From the sound of the conversation with Nola's mother, Wallace had indeed seduced Nola, and that had led to a breakup between her and Cowling.

If Cowling didn't have an alibi for two nights earlier, and if he could be placed in the neighborhood of Wallace's house, he would definitely be a good suspect for the murder, maybe a good enough suspect that the authorities would start to have some doubts about Forbes. It would be a hell of a lot simpler, Hallam told himself, to find Wallace's killer here in Hollywood than to have to keep digging into Forbes's past in Kansas. The possibility that he might actually have to make a trip to the Midwest to come up with anything solid had already occurred to him.

As he drove onto the lot where Neal Hart was working, Hallam hoped that things wouldn't get to that point.

The guard at the gate knew him, of course; practically all of the security people in town did. None of them were sticklers for regulations where he was concerned, either, considering him one of them. This one told Hallam that Neal Hart was filming in the big main studio, doing some saloon scenes this morning. Hallam nodded, thanked him, and drove on. He parked next to the big whitewashed building, saw that the light over the main entrance wasn't burning, and went inside.

As usual, the inside of the studio was bustling with activity. Arc lights illuminated the saloon set where filming had been going on. It consisted of a bar with a mirrored backdrop, tables and chairs scattered around in front of the bar. The massive camera was located off to one side so that it wouldn't show up in the mirror. Actors and actresses were clustered along the bar. A man was standing on one of the chairs next to a table, and he was haranguing the players in a harsh voice. Other members of the crew were standing around by the camera and the light standards, looking bored as the director continued his tirade.

Neal Hart was in the center of the group by the bar, his face heavily made up, as were the faces of the others. He pushed his hat to the back of his head and looked coldly contemptuous of the director and the tantrum he was throwing. Then he spotted Hallam standing in the shadows amidst spare equipment and painted flats, and he broke into a grin.

"You just keep right on going, Roddy," he interrupted the director. "Don't mind me."

Then he stalked off the set, paying no attention to the director's angry, dumbfounded look.

"Hello, Lucas," Neal said as he came up to Hallam. "Guess you got my message."

"Yep. Also some words of advice from Bill Gillis. Seems he thinks I ought to give up the detective business."

Neal chuckled. "That's like ol' Bill, all right. If it ain't something you can do from a saddle, it ain't honest work, leastways not to Bill." He sighed and shook his head. "I might be startin' to agree with him, though. The more I work in this business, the more I think I ought to get out while I still can, buy me a ranch somewhere."

"*Mr. Hart!*" the director suddenly bellowed. "You are aware that you're holding things up, aren't you?"

"Just waitin' for you to get finished, Roddy," Neal said with a grin. "I'll be right with you." He glanced back at Hallam. "See what I mean?"

"Sure do." Like Neal, Hallam ignored the director glaring at them. "Say, did you find that Cowling feller?"

Neal nodded. "He's working over at Quality Pictures as the A.D. on some African thing. Figure you could catch him there 'most any time."

"Thanks, Neal. Did you talk to him or just ask around?"

"Just asked around. He won't know you're comin', if that's what you're gettin' at." Neal shook his head. "I'm like Art, Lucas. I think you're makin' a mistake, too. Marty Cowling's no more a murderer than I am."

"Hope you're right. I've still got to check him out, though."

"Guess I can understand that."

The director was still standing on the chair, arms akimbo, foot tapping impatiently. "Mr. Hart," he broke in, his voice almost shaking with rage, "are you going to come back to work, or am I going to have to replace you?"

Neal said, "All right, Roddy, all right. I'm comin'." He turned back to Hallam for a final word. "Heard somebody took a potshot at you last night. You be careful, you hear, Lucas."

"You know me, Neal. I'm always careful."

Neal Hart nodded, the expression on his face showing full well how unlikely he considered Hallam's last statement. Then he went back onto the saloon set, grinning up at the furious Roddy.

Hallam wasn't surprised that Neal had heard about the shooting at the temple the night before. There was little that went on in this town that didn't get around in a hurry. Gossip was food and drink to Hollywood, which sometimes made a detective's job easier... but only sometimes.

Quality Pictures was a Poverty Row outfit only a few blocks away from Vitagraph. Hallam drove over right away, ignoring the fact that he was starting to get hungry himself. This time the guard on the gate was a little more reluctant to admit him without a pass, but Hallam talked him around to it and promised not to disrupt any filming that was in progress. The lot here was even smaller than the one Hallam had just left, and the studio was a converted barn. Hallam parked at the side of the building and walked around to the front entrance.

Two men were standing by the large sliding double

doors that had been installed in the barn. Both wore dark body makeup, had girdles made of dried grass around their waists, and teeth necklaces looped around their necks. Headbands with tall plumes attached made each of them taller. Each man was barefooted and carried a spear, and each had hand-rolled cigarettes drooping from their mouths. They grinned at Hallam as he walked up.

"Well, now," Hallam drawled, "if it ain't a couple of gen-u-ine aborigines."

"Howdy, Lucas," one of the phony natives said. Both of them were stuntmen who had worked with him on other pictures. The one who had spoken went on, "If you're looking for a job, I don't think we've got any openings left. Have to check with the casting director to be sure, though."

"No, thanks," Hallam said. "Think I'll stick to Westerns. They shooting inside?"

"Setting up," the other man said. "Thought we'd grab a smoke while they were getting things ready."

One of the big doors suddenly slid back about a foot, and a man poked his head out. He was sweating heavily, which was explained by the thick, moth-eaten gorilla costume he was wearing. He held the headpiece in one hairy paw.

"Will you guys get back in here?" he snapped. "You know how the boss is when everybody's not in place. We're going to be ready to shoot in just a few minutes."

"Okay, okay," one of the stuntmen said wearily. "Keep your shirt on." He and the other man looked at each other and broke into laughter.

"Very funny," the man in the gorilla suit said. "Now come on." He squinted at Hallam. "Do I know you?"

Hallam shook his head. "Reckon not." He jerked a callused thumb at the old barn. "Marty Cowling in there?"

"Where else? We're busy now, though. Come back later."

"You got the brains of an ape, that's for sure," one of the stuntmen said. "This is Lucas Hallam, Eddie. He ain't a good man to cross."

The man in the gorilla suit looked Hallam up and down, then said, "Okay, come on in. But keep quiet, and don't bother anything until after the scene's over, okay?"

"Sure thing," Hallam told him, not quite sure what to make of the situation. He hadn't had to deal with too many apes, at least not this kind. But that was Hollywood for you.

The four of them went inside, and one of the stuntmen slid the door closed. Hallam hung back as the others took their places. He stood off to one side as the director ran the cast through the scene, which involved several natives, a distraught heroine, a stalwart hero, and the gorilla. The tinny strains of a victrola provided mood music to help the actors emote. The whole thing struck Hallam as pretty silly.

He spotted Marty Cowling right away, a tall young man at the director's side, ready to follow any of his commands. He yelled for quiet when the director wanted quiet, worked the slate when the cameras started rolling, then ducked out of the way.

Hallam ignored the histrionics of the scene being filmed and concentrated on Cowling. The young man had a shock of blond hair and an appealingly homely face. He did his job competently enough, as far as Hallam could see, and seemed to be enjoying himself.

The scene went fairly quickly, the director wanting only three takes of it, and then the actors moved off the set so that it could be redressed. The "jungle" had consisted of several bushes and palm trees and a painted backdrop of some mountains, so changing it into something else wouldn't take long. Stagehands began to rearrange the foliage and bring in some grass huts that were built on balsa wood frames.

Hallam stepped up close to the set and said, "Marty Cowling?"

Cowling glanced over at him, surprised to hear his name called, and said, "Yeah? What can I do for you?"

"Wonder if I could have a few words with you? My name's Lucas Hallam."

Cowling came over to him carrying a notepad and a script. He took the hand Hallam held out to him, then said, "I don't have but a second, Mr. Hallam. What's this all about?"

Might as well get right to it, Hallam thought. "It's about the murder of Allan Wallace," he said.

Cowling caught his breath and took a step backward, grimacing. He stared suspiciously at Hallam. "What are you, some kind of detective?" he demanded.

"I'm investigatin' the killings," Hallam said. "Heard you had a run-in with Wallace a while back."

Cowling shook his head vehemently. "No, sir. I knew the man, but you're not pinning anything on me. That crazy preacher killed Wallace, everybody knows that."

"Not everybody, son," Hallam said softly. "Some of us think that preacher's been framed. You wouldn't know anything about it, would you?"

Cowling's fingers were tightly clutching the

notepad and script now. Actors and crew members were moving around the two of them, not paying any attention to Cowling or the big man talking to him. Cowling kept his voice low as he said, "I don't know what the hell you're talking about. I didn't have anything to do with Wallace's death. I wouldn't have any reason to kill him."

"No? What about Nola McGuire?"

Hallam was watching the young man intently as he threw the words at him, and he saw emotion flare in his eyes. There was regret there, but mostly there was anger.

"You leave Nola out of this, you understand?" Cowling hissed. "Wallace caused her enough trouble when he was alive. I won't have her name dragged into his death!"

"Take it easy, boy—"

"I *won't* take it easy!" Cowling's voice was rising now. "You cops just dig into everything, don't you? You won't rest until you ruin everything!"

People were starting to pause in their work and look over at the young man, who was now almost shouting.

"Didn't say I was a cop," Hallam cut in sharply. "They don't know about Nola, and maybe they won't have to if you'll talk to me."

"Blackmail, is that it?" Cowling's composure had completely deserted him now. He was shaking with anger.

"Just a few questions." Hallam reached out and put his hand on the boy's arm. "Why don't we step over here out of the way?"

Cowling slapped out at him with the papers in his hand. "Let go of me!" he yelled. He jerked his arm free from Hallam's grip, balled the fingers into a fist, and launched a punch at Hallam's head.

"Marty! No!" yelled one of the stuntmen who had been watching the altercation.

"Dammit!" Hallam muttered as he let his head move enough to one side to miss the blow. He held down all the instincts of the years that would have normally had him lashing back. Cowling was just a kid, and a damned upset one, at that....

Hallam reached up and caught Cowling's arm as the boy stumbled off-balance from the missed punch. He jerked Cowling closer to him, grabbed the other shoulder. "Told you to take it easy, boy," Hallam grated. "You settle down now."

Everything had come to a stop in the studio as cast and crew stared at Hallam and Cowling. There were a few mutters of protest from crew members who wanted to go to the aid of their assistant director, but the ones present who knew Hallam put a stop to that with some quiet, strategic words of caution.

Cowling's eyes were wide, his features warped by the emotions wracking him as he stared at Hallam from a distance of a few inches. Suddenly his eyes filled with tears, and he sobbed, "I'm glad he's dead!"

Hallam felt a surge of excitement. There was no telling what the boy might say next. A confession might clear things up in a hurry.

"I'm glad he's dead, but I didn't kill him!" Cowling went on, dashing that hope. "After what he did, I hope he suffered!"

Hallam released him with a little shove. Cowling dropped his pad and script to the floor but didn't even seem to notice. He lifted a trembling hand and passed it over his face.

"What did Wallace do?" Hallam asked in a low voice.

"He took Nola away from me, that's what he did. The no-good bastard *used* her!"

"And then you couldn't love her anymore after that, could you?" Remembering what Nola's mother had said, Hallam let a harsh edge creep into his voice. "You let that ruin whatever the two of you might've had, didn't you, boy?"

"I couldn't help it." Cowling closed his eyes and shook his head. "She should have known better... " he said pitifully.

Hallam took a deep breath. He didn't much like what he was doing to Marty Cowling, but he had an obligation to Forbes. And there was no denying, after this performance, that Cowling had plenty of motive for wanting Wallace dead.

"Where were you night before last?" he asked.

Cowling looked up at him with red-rimmed eyes. "Here." His words took on more strength as he went on. "I was right here. I told you that you couldn't pin those murders on me. We were filming." He flung an arm out to indicate the onlookers. "Anybody here can tell you!"

"He's right, Lucas," one of Hallam's acquaintances said. "We were here shooting until about nine o'clock."

Hallam looked around as some of the others nodded. There didn't seem to be any getting around it. Marty Cowling had an alibi, and Hallam had stirred up a lot of old hurts for nothing.

He'd had to give it a try, though. It wasn't fair to his client to overlook any of the possibilities.

The director stepped up to him, face set in angry lines. "Look here," he said. "Did I hear you say that you're not with the police?"

"That's right," Hallam rumbled. "I'm a private detective."

"Then what right do you have to come in here and harass one of my crew? I demand that you leave right now, or I'll call the guards."

Hallam eyed him and saw that he meant business. "Reckon you're right," he said slowly. "I'll be goin'."

"Mister..." Cowling said.

Hallam looked back at him.

"You said the cops don't know about Nola?"

Hallam shook his head. "Not so far as I know. I know I ain't told 'em."

"Please. Leave her out of it."

Hallam sighed and said, "If I can, son, if I can." Then he turned and stalked out of the studio.

"Oughta be damn proud o' yourself, Lucas," he muttered under his breath as he drove away from Quality Pictures a few minutes later. "You ruined that boy's day."

He wasn't solely to blame, though. Love, or what passed for it sometimes, had had a part, too. Cowling had been in love with Nola McGuire, or at least he thought he was, but that hadn't lasted. Wallace had put a stop to that. Wallace had gotten what he wanted, and Nola and Cowling had gotten all the pain that went with it.

Well, Wallace was dead now, and Nola seemed to have gotten a new start on her life, but the past was still eating away on Cowling. It had to have been lurking pretty close underneath the surface to come out as quickly and easily as it had when Hallam began questioning him. But the boy wasn't a murderer, not unless everybody back there at the studio was lying, and Hallam didn't believe that.

He wondered if Elton Forbes had ever loved anybody.

SEVENTEEN

HE SWUNG BACK ONTO SUNSET, stomach growling, and pointed the nose of the flivver toward the Waterhole. That scene back there with Cowling should have killed his appetite, but Hallam had discovered, to his surprise, that he was still hungry. So, he thought, Cowling had an alibi for the time

of the killings. So did Willard Riley. Nola McGuire had one, too, though he hadn't checked it out yet; all he had to go on was her mother's word that the girl was at home with her parents. Hallam's gut told him that Mrs. McGuire had been telling the truth, though. That left him without any good suspects.

Hell, it even left him without any unlikely suspects.

Or did it? Looking up ahead on the crowded sidewalks, Hallam spotted a familiar figure standing in front of a store, arms raised and head thrown back in an oratorical pose.

Hallam swung the flivver over to the curb.

"Repent, lest ye suffer the fires of damnation, the eternal blaze of God's wrath!" Jeremiah shouted. His voice was strong, rich, controlled, the kind of voice you expected from an evangelist like Elton Forbes, not some itinerant street preacher.

Jeremiah wasn't attracting much of a crowd. A few people were pausing to listen to him, but most of the pedestrians were in a hurry. The heat from the summer sun was bothering them more than the possibility of eternal damnation.

Hallam got out of his car and leaned against the fender, watching with a smile on his face as Jeremiah exhorted the passersby to heed his message. Occasionally—very occasionally—someone would hand him a coin. Jeremiah's expression never changed at these offerings, but he didn't turn any of them down.

Jeremiah had spotted him right off, Hallam knew. He had seen the man's eyes flicker in his direction and study him for an instant. But his presence didn't stop Jeremiah or even slow him down. He continued his preaching for at least ten minutes after Hallam got there, and it was good old-fashioned hellfire and brimstone, which made Hallam remember some of the brush arbor meetings he had attended as a boy back in Comanche County, Texas. That had been during a period of time when his father had decided to settle down, quit the lawman business, and give his family some stability. The elder Hallam had at least made an effort to be a peaceable man, and that included churchgoing from time to time, but like most noble intentions, they hadn't quite worked out the way they were intended.

Hallam shook off the memories. Jeremiah's only audience at the moment was a young woman who shook her head and went on her way. Jeremiah sighed at the lack of receptiveness in the average Hollywood citizen and came across the sidewalk.

"Good afternoon, brother," he greeted Hallam. "Have you returned to hear the word of God?"

Hallam shook his head. "Not right now. Thought I might ask *you* a question or two, though."

Jeremiah's smile was weary and put-upon. "Of course. I expected as much. I am, after all, not nearly as wealthy as Elton Forbes. At least, not wealth as the world reckons it."

"Got nothing to do with it," Hallam told him. "You ain't the only bird whose feathers I been rufflin'."

"I'm sure of that. What do you want to know, Mr. Hallam?"

"For starters, where were you night before last?"

"The proverbial alibi is what you're interested in, I see. Very well, I'll tell you. Though I am disappointed in you."

Hallam raised an eyebrow quizzically. "Disappointed in me?"

"That you think I would break one of God's commandments. Remember, I told you, 'Thou shalt not kill.'"

"Reckon somebody didn't pay enough attention in Sunday school," Hallam said grimly. "'Cause Wallace and Berlund are sure enough dead."

"Perhaps their punishment matched their sins."

"You were goin' to tell me where you were two nights ago," Hallam pointed out, not wanting to let Jeremiah steer the conversation into theological questions.

Jeremiah smiled at him. "I was in church," he said.

Recalling what Jeremiah had said the day before

about the whole world being his church, Hallam asked, "You mean you were out here on the street?"

"Not at all. I was in a mission run by one of the local churches. They see it as their Christian duty to help provide food and shelter for those of us not fortunate enough to have a real home."

Just like before, there was nothing but sincerity in Jeremiah's voice. Hallam lifted a hand, rubbed at his jaw, said, "Reckon you can prove that?"

"Indeed I can. I'll go with you to the mission right now, if you like." He glanced up and down the street and let a slight expression of disgust creep onto his face. "I don't seem to be having much success at spreading the word today."

"Reckon you mean the pickin's are kinda slim."

Jeremiah's dark eyes snapped over to lock with Hallam's, and for the first time, Hallam saw anger there. "I am not a panhandler," Jeremiah said stiffly. "I am a messenger of God's holy word, and if people choose to help me in my quest, it would be a sin to refuse them the opportunity. Do you understand, Mr. Hallam?"

Hallam understood, all right. He understood that despite his controlled air, there was a fanatic lurking inside Jeremiah. And fanatics could be damn dangerous when someone intruded on their own private world.

"No offense," Hallam said, not wanting to set Jeremiah off right here in public. "Guess I did misunderstand, at that."

Jeremiah looked slightly mollified. "Well, shall we go check out my story, Mr. Hallam?"

Hallam thought about the look that had flashed from Jeremiah's eyes, and said, "Reckon that might be a good idea."

JERMIAH'S STORY CHECKED OUT. At this point Hallam wasn't surprised. He was hitting so many dead ends in this case that one more came as no shock.

The soft-voiced minister who was in charge of the mission drew Hallam aside as Jeremiah joined a line of men much like himself to receive a bowl of soup, a plate of beans, and some bread.

"Are you a friend of Jeremiah's, Mr. Hallam?" the minister asked.

"Don't reckon you could say we're friends. Acquaintances, more like."

"Do you mind if I ask why you're checking up on his whereabouts?"

"I'm a detective, Reverend," Hallam told the man. "I thought Jeremiah might've had something to do with a case I'm workin' on, but it's startin' to look like I was wrong."

The preacher nodded. "I thought as much. You have the look of a man who has seen much."

"I've rode a few miles," Hallam admitted.

"I have to be a good judge of character in my business," the minister said with a slight smile. "Please take my word for it that Jeremiah couldn't have been involved in any crime, Mr. Hallam. He's one of the most peaceful men I know."

"That's not the way I heard it. Heard tell he's busted up some church services in his time."

"That is, unfortunately, true. He takes his calling quite seriously. And he's good at it." The smile grew wider. "I hate to think it, but he may lead more sinners to God than I do. He does get involved in shouting matches from time to time, but that's a far cry from being a criminal."

"Even if he was pushed too far?" Hallam asked.

"Maybe there was a time in his life when I would have said yes, that he would break and become violent if he was pushed far enough. But no more."

"Reckon I'll just have to take your word for that, Reverend. If he was here night before last, it's none o' my business what he might've done any other time."

"He was here all night. We have a small dormitory; the men pay for their food and the use of the cots by doing whatever manual work we need done around here. Jeremiah went right to bed after supper."

Hallam glanced over at the serving area. Jeremiah had gotten his meal and was taking a seat at one of the tables that took up most of the floor space in the old building.

"Any chance he could have left later without anybody knowing?"

The minister shook his head. "We always have someone on duty here at night. These men..." He sighed and shook his head. "These men cannot be trusted, most of them. I don't mean they're dishonest. I mean that they sometimes can't take care of themselves properly. They might accidentally start a fire or injure themselves in some other way, and we have to have someone here to keep an eye on them. The back doors are always locked after dark, and no one can get out the front door without going past our volunteer. No, Mr. Hallam, I don't think Jeremiah could have left without us knowing about it. I suppose nothing is impossible, but..."

"You don't try to stop the men if they start to leave at night?"

"This is not a jail, Mr. Hallam. We're here to help these men, not imprison them."

Hallam nodded. "Reckon I understand. Appreciate you talkin' to me, Reverend."

"I want to help Jeremiah if I can. I don't want to see him in trouble."

"He's not, far as I'm concerned." Hallam looked again at the food line, relishing the rich aroma of the food as it drifted through the room. "Say, Reverend, if I was to make a donation..."

The minister smiled broadly. "You're quite welcome to join us, Mr. Hallam. A donation isn't required, but I can promise you, anything you care to give will be put to good use."

"Reckon I'll take you up on the invite, Reverend," Hallam grinned.

Alibi or not, he was glad the trail had led him here. It was too damn long since he had had a big plate of red beans and cornbread....

———

THE BENTLEY INSURANCE AGENCY was tucked away on a side street in the business district of Glendale, the only occupant of a neat little bungalow with a small lawn. A sign in the yard gave the name of the company. Hallam was able to park directly in front; looked like the insurance business was a mite slow this afternoon.

All during the meal at the mission, he had wrestled with his conscience. Part of him said that the McGuires had had enough trouble in their lives and that his visit to their home the day before had been enough of an imposition. Years of being in the detective game had taught him not to accept anything at face value, though. Mrs. McGuire had seemed like an honest, God-fearing woman, but Hallam had seen the most innocent-looking folks turn out to be liars and worse. Much as he wanted to, he *couldn't* just take her word that Nola had been home on the night of the murders.

So here he was in Glendale again, trying to check out one more possibility. If Nola McGuire did turn out to be in the clear, that left him with only one more place to turn.

Holloway, Kansas.

Hallam got out of the flivver and shut the door quietly. A concrete walk led across the lawn and up to a small porch. Hallam paused for a moment and looked around before he started up the walk.

It wasn't quite two o'clock. He hadn't stopped by the McGuire home this time, but had instead driven directly downtown, pulling into a gas station to ask directions to the insurance office. The town seemed sleepy on this hot summer afternoon, despite its growth. A block away from the insurance office was an elementary school, closed now for the summer, but when Hallam looked in that direction, he saw one little boy on the playground, sitting by himself on a swing and going back and forth in the sun-washed glare. He saw Hallam looking at him, lifted a hand, and waved without ever slowing down. Hallam waved back, then went up the walk.

A sign on the front door said Open—Come In, so Hallam did. He stepped inside and let the door swing behind him. The bungalow was a converted residence, and the front room contained a desk, several chairs, and a short sofa against the wall opposite the desk. An open archway to the left led into another office, this one a little more comfortably furnished. Hallam figured that Nola worked in the first office and that the other one belonged *to* Mr. Bentley. A hall ran toward the back of the bungalow from the first office, and there were more doors opening from it, leading to storage rooms and maybe a kitchen, Hallam thought. There was also a closed door in Bentley's office.

Both offices were deserted.

Hallam stood there for a moment and thought about calling out. This Bentley fellow must not be much of a businessman, to go off and leave his place wide open like this. Anybody could walk in and—

A bumping noise behind the closed door in Bentley's office drew Hallam's attention. He turned in that direction, and a low moan came to his ears.

His hand dropped to his right leg, yanked the pants up, and plucked the Bowie from his boot top. Wearing it there was a little uncomfortable, but it was too hot for a coat, and even in Hollywood, folks looked at you sort of funny when you carried twelve inches of cold steel on your hip.

Hallam moved across the inner office with speed and quietness surprising for a man of his bulk. He remembered the attempts on his life and his theory that he might have come closer to the actual killer than he even realized.

If Nola McGuire was involved some way, it could be that somebody had decided to put an end to the threat of her talking... along with anybody else who was unlucky enough to be with her.

Hallam paused in front of the closed door and

leaned closer to it. Now he heard harsh breathing from the room inside. Sounded like somebody in pain. Could be the killer was still inside, he thought. And if not, maybe at least he was in time to keep anybody else from dying, if he could get help to them in time....

The Bowie in his right hand, Hallam lifted his leg and drove his booted foot against the door with a crash.

It slammed open, the facing splintering. Hallam dove through, ready for anything as a scream rang in his ears.

He stopped in his tracks, the Bowie held low, ready to thrust and slash—

And then said explosively, "Ah, *hell*...!"

"Omigod, don't kill us!" the girl who was sprawled on a table shrieked as she covered her eyes with her hands. Her dress was up around her waist, and she sure as hell wasn't covering anything else. In one corner of the room, a man in coat, tie and shirt was struggling desperately to pull his pants over his shoes, all the while darting terrified glances at the big man with the Bowie knife.

Hallam felt just about as stupid as he ever had in his life.

He bent and slid the blade back in its sheath. "Take it easy," he growled. "Ain't nobody goin' to get killed, not less'n one of you has a heart attack." He was carefully avoiding looking at the girl, who was only now becoming aware that she wasn't in any immediate danger of losing her life. She yanked her dress down and sat up on the table, glaring at Hallam.

"Who the hell are you?" she demanded.

"Lucas Hallam," he said. "Reckon you'd be Nola McGuire. And this feller"—he waved a hand at the man in the corner, who by now had climbed into his pants and was hastily buttoning them up—"must be Bentley."

"Donald Bentley," the man replied, his voice shaking with a mixture of anger and leftover fear. "And you had no right to come barging in like—"

"Door was open," Hallam cut in. He said to the girl, "You *are* Nola McGuire?"

"That's right. What business is it of yours, mister?"

Hallam looked at her for a moment before answering. He saw a pretty girl, more than pretty enough to have been in the movies, with honey-blond hair worn in short, tight curls. Her skin was pale, her eyes blue and large and expressive. There was a hardness in those eyes, though, that told a story of troubled times in the past, problems that had beaten her down until she had decided to become as tough and cynical as the rest of the world.

"I talked to your mother yesterday," Hallam said. "Figured I'd better talk to you, too."

"You're that damn detective!" she said as she rolled off the table with a flash of stocking tops. "Mama told me you came around bothering her." She advanced a step toward Hallam, those hard eyes blazing now. "Get this straight, mister. I don't give a damn that Allan Wallace is dead. He can burn in hell for all eternity as far as I'm concerned. But I didn't have anything to do with it!"

"Reckon you can prove that?" Hallam asked softly.

"Nola doesn't have to prove anything!" Bentley exclaimed. He was a middle-sized man, in his forties, with graying brown hair and a considerable bald spot at the back of his head. He stepped forward and put an arm around Nola's shoulders. "I insist that you leave us alone and get out of here, or I'll call the police."

Hallam's eyes raked over him in contempt. "You just shut your mouth 'fore I bounce you off a wall. I got no use for men like you."

"Why?" the girl asked with a sneer. "Because he sees what he wants and goes after it?"

Hallam took a deep breath and ignored the question. "I asked you if you could prove where you were night before last."

"I was home with my parents. They can tell you."

"Anybody else see you there?"

"One of the neighbors dropped by." Her lips drew back from her teeth in what passed for a smile. "We live in a friendly neighborhood."

"You recollect what time that was?"

Nola shook her head. "No, I don't. I just know it was in the evening."

Bentley swallowed and tried to summon up more courage. "Haven't you asked enough questions? Now, I've requested that you leave my place of business. Are you going to do as I ask?"

"Told you to shut up," Hallam said, and Bentley took another step back from the bleak look on Hallam's face. Turning back to the girl, Hallam said, "Reckon you're tellin' the truth."

"Well, gee, thanks," Nola bit back.

"Mind tellin' me that neighbor's name?"

The girl's features tightened. She told him the name, then said, "I don't want you going around spreading stories about me."

"Gossipin' ain't my business. I'm just lookin' for a killer."

"'The police already have that preacher. It seems to me he did the world a service by getting rid of Wallace."

"He says he didn't do it," Hallam pointed out.

"Wouldn't you say that, if you were guilty?"

Hallam shook his head. "Never shot nobody I didn't own up to if asked. Nor anybody that didn't deserve it."

Bentley swallowed again.

"You're one tough cowboy, aren't you?" Nola said. "Well, you don't scare me. I've told you my story; you can go check it out. And leave me the hell alone."

"If you're tellin' the truth, you won't ever see me again." Hallam grimaced. "You got my word on that."

She gritted her teeth and spoke angrily past them. "What's the matter, cowboy, you never saw anybody doing it before? Are you that disgusted by me?"

Hallam went to the door and paused there. "Reckon you just didn't turn out like I expected you to," he said, wondering why he was even bothering to try to explain. He glanced over at Bentley, who was still pale. "Lock your damn door next time!"

Then he stalked out through the offices and left the bungalow.

He headed back toward Hollywood a half hour later, after checking with the neighbor and finding that Nola had been telling the truth, at least about her alibi. He'd learned a lot about Nola McGuire the last two days, he thought. He'd heard about the girl from Frank Sheldon and Art Acord, from her mother, and from Marty Cowling. Looked like none of them had had her figured just right. Maybe at one time she had been like they described her: young and fresh and innocent. Maybe he was just a damned old fool passing judgment on somebody he had no real right to judge. Nola

McGuire was a grown woman and had a right to do as she pleased.

And she wasn't a killer. Hallam sighed. He was sure of that. Looking in her eyes, he had seen that she wasn't the type to pick up a gun and shoot a man. She had other weapons.

EIGHTEEN

HALLAM LIKED UNION STATION. It was a mix of old and new, its red tiled roof and its patios paying tribute to the rich Spanish heritage of Southern California while the ever-present bustle of people coming and going told how the area was growing by leaps and bounds. Close by was Chinatown, representing yet another aspect of Los Angeles.

And there were always the trains. Hallam liked the trains. As a boy, he had heard old-timers cuss the coming of the railroads. He had to admit, nothing could replace a good horse, but as far as he was concerned, the railroads had helped to open up the West, and that was a good thing. One of his earliest memories was riding the narrow-gauge train up alongside the Animas River from Durango to Silverton. To this day he remembered the pungent smell of the coal smoke from the engine, the way ashes and soot would sometimes blow back through the windows of the passenger cars. The tang of the clear, cool mountain air more than made up for the occasional inconvenience, though, as did the sweeping vistas of pine-covered heights. There were few things lovelier, to Hallam's mind, than the sparkle of sunlight on a mountain stream as it leaped and raced through deep valleys.

Normally, the prospect of a cross-country train trip would have appealed to Hallam. Now, though, it was just work.

The train to Kansas pulled out at eight o'clock in the morning. Hallam was at the station at seven. He stood in line to buy a round-trip ticket, then made a note of the cost to add to his expense sheet later. He could have gotten a berth in a sleeping car, since Forbes would wind up paying for it later, but for some reason he had never been able to sleep very well on trains. Instead, he bought a seat in a regular passenger car; what sleeping he did he could do sitting up.

That left him with enough time to stop at the station grill for some breakfast and coffee.

He had studied the schedules and figured that it would take about forty hours to reach Holloway, Kansas. This was Thursday morning. That would put him in Holloway about midnight Friday. Not just a real good time to be starting an investigation. He was hoping he'd be able to get something accomplished over the weekend, though, so that maybe he could get back here by sometime Tuesday.

He hadn't told Ben Dunnemore that he was leaving town; Ben probably wouldn't have been too fond of the idea. With any luck, though, Hallam thought he could be back before anyone missed him. He had left word at the Waterhole where he was going, so that he could be reached in an emergency.

As far as Hallam could see, this step was a necessary one. He was convinced that whoever was behind the attempts on his life was right here in Los Angeles, but the key to the thing was somewhere else, most likely in Forbes's old home town.

He might even run into the girl called Emilie...

He had just finished off a big plate of eggs, bacon, and flapjacks and was starting on his second cup of coffee when a hand came down on his shoulder. Hallam glanced up sharply, ready for trouble, then relaxed when he saw Frank Sheldon standing beside him.

"Skipping town, Lucas?" Sheldon asked with a smile.

Hallam waved him into the other chair at the little table and said, "That ain't funny, Frank. The cops won't think so, either, if they find out I'm leavin'."

Sheldon frowned as he sat down. "I was just kidding, Lucas. Are you really leaving?"

"Not for good. I'll be back next week, I hope. Just doin' a little work."

"The Forbes case, eh?" Sheldon leaned forward and lowered his voice. "I heard somebody took a shot at you a couple of nights ago. Are you sure it's a good idea to keep on with this case?"

Hallam sipped his coffee. "Don't have much choice. Can't leave Forbes danglin' in the breeze, now, can I?"

"Knowing you, Lucas... no, I guess not. You're a dedicated man, you know that? Nothing means more to you than duty and honor and the law."

"Hell, don't know about that," Hallam growled. "I like eatin' and a good drink now and then, too."

Sheldon laughed. "I didn't mean to embarrass you,"

he said. "It's just that you're a pretty impressive individual."

"Just an old cowboy."

"Yeah, sure."

"Say, what're you doin' down here this early in the morning? I thought you Hollywood producers didn't get up 'til noon."

"I was seeing a friend off," Sheldon said. "I didn't think I'd get to see another one off on the same visit. Anyway, I like coming down here." Sheldon looked around at the busy depot. "It always reminds me of the first time I came to L.A."

"You're not from around here? Always figured you for a native."

Sheldon's chuckle was sardonic. "Nobody's a native in Hollywood," he said. "We're all from somewhere else. In my case, Arizona."

Hallam looked across the table at the producer, murder cases and suchlike forgotten at the moment. "Arizona? Hell, I didn't know that. Spent some time there myself."

"Yeah, my dad was a ranch hand. My mother died when I was a baby, so Pop and I knocked around the whole state together. He got work wherever he could, and I never had to go to school much. Melinda says I'm a self-made man; I guess maybe she's right. I never made it past the seventh grade."

Hallam looked at him, at the expensive suit and the heavy ring sparkling on his finger. "Reckon you did some climbin' up the ladder."

"I had to," Sheldon said quietly. "I had something to prove."

"Reckon we all do," Hallam agreed. "How'd you come to wind up in Hollywood?"

"My father died." Sheldon's voice was flat and expressionless now. "I was fourteen. I scrambled around Tucson for a few years, doing whatever I had to to survive, then saved up enough money for a train ticket out of there. I didn't care where I went, as long as it was someplace else." He grinned now, shaking off the unpleasant memories. "It wound up being some weird place called Hollywood. Ah, I tell you, Lucas, as soon as I saw the place, I knew I was home. I got a job sweeping out a movie studio." He pulled a cigar from his vest pocket, lit it with a match, and blew smoke toward the high ceiling. "Fifteen years later, I owned the place," he finished dramatically.

"Sounds like it'd make a pretty good picture," Hallam said.

"You know, it might at that." Sheldon flashed a grin again. "I'll have to get some of my story people on it, polish it up a little."

"You do that." Hallam pulled his turnip out of his watch pocket and flipped it open. "Got me a train to catch. Glad I ran into you, Frank."

"I don't talk about the past much," Sheldon said, looking off as if his thoughts were still elsewhere. Then he glanced at Hallam. "Maybe you're just one of the few people who really understand about the past, Lucas. After all, you were *there*."

"That your way o' tellin' me I'm old, Frank?" Hallam asked with a grin as he stood up.

"No offense, Lucas, no offense." Sheldon stuck the cigar in his mouth and stood up as well. "I'll see you off."

"No need for that."

"I insist." Sheldon took Hallam's arm. "Come on."

They joined the throng of passengers and friends that filled the big building practically every hour of the day and night. According to Hallam's ticket, the train he wanted was departing from Track Seven. He and Sheldon made their way to that platform. Hallam's only baggage was his war bag, and he would carry that on board and stow it below his seat.

It was only a couple of minutes before eight when they reached the car where Hallam's seat was located. Evidently the train would be leaving on time, because the conductor was striding hurriedly along its length, bawling, "Booooard! All abooooard!"

Hallam stuck out a hand and shook with Sheldon. "So long, Frank."

"Be careful, Lucas. I've told you all along, this private eye business is dangerous."

Hallam grinned as he started to step up onto the platform at the rear of the car. "Shoot," he said. "Ain't nothing like the old da—"

He looked up, saw the man on the platform with the gun.

Hallam swung the war bag and dove forward at the same time.

The war bag smacked into the gunman's hand as the pistol went off, the explosion deafeningly close by Hallam's ear. His right shoulder slammed against the man's stomach and drove him back into the railing around the platform. Hallam dropped the war bag, got his hands on the man's wrist, and twisted. The two of them swayed there on the platform, their grunts of exertion lost amidst the never-ending uproar of the busy station.

Hallam didn't know where the bullet had gone, but he didn't have too much time to worry about it. This particular car must have been almost full already, because no one else had been loading as Hallam went on board. Frank Sheldon was the only other person nearby, in fact. Hallam hoped he had had sense enough to duck when the shooting started.

The gunman's free hand flailed around for a few seconds, then found what it was looking for. Hard, blunt fingers caught Hallam by the throat, dug savagely into the sensitive flesh.

Hallam let go of the gun wrist with his right hand, balled the fist, drove it into the man's stomach. He hadn't had a chance to catch a breath before the man got his chokehold, and things were already starting to get a little fuzzy. The man gasped as Hallam's knobby fist slammed into his belly, though, and the grip eased a little.

Putting all of his strength into his left arm, Hallam suddenly crashed the man's wrist into the railing around the platform. The man gave a sharp cry of pain, and the gun slipped from fingers that had gone numb with agony. It clattered to the tracks below the train.

Hallam hit the man in the stomach again, then again. He knocked the grip on his throat completely loose now, stepped in and drove a hard left to the man's jaw, staggering him against the railing once more. Sensing victory, Hallam moved in to finish off the would-be killer. With this man in custody, the trip to Kansas might not be necessary after all. There was no doubt in Hallam's mind that this was the man who had tried to kill him outside the temple.

A fraction of a second too late, he saw the fist coming at him in a desperation swing.

He ducked, but the blow still caught him above the ear, the same ear that the pistol had almost blown off. Pain surged through Hallam's head, and for a second he couldn't see anything but a red haze. He groped for his opponent, but then a shoe smashed into his kneecap and his balance deserted him. Hallam went down.

He shook his head to clear it, looked up in time to see the gunman leap down from the platform on the other side of the train and go stumbling off into the crowd. He wasn't moving too well, and Hallam at least had the satisfaction of knowing that he had done some damage. He put his hands down to brace himself and started to heave to his feet.

The sudden arrival of Frank Sheldon put a stop to that. "Lucas!" Sheldon exclaimed, clutching at him. "Are you all right? My God, what was that all about?"

Hallam shook off Sheldon's hand and glared at the crowd. The gunman had disappeared. Hallam sighed, gave his head a shake again.

"Reckon somebody don't want me goin' to Kansas," he rumbled. "Looks like I'm on the right trail."

"He tried to kill you!"

Hallam looked at the shocked producer. "Damn right. And somebody hired him."

"I'll get the conductor—"

Hallam put out a hand to stop him. "Conductor's already comin'," he said, nodding toward the front of the train. "Don't want you sayin' anything to him about this, Frank."

"But you've got to report it," Sheldon insisted.

"If I report it, that'll mean the conductor will call

the cops. Then the train gets delayed and I don't even get to go." Hallam's hand tightened on Sheldon's arm. "As a favor, Frank, don't say anything."

"Well, all right," Sheldon agreed grudgingly as the conductor appeared in the door at the rear of the car.

"What's going on here?" the uniformed man asked. At the front of the train, a whistle rang out, and the sharp hiss of steam was audible all through the depot. "We're pulling out, gentlemen. Is there some problem?"

Hallam adjusted his coat and ran his fingers through his disheveled mane of hair. "Tripped gettin' on board," he said with a sheepish grin. He turned to Sheldon as the train gently lurched into motion. "You best get a move-on, Frank, 'less you want to go to Kansas, too."

"Damn, I can't do that." Sheldon swung down from the train as it started to gather speed. Hallam lifted a hand and waved in farewell. Sheldon waved back and called, "Watch out for that tripping, Lucas!"

Hallam grinned and bent to pick up the fallen war bag. The conductor said, "You all right, mister?"

Hallam thought about what had just happened and got that old familiar feeling of being hot on the trail. "Never better," he told the conductor.

It was a good feeling.

NINETEEN

THE TRAIN CUT across the southern part of California, through deserts and scrubby flatlands. Hallam had taken a seat by a window, and as the cars clicked along the rails he looked out to the north and saw the dim blue haze of mountains.

Chuckwalla was up yonder, he thought, and he still hadn't looked in on Liz Fletcher again. He had been so caught up in the case that other things just hadn't entered his mind except on stray, fleeting occasions.

Liz knew how to take care of herself, though. She'd been managing all right for a long time, at least to hear her tell it.

Hallam promised himself that he would take a run out there whenever he got back from Kansas, though.

He stretched his legs and tried to get comfortable. Train seats weren't really built for people as long-legged as he was. He was used to that, however. Over the years, he had taken plenty of train rides, and he knew when to get up and move around so that he wouldn't cramp up too bad.

There wasn't much scenery for a while, just miles and miles of flat and dry land with a few little trees and the endless string of telegraph poles to break the monotony. Hallam dozed in his seat, his head dipping forward onto his chest. The train crossed from California into Arizona in the early afternoon. Hallam didn't notice.

A young woman was sitting beside him for the first part of the trip. Hallam figured she had chosen that seat because he looked like the kind of man who wouldn't bother a girl traveling alone. Harmless, in other words, he thought with a wry grin as he looked out the window. The girl didn't talk other than to say a quiet "Hello" when she first sat down, and Hallam didn't feel much like talking himself.

Even though he had thought out all the different facets of the case during the last couple of days, he found himself running them through his head again, looking for that one connection that would unravel the whole thing. Up ahead, in Holloway, he would find the answers. He was sure of that.

And if he didn't... ?

Hallam didn't like to think about that. But maybe all the answers *weren't* in Kansas. He might have to face that fact. And there was something nagging him far in the back of his mind, something that he had overlooked, or something that he had seen from the wrong perspective.

He shook his head and muttered to himself, then glanced over to see the young woman casting furtive looks at him. She must have decided that she made the wrong choice about a seatmate after all. Hallam smiled at her, as reassuringly as he could, then turned his attention back to the vista unrolling outside the window.

The train passed a road that led off to the old town of Backsight. Hallam recognized the road, remembered when it had been just a trail. He had ridden up that trail about twenty-five years before, a young cowhand looking for work. Instead, he had found trouble.

Over the years, he had gotten used to that particular turn of events.

The girl got off the train at Flagstaff. Hallam barely noticed when she left.

Around the middle of the afternoon, his stomach reminded him that he hadn't eaten since early in the morning, so he hefted his war bag and went up to the club car for a sandwich. As he looked out at the arid landscape, he wished he had a cold beer to go with the food, but settled for coffee instead.

Slowly, the country changed. Hills appeared, turned into mountains farther on. Hallam opened the window next to his seat. The air outside was cool now.

Far in the distance, somewhere along the Arizona-New Mexico line, he spotted a saw-toothed crag that looked familiar. For a moment he couldn't remember its name, and the memory lapse bothered him. Medicine Peak, he suddenly recalled. That was what it was called.

A winter's day, so different from what was outside now. Air so cold you felt like your lungs were going to frost right up with every breath you took. Hallam lay crouched in the snow, the peak towering above him. His right leg was numb from the bullet wound, but that was better than the pain that had been in it earlier. He listened for the slightest sound in the crystal-clear mountain air, knowing that if the other man moved and he didn't hear him, chances were that Lucas Hallam would die on this desolate height.

Snow fell from a branch of a nearby pine. Hallam's taut-stretched nerves made him swing around sharply, his Colt coming up. With a sick feeling in the pit of his stomach, he realized that he had jumped at the wrong sound. There was a crunch in the snow behind him.

He went down, twisting as a shotgun roared. Pain lanced into his arms and legs and torso, but he ignored it as the bulk of the other man loomed in the sights of the Colt. Hallam squeezed the trigger, once, twice, three times, saw the man jerked backward by the impact of the bullets. Drops of blood spattered redly on the snow.

Hallam hauled himself to his feet. He was wounded in at least half a dozen places from the shotgun blast, but he was just thankful that the man he had been hunting hadn't been a little closer. Limping badly now, he stepped over to the sprawled corpse. He knelt awkwardly, rolled the man over, saw for sure that he was dead.

Now all that was left to do was pack him back down the mountain. Maybe if Hallam was lucky he'd get back to what passed for civilization before the snow started again. If it caught him on the mountain, he reckoned that would be the end of it.

The thought had started occurring to Hallam off and on that this was damn hard work to do for a U.S. marshal's salary....

Well, that was a long time back, he reflected now as the train clattered along toward Albuquerque.

It was early evening when the train swept down out of the mountains. The lights of the city sparkled prettily in the valley. Quite a few years had passed since Hallam had visited Albuquerque; that last visit had been a pleasant one, a time when trouble hadn't come looking for him. He had been able to spend a few weeks there just relaxing, sipping beer in the cantinas and watching the señoritas swaying by. It had been a nice time.

The train stopped there for thirty minutes. Hallam swung off and got some supper at a Mexican place a block from the depot. The fiery food and the cold beer only reinforced the memories he had of that earlier visit.

Back on board, he watched out the window for a while longer as the route turned north. There wasn't much to see, though; long stretches of blackness broken only by an occasional light from an isolated ranch house. By the time the train was moving across the Texas panhandle, Hallam was asleep.

He awoke in Oklahoma. Indians and oil wells, he thought as he shook the cobwebs from his mind. And Sooners. A more fractious bunch of people he had yet to see. He'd been a deputy sheriff in an oilfield town at one time, and the only thing he'd ever come across to compare it with were the old-time mining camps. When the roughnecks came off the rigs, they wanted to play as hard as they worked, which meant prime opportunities for gamblers, grifters, and whores. Hallam thought back to the night when he and a couple of other deputies had been called to one of the saloons on the fringes of the oil patch. There had been a full-fledged riot going on inside, the results of a tinhorn being stupid enough to bottom deal and get caught at it. The other deputies hadn't wanted to go in, preferring to wait until the fighting played itself out. Then they could move in and arrest anybody still on his feet.

"That ain't the kinda job I'm bein' paid for," Hallam had said, and then he waded into the fracas, busting chairs and swinging table legs with the best of them. He was bruised and bleeding by the time it was over, but he was still on his feet and over a dozen prisoners were taken into custody.

Unfortunately, quite a bit of damage had been done to the place, and the owner accused Hallam of making the situation worse instead of trying to stop the property destruction. The man had enough political pull to insure that Hallam's boss saw things the same way.

What the hell; he had been ready to move on anyway.

And he was still moving on, more than twenty years later. Hollywood was the only place in which he had spent more than a couple of years since he had left home almost thirty years before. He supposed it was the closest thing he had to a home now. He enjoyed the movie work and the cowboys he worked with, and enough interesting cases came along that he could keep his hand in the detective business.

This train ride had him thinking, though. Memories kept crowding in on him, recalling both good times and bad as he retraced his trails across the Southwest. He'd seen and done a hell of a lot. He didn't know if he was ready to settle down and spend the rest of his days in one spot.

Yet, what else was there for an old man to do?

Hallam gave a shake of his head. Bein' old was just a

matter of the way you looked at things, he thought. And right now he didn't have time for any maundering or feeling sorry for himself.

He had a murder case to solve and an innocent man to set free, by God! Didn't matter if he had ridden these trails before and seen some downright wild times in the old days.

Hallam smiled. There were wild times yet to come....

THE TRAIN MADE GOOD TIME. It pulled into Holloway, Kansas, a little before ten o'clock on Friday night.

TWENTY

HOLLYWOOD, California, to Holloway, Kansas, in thirty-eight hours. The distance between the two places was much greater than could be measured in miles or hours. The similarity in names had struck Hallam more than once during this case, but that was where the similarity ended.

Hallam had trouble imagining two places less alike.

He stepped down from the train, onto the station platform. No one else was waiting to board, and no one else got off. He stood there for a moment as the conductor hurried into the depot and then came back out after conferring with the stationmaster or whoever was on duty. Evidently they decided it would be all right for the train to proceed, even though it was ahead of schedule, because with a hiss of steam it slid out of the station. Hallam watched the red light on the caboose disappear into the darkness; it dwindled steadily until it was gone from sight.

Then he turned and surveyed the station and the town beyond.

The depot building was native stone, great blocks of it hewn from the earth. It had a shingled roof that overhung the platform. Inside the building a single light burned. Looked like there wasn't much traffic in or out of Holloway. Hallam went inside, saw a sleepy-faced young man standing behind a window in the partition that separated the office from the waiting area. Some hard wooden benches that reminded Hallam of church pews —and of Elton Forbes—were the only furniture in the waiting area.

The young clerk looked surprised to see Hallam walking toward him. No doubt it was unusual to see anybody here at night, let alone somebody as big and distinctive as this lone traveler.

"Yes, sir?" the clerk said as Hallam put the war bag on the floor at his feet. "Could I help you?"

"Reckon you ain't the stationmaster." It was more statement than question.

"No, sir. I'm the night telegrapher. Jimmy Daniels."

Hallam nodded. "Pleased to meet you, son. Think you could give me some directions?"

"Be glad to." The young man grinned. "I suppose I know every street and alley in Holloway. I grew up here."

Hallam had the feeling that Jimmy Daniels was glad to have somebody to talk to. Sitting in an empty depot night after night with nothing but a chattering telegraph key to keep you company was bound to get boring.

"There's still a college here, ain't there?" Hallam asked.

"Yes, sir. The teachers college. It's clear on the other side of town, though."

"And how far's that?"

"Nearly a mile."

Hallam grinned. "Reckon I can hoof it that far."

"Ol' Davey has a jitney he hires out... ," the young man began. "He's probably asleep by now, though."

"No need to bother him. I'll walk. Now, is there a rooming house close by that college?"

"Several of them. Most of the students live in the dormitories, but the professors have to have some place to stay, those that aren't married, I mean."

"Been here all your life, you say?" Hallam asked, rubbing his jaw.

"Yes, sir. Eighteen years."

"Remember a man name of Elton Forbes? Taught at the college for a while?"

Jimmy Daniels frowned. "Elton Forbes," he repeated thoughtfully. After a moment, he shook his head. "Sorry. I don't think I know him. I haven't attended the college yet, though. Thought I might start in the fall."

Well, it had been worth a try. Hallam said, "Thanks anyway. Have any idea which o' the roomin' houses is the best?"

"Mrs. Bondurant's is the most popular." Jimmy grinned. "Leastways, she sets the best table, from what I hear."

"How do I go about findin' it?"

"I'll show you." Before Hallam could tell him not to bother, Jimmy had ducked out of the window and come around to a door in the partition.

He didn't mean to leave the depot, though. He just went to the front door of the building, which someone had propped open with a loose brick, and pointed down the street that led away from the station.

"You just follow Elm Street right there through downtown until you get to March Avenue. Turn left on March, and it'll take you right by the college. Mrs. Bondurant's place is just across the street from the administration building. Real handy for the professors."

Hallam picked up his war bag and said, "Thank you, son. Reckon I'll stroll on over there."

"You're welcome, sir."

Hallam went down the three wooden steps that led to the street, going beneath a swinging plank sign that said HOLLOWAY.

Elm Street was hard-packed dirt. The first couple of blocks were lined with warehouses that were dark and deserted at this time of night. Hallam passed a grain elevator, a farm implement dealership, a set of public scales, and a feed store before he came to a residential area. His way was lighted by widely spaced gas lamps that cast circles of yellow, flickering illumination. There were no lights in the houses that he passed. It looked like Holloway went to bed early, at least compared to what he was used to back home.

The houses were all whitewashed frame buildings, from what he could see in the shadows. Some of them had picket fences enclosing their front yards. There were shade trees in the yards, and Hallam reckoned it hadn't been too many years since Jimmy Daniels had been climbing in those trees.

The hospital was the first building that had shown any lights since Hallam left the depot, and those were dim. A large, two-story structure, it looked to have been a private residence at one time, before being converted into a hospital. It was only a block off the main street, which was also the highway that ran through Holloway. Hallam had yet to see a car pass on that highway, though, as he walked toward downtown.

The highway wasn't paved, just oiled. Hallam paused before crossing it, not to check for traffic, since there wasn't any, but to take a better look at this town that had produced Elton Forbes. The business district ran for several blocks on both sides of the highway, sturdy stone buildings with concrete sidewalks raised several feet above the level of the street. There were more lamps here downtown, and Hallam could make out the bank, a couple of general mercantile stores, a barber shop, a candy store, a domino parlor, and a post office. Down on the edge of town, he thought he saw a stable, and glancing the other way, three blocks down the highway, he saw a building with a startlingly familiar shape.

It was a big building with a steeple-like structure in front, but it wasn't a church. There was a star at the top of the steeple, and big letters running up and down it that spelled RIALTO.

Damned if Holloway didn't have a movie theater, Hallam realized with a grin. He squinted to read the title of the picture that was displayed on the marquee beneath the steeple.

His grin got wider. *Travelin' On,* the marquee read, "with Wm. S. Hart." And in an uncredited appearance, one Lucas Hallam...

Hallam doubted if anybody in Holloway would recognize him from his part in the movie. He'd been one of the dog heavies and had been killed off fairly early. Anyway, wardrobe had given him some God-awful black outfit to wear, instead of letting him wear his own buckskins, and he hadn't looked like himself at all. Of course, he thought wryly, some folks wouldn't say that that was such a bad thing.

He walked on across the highway and followed Elm to March. As Jimmy Daniels had directed him, he turned left and started that way and almost immediately saw the buildings of the college bulking up out of the darkness on the right.

The administration building was the largest, a forbidding three-story structure complete with turrets and cupolas and a steep roof. Ranged on either side and behind it were boxlike classroom buildings, none of them more than two stories.

Beyond the school was prairie, a seemingly endless stretch of flatland. Hallam wondered if the students in the rear classrooms sometimes stared out at that level expanse and saw their own future in it.

Mrs. Bondurant's rooming house was right across the street from the administration building, Jimmy had said. Hallam paused in front of the house that he took to be the correct one and studied it. There was a light on inside, the first one he had seen in a residence since arriving in Holloway. Mrs. Bondurant probably left a light on for boarders who were coming in late, and also to encourage any travelers who might want to stop. Like most of the others in town, the house was a whitewashed frame two-story, with several nice trees in the front yard, a hedge bordering the sidewalk, and a big front porch. In the light of day, the grass and the trees and the hedge would probably have a slightly brown wilted look to them due to the heat and dust in this part of the world; but now, in moonlight and shadows, the place was downright pretty.

A flagstone walk led from the opening in the hedge up to the porch. Hallam strode up it and climbed the four steps to the porch, his boots clumping on the boards despite the fact that he tried to walk softly. The screen door was closed, but the inside door was open and a soft patch of illumination fell onto the porch from the house.

Someone inside must have heard Hallam coming, because a woman appeared at the door almost before he got through rapping softly on it. In a quiet voice, she said, "Yes, can I help you?"

Hallam took off his hat and let it dangle from his fingers, brushing against his leg. "I'm lookin' for a place to stay, ma'am," he said. "Would you be Mrs. Bondurant?"

"I would. It's sort of late to be looking for a room, isn't it?"

"Well, yes, ma'am, it is. But I just got into town on the train, and I didn't have a chance to write ahead or anything."

"I see." The woman looked at him for a long moment through the screen, no doubt studying him and trying to make up her mind whether or not she wanted to let him in.

Hallam couldn't see her very well since the light was at her back, but her silhouette was slim and straight, and she didn't seem to be an old woman. After a moment she nodded and pushed the screen door open, stepping back to let him in.

"I was sitting up reading," she said as he came in. "A vice of mine, I'm afraid. I'm Irma Bondurant."

Hallam turned and got a better look at her now. She was older then he had first thought, in her forties perhaps, with straight, dark brown hair only lightly touched with gray. And she was a damned handsome woman, too.

"Name's Lucas Hallam," he introduced himself. "The boy down at the train station said you set the best table in town, ma'am."

She laughed lightly. "That would be Jimmy Daniels, I'd wager. He lives here."

Hallam raised an eyebrow and said, "Reckon he forgot to mention that."

"Oh, yes, Jimmy's been with us since his own folks passed away several years ago. He must have liked you, Mr. Hallam, or he wouldn't have sent you here."

"Seemed like a nice boy."

"He is." Irma Bondurant gestured at the war bag. "Is that all of your luggage?"

"Yes, ma'am, I travel light. Hope that's all right."

"Perfectly all right with me, Mr. Hallam." She tightened the throat of her housedress, and Hallam wondered if he was making her nervous. The rest of the house was quiet, as if all the other boarders had gone to bed. Mrs. Bondurant asked, "Have you come to Holloway on business or pleasure, Mr. Hallam?"

"Reckon you could say it's business. Been thinkin' about buyin' a farm hereabouts." Hallam had decided that would be a believable story and would also give him an excuse for asking questions about the area.

"Well, I hope you're successful in what you're looking for." Her tone became more businesslike as she went on, "Rooms are five dollars a week, and that includes supper. Will you be staying at least a week, Mr. Hallam?"

"That all depends," he said as he reached in his pocket and pulled out a worn wallet. "Reckon the best thing would be to go ahead and pay for a whole week and then we can go from there."

"That'll be fine," she said, taking the money from him. "Top of the stairs, turn left, third door on the right." She smiled again, and her voice softened. "You're lucky we happen to have an empty room. It's summer, you know. All the rooms will be filled again when the fall term starts at the college. Not many people attend during the summer."

"Yes, ma'am." Hallam nodded, wondering if he should go ahead and ask her about Elton Forbes. He didn't want to put her on her guard right away if she did know anything about Forbes.

She helped him make the decision by asking, "What made you decide to look for a place around Holloway, Mr. Hallam? Have you been through here before?"

"Nope, this is my first time. Friend o' mine told me about your little town, though. Said it was a good place to live and had plenty of good farm land in the area. Name of Elton Forbes; maybe you know him?"

"Professor Forbes? I think I remember him."

The woman had made a good recovery, but Hallam had seen the slight widening of the eyes, heard the tiny catch in the voice.

Mrs. Bondurant had known him, all right. Hallam had been lucky on his first try, and he decided quickly to push it just a little further.

"Maybe he stayed here," he said. "Ol' Elton used to teach right there across the road."

"Yes. Yes, I remember him now. He was a good boarder, quiet and no trouble. I think he gave up teaching a few years ago, though. What's he doing now?"

Hallam's mind was working rapidly. She wasn't just now remembering Forbes; she had known him as soon as Hallam mentioned his name. There was a chance she knew what Forbes was doing these days, too, and a lie might just land Hallam in a lot of trouble.

"He's gone to preachin' out there in California," he said truthfully. "That's where I met him."

"How interesting." Mrs. Bondurant's tone made it clear, though, that she didn't consider the topic interesting enough to continue with it. "Well, I believe I'll say good night to you, Mr. Hallam. Breakfast is at seven o'clock and costs a quarter extra, but I'm told it's worth it."

"I'm sure it is. Good night."

Hallam left her standing in the parlor and went up the stairs, turning as she had told him to do and finding the unlocked door of the room she had assigned him. It was comfortably if not luxuriously furnished with bed, armchair, and dresser. A small closet opened off the room. A kerosene lamp sat on the dresser. Hallam lit it with a kitchen match from his pocket.

He didn't unpack anything from his war bag, doubting that he would need anything during his brief stay except a change of clothes and his straight razor. He peeled down to his summer long johns and blew out the lamp, then went over to the single curtain-covered window.

Sweeping back the curtain with a big hand, Hallam peered out into the night. From this vantage point he could see the sleeping town spread out before him. There was nothing moving, no sign of life. He began to wonder if Holloway was going to yield any answers at all to the questions that plagued him.

But there had been Mrs. Bondurant's response to his mention of Forbes. He wasn't going to let go of that just yet.

He let the curtain drop closed, went to the war bag on the dresser, and pulled out his Colt. He didn't need light to check it and know that it was in good working order and ready if he needed it.

He tucked the gun under the pillow and stretched out on the bed.

Hallam had thought that he would fall asleep as soon as his head hit the pillow. After all, he hadn't slept much on the train, and there was no denying that the bed was one of the most comfortable he had run across.

But instead of sleeping, he found himself listening to the night. He could hear insects singing, the occasional bark of a dog, the sighing of a light breeze in the trees. But that was all.

There were no artificial noises. No car engines, no trolley cars bumping and clanging, no orchestras playing, no brittle laughter and hot words. It wasn't like Hollywood.

Hallam drew a deep breath and let out a long, satisfied sigh.

The quiet lasted maybe another ten seconds.

Then Hallam heard the sputter of a car coming down the street. The sound seemed to stop in front of the house, and a moment later the slam of a car door came drifting to him.

The house was still silent enough that he had no

trouble hearing the sudden patter of footsteps on the floor below. They were followed by the creak of the front door opening, heavy steps coming across the porch and into the house. Voices floated upstairs, unintelligible, one masculine and sullen, the other female, soft, hissing.

"Leave me alone, Ma!"

Hallam heard that plain enough. A young man's voice, harsh and slurred. Another door opened, this one on the back of the house, almost directly under Hallam's window.

Hallam swung his long legs out of bed and padded to the window. He pulled back the curtain enough to look out, saw a shadowy figure moving across the back yard toward the outhouse. The figure wasn't moving any too well, either, swaying back and forth, stumbling, almost losing its balance and falling to the grass. As Hallam watched, the young man disappeared unsteadily into the outhouse.

Hallam closed the curtain and went back to bed. He could imagine what was going on out there in the little building. Too much bathtub gin would do it to you every time, especially when you were young.

Hallam closed his eyes, listened to the night awhile longer, and then went to sleep.

TWENTY-ONE

HALLAM WAS awake before dawn the next morning, despite the late hour at which he had gone to sleep the night before. Getting up early seemed to be a natural thing with him, an instinct ingrained by years of not wanting to burn daylight. One good thing about getting older—a man didn't seem to need as much sleep.

Nobody was stirring in the house as he dressed and slipped out to visit the facilities. The early morning air was cool on his face, with just a hint of dampness about it. Right now was probably as comfortable as the weather got around here in summer, he thought on his way back to the house.

Jimmy Daniels came out the back door, obviously bound on the same errand Hallam had just taken care of. He was rubbing his eyes sleepily, and a huge yawn cracked his jaws. Pausing to stretch tired muscles, he said, "Morning, mister. See you found the place."

"Sure did. You didn't tell me you lived here, too, son."

Jimmy grinned. "I like to drum up business for Mrs.

Bondurant. She and Ted have been pretty good to me the past few years."

"Ted? That'd be Miz Bondurant's husband?"

"Nah. Ted's her son. He and I are pals."

"He fixin' to start to college, too?"

"Oh, no." Jimmy shook his head. "Ted's older than me. He's twenty-three. But we're still chums."

Hallam nodded. "That's good." He stuck out his hand. "By the way, name's Lucas Hallam."

Jimmy returned the handshake. "Glad to know you, sir." He gestured toward the outhouse and went on, "Now, if you'll excuse me, I need to attend to a few things and then get to bed. I sleep during the day since I work at night."

"Sure thing. See you around, son."

Jimmy hurried on while Hallam strolled leisurely into the house. He found Irma Bondurant standing by the stove in the kitchen. The smell of coffee brewing had drawn Hallam there, and he inhaled deeply as he entered the room.

"Good morning, Mr. Hallam," she greeted him with a slight smile. "You're up early this morning. Most of the boarders are still asleep."

"Force o' habit, I reckon." Hallam gestured at the coffeepot. "I'd surely admire a cup of that coffee, ma'am."

"It's ready." She turned and got down a heavy chipped cup from a cabinet. She filled it and said, "Anything in it?"

Hallam shook his head. "Just like that." He took the cup from her, sipped the strong, steaming brew, and closed his eyes in appreciation. "Best I ever tasted," he said.

"And you're a flatterer," Mrs. Bondurant said with a laugh. "I'll get started on breakfast. I imagine you'll have first crack at it this morning."

"I'll try to leave enough for the other folks," Hallam said solemnly.

Without being asked, he pulled out a chair at the kitchen table and sat down, nestling the coffee cup in his big hands. Mrs. Bondurant glanced over at him, then started going about her work. There were biscuits to cook, bacon, eggs, flapjacks to prepare. She seemed to be a bit uncomfortable about having another person in her kitchen while she worked, but Hallam didn't say anything, just sipped his coffee. Gradually she seemed almost to forget that he was there.

When she had the food ready, she said, "Since no one else has come down yet, why don't we eat here in the kitchen, Mr. Hallam? Then I'll take the rest of the food out to the dining room."

"Sounds good to me. I could use a refill on this coffee, too."

She refilled the cup and then set a big platter in front of him. Hallam dug in, savoring the crispness of the bacon, the flakiness of the biscuits, the rich taste of flapjacks and honey. He didn't say much for a while, his mouth being otherwise occupied.

Finally, when the platter was clean and the coffee cup was drained, Hallam sighed and said, "Sure beats trail cookin', ma'am."

Irma Bondurant smiled. She had been eating, too, though her plate hadn't been nearly as full to start with as Hallam's. "I'm glad you enjoyed it," she said. "I like cooking for a man who likes to eat. My husband always enjoyed a good meal."

Hallam hesitated, then said, "If you don't mind my askin', ma'am..."

"I'm a widow, Mr. Hallam," she said, answering the question before he could ask it. "My husband was killed seven years ago in an accident." Her voice was brisk, with no real emotion, as if it was a question she was used to answering, one that no longer really bothered her.

"I'm sorry to hear it," Hallam said truthfully.

"He built this house. Ted and I decided that he would have wanted us to use it to take care of ourselves. That's why I started taking in boarders," She paused. "Ted is my son."

Hallam nodded. "I know. I ran into Jimmy Daniels again, and he told me about Ted. The two of 'em seem like good friends."

Her smile was a bit rueful. "I'm afraid Jimmy tends to idolize Ted more than he should. Ted's a good boy, though; I wouldn't want you thinking he's not."

"I'm sure he's a fine boy, with you for a mama."

Looking embarrassed, Mrs. Bondurant suddenly stood up and started clearing away their dishes. "My goodness," she said, "I've got to get the dining room ready. I'll have some unhappy boarders clamoring for their breakfast before you know it."

Hallam stood up. "Anything I can do to help?"

"Oh, no, that's fine. Thank you anyway, though."

Hallam leaned against the counter. "Reckon I should get on about my business, then. A meal like that makes me move a little slow, though." He rubbed his jaw and nodded. "I recollect now that Elton told me how good your cookin' was."

"Oh. Is that right? I'm surprised he'd remember. It

has been a while." She didn't look at him. Her movements seemed to get a little more hurried as she dished out the food.

"Yep, but ol' Elton remembers a lot about Holloway. Seemed to really like it here."

"If that's so, then why did he leave like he did?"

The question burst from her with more force than she intended. Hallam could tell that by the way she suddenly put her hand to her mouth, as if she wanted to catch the words and pull them back in. He took a deep breath and said, "Wouldn't rightly know about that, ma'am. Maybe you could tell me?"

She looked at him for a long moment without saying anything, and he saw the birth of suspicion in her eyes. "I have to get breakfast ready for the others," she said abruptly. "You'll have to excuse me, Mr. Hallam."

"Sure," Hallam nodded. He'd gone as far as he could... for the moment.

He stayed where he was while she carried some of the plates into the dining room. While she was gone, Hallam heard footsteps behind him and turned to see a young man with dark, curly hair coming into the kitchen from the rear hall of the house. He wore work clothes, but he didn't look too enthusiastic about getting to work. His head drooped and his step was slow. He walked almost all the way past Hallam before realizing that someone was there.

The young man looked up and frowned. "Who the hell are you?" he muttered.

Hallam knew he was looking at the person who had come home late last night—Ted Bondurant. Even if Hallam hadn't seen his shakiness on the way to the outhouse, he would have known that Ted had been drinking the night before. The signs were all there: the bleary, bloodshot eyes, the faltering step, the fuzzy, thick-tongued voice. Ted had a beaut of a hangover.

"Name's Lucas Hallam. New boarder."

"Oh." Ted closed his eyes, swayed for a moment. Then he headed for the coffeepot without saying anything else.

His mother came back into the kitchen and stopped when she saw that Hallam was still there. "Can I get you anything else, Mr. Hallam?" she asked.

"No, thanks. I'll be gettin' on about my business, I reckon." He nodded to her and left the kitchen, heading down the hall toward the stairs, intending to go back up to his room. He paused, though, as he heard voices coming from the kitchen behind him.

"Really, Ted," Mrs. Bondurant said sharply, "do you have to let the boarders see you like that? It's bad enough when you come in late at night after everyone's gone to bed."

"How'd I know the old geezer would be here in the kitchen?" Ted returned truculently. "I figured you'd be down here by yourself, as usual. Who is the old guy, anyway?"

"He says he's come to town to look for a farm to buy."

Hallam grimaced at the uncertainty in Irma Bondurant's tone. She was starting to doubt his story, all right.

"Fine," Ted slurred. "Long as he's not going to be my new daddy."

"Ted! I swear, I don't know what makes you say such things!"

"There's not very many unattached men around here, Ma, you know that. Not since the prof left." Ted laughed unpleasantly. "I'm just trying to look out for you."

"I can take care of myself, thank you," his mother said tightly. "Hadn't you better be getting down to the elevator?"

"Sure, sure. Fix me something to eat, all right?"

"Of course. As if I don't have my hands full already, you decide you have to start taking your lunch instead of eating in the diner like you used to do."

"Ah, Ma," Ted said in a plaintive voice. "Do you have to complain about *everything?*"

"If you think it's been easy, raising you and running this place with no help—"

"You had help," Ted cut in coldly. "Your boyfriend changed all that, didn't he?"

Standing in the hall, Hallam heard the sharp ringing sound of a slap, followed immediately by sobs and Irma Bondurant saying, "I'm sorry, Teddy, I'm sorry. I didn't mean to hurt you. You just made me mad..."

"I need that lunch," Ted said, his voice strained.

"I'll fix it for you right away."

Out in the hall, Hallam listened for a few moments more, but neither of the people in the kitchen were talking now. He finally shook his head and moved on to the stairs, walking quietly enough that neither Mrs. Bondurant or Ted would have been able to hear him.

He was glad he had eavesdropped. That conversation had given him plenty of things to think about. He wasn't sure yet just what all of it meant, but at least he was confident that he *would* find some of the answers here in Holloway.

There was more brewing in this old house than coffee.

HALLAM WAS on the front porch when Ted brushed past him and went to a Model T parked at the curb. Ted paid no attention to him, but Hallam saw the good-sized paper sack in his hand. Looked like he ate a big lunch, Hallam thought. Ted got out the crank and started the Ford, then drove off in the direction of downtown. His mother had said something about him having a job at one of the grain elevators, and Hallam knew that must be where he was heading.

Hallam left the house himself when Ted's car was out of sight. He walked downtown, noting that Holloway was a lot busier place on Saturday. There were Model T's parked up and down Main Street, along with a few horse-drawn wagons tethered here and there. People bustled in and out of the stores, the men wearing suits that were showing their age but were clean and well taken care of, the women wearing dresses made from store-bought cloth rather than feed sacks. Children ran up and down the sidewalks, yelling and playing but not *too* rambunctious, stopping and behaving for a moment whenever some adult looked at them too hard and then rejoining their comrades as soon as the coast was clear. There was nothing quite like Saturday in a small town.

During the afternoon, Hallam knew, the picture show would do a good business, as most of the kids and some of the adults watched spellbound while Bill Hart dourly cleaned up the bad men. Hallam grinned, wondering what these folks would do if they knew that one of Hart's opponents in that movie was walking here among them. At the same time, he hoped that they wouldn't find out.

He spent the morning wandering from place to place, striking up conversations with storekeepers and customers alike. He stuck to his story about looking for a farm to buy, and if it had been the truth, he would have had at least a dozen possibilities to check out. Along the way, he managed to drop Elton Forbes's name, and though he ran into several people who remembered him as a professor at the college, no one had anything to say that tied in with the case. The only remembrances of Forbes seemed to be vague ones.

When it got to be lunch time, he asked a clerk in the hardware store where the best place to eat was. The fellow bent over to pick up a loose nail from the floor and drop it in a pocket of his apron, then said, "Miz Farris over to the cafe does a right nice job. Then there's Curley's Diner. Ol' Curley can whip up a good meal, too."

Hallam remembered that Irma Bondurant had made some comment to Ted about eating in the diner. He nodded and said "Thanks" to the clerk, then went in search of the establishment.

The diner was in a low, flat-roofed building by itself, down close to the livery stable. There were several customers sitting on stools by the counter when Hallam came in. The place was doing good business without being actually crowded. He found an empty stool and ordered steak, potatoes, and beans from a chunky man in a white shirt. "You must be Curley," Hallam said to him.

The man shook his head and jerked a thumb at the opening in the wall between the kitchen and the dining area. "Curley does the cooking," he said in a gravelly voice. "I just run the counter."

Hallam nodded. "Heard a lot about this place. Supposed to be real good food."

"We do our best, mister. You want anything else to go with that?"

"Could use a glass of water. Gettin' warm out there today."

"Does that this time of year," the counter man grunted.

"My friend Ted Bondurant told me to come down here if I wanted a good meal. Reckon from the way he talked he used to eat here a lot."

"No used to about it," the counter man said. "Ted's a regular, buys his lunch here every day he's working."

"That so?" Hallam nodded thoughtfully. "Didn't think he'd been here in a while."

"He was in just a little while ago. Had a big meal, just like always." The man cocked his grizzled head and stared at Hallam. "Say, why all the interest in Ted's eating habits? I thought you said you were a friend of his."

"Haven't talked to him in a while," Hallam admitted. "Been travelin' some."

"Oh." The counter man looked dubious, and he seemed glad to move off down the counter to take an order from another just-arrived customer. He came back a moment later, poured a glass of cold water from the pitcher, and handed it to Hallam without a word.

Hallam sipped the drink, enjoying the coolness. He was turning things over in his mind. An idea had suggested itself to him, and he was trying to decide if it made any sense or not. For the moment, it just raised more questions than it answered, he thought.

Curley's food was all right, Hallam discovered when it was ready, but no better than at any other greasy-spoon diner. When he left the place a half hour later, he went back to the routine he had followed before dinner, but now he managed to work Ted Bondurant into his conversations as well as Elton Forbes. The opinion of the town was pretty well unanimous—Ted was a good boy, a little wild sometimes, but he was helpful to his poor widowed mother. Maybe he drove out to Jess Crider's place for some moonshine whiskey now and then, but that was just a young man letting off steam, now wasn't it?

Hallam had been right about one thing: the Rialto was doing the business. People were lined up on the sidewalk outside, waiting to get in and see the show. The stores emptied out somewhat. Hallam knew he had found out just about all he was going to do with his innocuous pumping of the townspeople.

He was going to have to cut through the curtains hiding the truth from him. Some feelings might get bruised along the way, but he had a client in jail back in California, not to mention someone worried enough to try to kill him. So far, he hadn't come across anything to tie anyone from Holloway to Hollywood, except for Elton Forbes. His instincts told him that there was more to Forbes's stay in this town than what was on the surface, though. Maybe once he knew what it was, he'd have that thread that would lead him all the way back to California and two dead men.

He was on his way back to the Bondurant house,

walking down March Avenue, when he saw Jimmy Daniels coming toward him. Jimmy greeted him with a grin and said, "Howdy, Mr. Hallam. Find you any good places to buy?"

"Well, I talked to a lot of folks. We'll just have to wait and see." Hallam pulled his turnip from its pocket and flipped it open. "Only five o'clock. You're not goin' to work this early?"

"No, sir, I don't go on until ten o'clock." Jimmy's grin got wider. "Thought I'd walk down to the show. There's a new William S. Hart picture on."

"You like Western movies, do you?"

"Sure do. Shoot, there's more excitement in one picture than you get in a year around here."

For a moment, Hallam was tempted to tell the boy who he really was, then decided against it. He still hadn't found what he came to Kansas for, and giving away his real identity would only complicate things, even if he swore Jimmy to secrecy.

Instead, he yielded to another impulse and said, "Reckon you could stand some company at that picture show?"

"You bet," Jimmy said quickly. "Be glad to have you come along, sir."

Hallam nodded. "You can forget about that sir business, too. Call me Lucas."

"All right... Lucas."

As they walked back down March toward Elm, Hallam said, "I met your pal Ted at breakfast this morning."

"He's a great guy, isn't he? He and his ma sure were nice to take me in. I guess you know my folks died a while back."

"Heard about it. I'm sorry, son."

Jimmy shrugged. "I try not to think about it. Anyway, the Bondurants have been like another family to me. Miz Bondurant's like my own ma now, and a fella couldn't want a better brother than Ted. When Emilie was there, it was like having a sister, too."

Hallam stopped dead in his tracks.

For a second, he seemed to have trouble getting air into his lungs. Then the tight band around his chest eased and he was able to say in a fairly normal voice, "Emilie?"

Jimmy didn't appear to have noticed Hallam's initial reaction to the name. He nodded and said, "Yeah, Emilie Masters. I told you that Miz Bondurant and Ted were nice folks. She didn't have any parents, either, but they took her in and gave her a place to live. She helped Miz Bondurant around the boardinghouse and earned her keep, but she wouldn't have had to. They'd have let her stay there anyway."

The two of them were strolling down the street again now. Keeping his voice casual, Hallam said, "When was this?"

"A few years back. Emilie had been living at the boardinghouse for a while already when my folks... well, when I came to live there. I really liked her. But then she moved away." Jimmy shrugged again. "She was older'n me, you understand, about Ted's age. I guess she just decided that she wanted to see what it was like to live somewhere else." He sighed. "I guess I can understand that. Holloway's a nice place, but not much happens. That's why I go to the picture show every week. A fella's got to have some excitement in his life."

Hallam nodded slowly. "Reckon that's so. Say, did

you ever remember that other feller I asked you about? Elton Forbes?"

"Didn't know I was supposed to be trying to remember him." Jimmy frowned at Hallam. "I told you last night I didn't know him, sir."

Hallam grinned, trying to allay any suspicions the boy might be forming. "Thought I told you to forget that sir stuff," he said. "Reckon it don't matter about Forbes anyhow. Met him a while back and just thought I'd look him up if he was still around here."

That was a different lie than the one he had been telling, but it didn't matter now.

The two of them walked on downtown, talking less now, and got in line at the Rialto for the six o'clock show. Hallam began to feel more conspicuous, standing there on the sidewalk in the crowd of townspeople. He was bigger than most of them, after all. No one paid any attention to him, though.

As he stood there peering off down the street to the west, he saw a low gray line of clouds on the horizon; a storm brewing up maybe. They could come up in a hurry out here on the plains.

The movie was better than he remembered it. Or maybe it was just the experience of sitting there in the theater with the people of Holloway and sharing with them their excitement at being able to get out of their own accustomed lives for a while. When things looked bad for Bill Hart and the audience leaned forward in tense anticipation, Hallam was drawn along with them to a certain extent.

But his mind kept going back to what he had learned on the way here. From the time he had stepped off the train the night before, Jimmy Daniels had been his best source of information.

And now Jimmy had given him what he needed to solve this case.

Hallam had been lied to. He knew that now. He knew who had lied, and what they had lied about. He had found the trail, and one part of it was leading to another. There were still questions, but now he knew where to go for the answers.

The trip to Kansas was going to pay off after all.

Hallam sat in the darkened theater and watched himself on the screen getting holes blown in him by Bill Hart's big Colts. He didn't really see the flickering shadows of life up there, though.

He was thinking about a killer.

TWENTY-TWO

NIGHT HAD FALLEN by the time the movie was over. Hallam and Jimmy stepped out of the theater onto the sidewalk with the rest of the audience, and Hallam knew immediately that he had been right about a storm blowing up. There was a hot, sticky wind starting to blow, a whirling wind that whipped up dust devils here and there on the side streets.

Jimmy lifted his head and made a show of sniffing the air. "Liable to be a big blow tonight," he said knowingly.

"Reckon you get a lot of storms through here," Hallam said.

"Not as many in the summer as in the spring. But we get our share, I suppose."

"I remember some of the cyclones I've seen," Hallam said. "They can do a heap o' damage in a hurry. Must be pretty scary when one blows up, especially for a woman livin' alone like Miz Bondurant."

"She's not alone," Jimmy said in surprise. "There's boarders there, and Ted's always around."

They were strolling down the sidewalk now, and Hallam cast a glance over at Jimmy. "Ted sticks pretty close to home, does he?"

"Well... as much as anybody, I'd say. Of course, he has his own life to live, too." Jimmy grinned. "He goes out to ol' Jess's place some to pick up some hooch. Promised he'd take me with him one of these days. He said he'd take me down to Wichita with him next time he goes, too."

"Been to Wichita here lately, has he?"

"Yeah, he told me all about it." Jimmy's voice was filled with vicarious excitement. "Had him a fine old time, he did."

"When was this?"

"About a week ago. Least he got back about a week ago. He was gone a couple of weeks before that."

"How'd his mama feel about that?"

Jimmy whistled. "She didn't like it one bit. Ted doesn't usually go against his mother, but like he said, everybody needs a vacation now and then." He frowned at Hallam. "You're asking a lot of funny questions again."

"Bad habit o' mine," Hallam grunted.

They crossed the street, and the first drops of rain began to fall. The raindrops were fat and heavy and far between, and when they landed they made craters in the dust. Hallam didn't even notice them. He was too busy thinking.

He had nearly all of it now. Some of it was still guesswork, but the answers could be filled in fairly easily now that he knew the right questions to ask. He wished there was time to wait, time to fill in more of the picture and get some proof lined up before he took action.

But every minute that Elton Forbes sat in jail in California was galling to Hallam. Not that Forbes was one of his favorite people—he wasn't and never would be—but he was a client, and more important than that, he was no murderer.

Hallam was sure of that now.

And it was time to bring the real killer to justice.

The two of them reached the intersection of Main and Elm, and Jimmy stopped. "Guess I'd better head on down to the depot," he said. "It's not time for me to be on duty yet, but there's nothing else to do in Holloway, even on a Saturday night."

Hallam had noticed that the town was kind of quiet. There was a little traffic passing by on the highway, but not much. All the stores were closed now, and once the picture show had let out, the audience had dispersed rapidly. Hallam saw a couple of other people strolling on the sidewalk a few blocks away, but they were the only other pedestrians.

"You've got a couple of hours before you have to be at work," Hallam said to Jimmy. "Why don't you come on back to the boardin' house with me."

"Sure. Why not?"

They turned toward the college and the boardinghouse. Hallam didn't say anything for a few moments as they walked along, not sure how much he could trust Jimmy. The boy seemed to be all right, but Hallam had seen a lot of deception in his time. Life made a man suspicious. That was a shame in a way.

They were passing a house on Elm when Jimmy

suddenly stopped and called out, "Howdy, Davey. How you doing?"

A young man was standing next to a jitney in the driveway of the house. He had one side of the hood up, and a kerosene lantern was balanced on the fender so that its light shone into the engine. He looked up and saw Jimmy in the faint glow from a streetlight, and said with a grin, "Hi, kid."

"Come on, Mr. Hallam," Jimmy said. "I'll introduce you."

Hallam followed Jimmy down the sidewalk, thinking that the boy was right about knowing everyone in town. And everyone in town seemed to look on Jimmy as an adopted son. It happened that way sometimes when a child was left an orphan, especially in a small place like Holloway that had a strong sense of community.

"Mr. Hallam, this is Davey Jenkins. Davey, this is Lucas Hallam. He's staying at Miz Bondurant's and looking to settle around here."

Jenkins put the lantern on the ground, slammed the jitney's hood shut, and wiped the grease off his hands with a rag. Then he extended the right one to Hallam and gave him a strong handshake. "Glad to meet you, Mr. Hallam. Holloway's always on the lookout for new citizens."

Hallam remembered that Jimmy had referred to Jenkins as "ol' Davey" the night before, but the man couldn't be more than twenty-seven or twenty-eight. Maybe that was old when you were eighteen. Hallam grinned and said, "Pleased to meet you. Hear you hire out this old bus."

Jenkins patted the jitney's fender. "Sure do. Just got

through tuning her up a little bit. You need to look over any of the country around here, Mr. Hallam, you just come get Betsy."

Hallam was about to make a reply when he heard the sound of a car passing by on the street. He glanced up and caught a glimpse of Ted Bondurant's Model T, with Ted behind the wheel. Hallam said quickly, "How much to hire her right now?"

Jenkins frowned in surprise. "Now? But it's night, you couldn't see much—"

Hallam had a five-dollar bill out of his pocket by then and was pressing it into Jenkins's hand. "I can see all I need to," he said as he swung up through the open doorframe onto the front seat of the bus.

"Gee, Mr. Hallam, what's gotten into you?" Jimmy asked.

Hallam jerked a thumb at the seat on the passenger side. "Come along and I'll explain it. I ain't got time to argue now, though."

There was a sudden rattle of wind and rain in the trees as Jenkins said, "Now look here, I don't know if I like this."

Hallam swept his coat back and jerked a badge out of his pocket. "I'm a lawman," he growled, "and I need this bus right now. I'll pay you more later if you want it, but for now, start the damned thing!"

The badge didn't really mean anything, of course, even back in California, but it had an effect on the two Kansans. Davey Jenkins's eyes widened, as did Jimmy's. Jenkins swallowed and said, "Yes, sir," as he reached inside the jitney, got out the crank, and ran to the front of the vehicle.

Staring at Hallam, Jimmy said slowly, "You want me to come along?"

Hallam nodded. "Figure there's some things we need to talk about."

Jimmy licked his lips and looked nervous. The rain was getting a little heavier now, but not many of the drops penetrated the cover of the trees above them. Finally Jimmy said, "Sure, why not." His face suddenly broke out in a cocky grin. "Nothing else to do in Holloway on a Saturday night."

Jenkins had the crank ready and turned it as Hallam stepped on the starter. The engine ground over for a few seconds, then caught with a throaty roar. The jitney sounded like it was in good running condition, for which Hallam was thankful.

Jimmy ran around the bus and jumped in on the other side. "I'll bring her back to you," Hallam promised Jenkins. Then he backed the car into the street and turned to follow Ted Bondurant.

Hallam could see taillights several blocks ahead, and given the amount of traffic on the roads tonight, he felt sure they belonged to Ted's Model T. He left the jitney's lights off as he pressed down on the accelerator and felt the vehicle lurch forward with more speed.

"You sure know how to spring a surprise, Mr. Hallam," Jimmy said. He was leaning forward, holding on to the edge of the doorframe. "I never would have guessed that you were a policeman."

"Well, actually, I'm a private detective," Hallam said as he searched for and found the switch that started the windshield wiper. As the wiper began to flick back and forth across the glass, it cleared away some of the rain that was splattering there but left a filmy smudge from the dust accumulated on the windshield. The rain wasn't hard enough yet to wash it away.

"A private detective? I never heard of such. They have a lot of 'em in California?"

"More'n enough," Hallam grunted.

There was more than a hint of accusation in Jimmy's voice as he said, "You know, you lied to me."

"No more than you lied to me, son." Hallam's voice was harsher than he had intended it to be, but dammit, it was the truth.

"When did I lie to you?" Jimmy demanded.

"When you told me you didn't know Elton Forbes." Hallam slowed down at Main Street just long enough to glance in both directions on the highway, then speed across. The lights of Ted's car were a little closer. The jitney was gaining, but only because Ted didn't know he was being followed.

"I don't know what you're talking about—" Jimmy started to say, but Hallam cut him off before he could go any further.

"Don't make it worse, boy. Forbes lived at the Bondurant house the same time as you did. You must have known him." Hallam shot a glance over at him, but the shadows in the bus were too thick to tell anything about the boy's expression. "Ted Bondurant told you what to say if anybody asked about Forbes, didn't he?"

"I still don't know what you're talk—"

" Dammit, don't keep lyin' to me, boy!" Hallam exploded. "You and Ted are friends, leastwise *you* think so, and you'd do anything he asked you to. We both know that."

"He is my friend," Jimmy said in a low voice. "But I'm starting to think you aren't."

"I never tried to get you in trouble with the law."

"Neither did Ted! I don't know what you're thinking, Mr. Hallam, but you're wrong about Ted. He never did anything bad!"

In a cold, flat voice, Hallam said, "He killed two people in Hollywood and let Forbes take the blame."

Jimmy shook his head violently. "No! You're wrong, you've got to be wrong!"

He didn't say anything else for long moments, and neither did Hallam.

The lights of Ted's car turned in front of the railroad depot. The jitney was a couple of hundred yards behind but got there in time to see the Model T take another road that bumped over the railroad tracks and then headed out across the fields. Hallam followed, the rough tracks rattling his teeth. But then the dirt road smoothed out some as it ran between the fences that bordered the fields.

"He did tell me not to say anything about Forbes," Jimmy said softly, so softly that Hallam almost didn't hear him.

"Is this the way to that Jess Crider's I heard about?" Hallam asked.

"No, Jess's place is out the other way from town. I don't know where Ted's going."

"I think I do," Hallam said.

The rain was still teasing, coming down hard for a few seconds and then slacking up almost to nothing. Lightning flickered ahead of them, low to the horizon, and thunder rolled across the plains. There was a storm coming that was a lot worse than what they were getting now.

Hallam drove as fast as he dared without lights.

The night was almost pitch black now with the clouds moving in, but the road was straight and flat and not hard to follow. The jitney bounced over the rough places, since Hallam couldn't see to slow down for them. The two red specks of light from Ted's car stayed in sight, though.

"I don't think Ted's a murderer," Jimmy said abruptly.

"Maybe I'm wrong," Hallam replied. "Don't think so, though. Reckon we'll find out before the night's over." He took one hand off the jitney's wheel and rubbed at his jaw. "Shouldn't have brought you with me, I suppose, but I wanted to ask you about Ted and Forbes. How'd they get along when Forbes lived in the house?"

Jimmy didn't answer for a moment, then said, "Ah, hell. There's no point in lying to you. They didn't get along at all. Ted always... liked to have fun, I guess you could say. No more so than any of the rest of us, you understand, but with Forbes right there in the house, he saw what Ted was doing and didn't mind letting him know that he didn't approve. Wasn't any of Forbes's business what Ted did, though. It wasn't like he was his daddy."

"At least not yet," Hallam said pointedly.

"Well, there is that. I thought that Forbes and Miz Bondurant might have been interested in each other, her being a widow and all and him never being married. They both liked to read, and they could go on for hours about books they'd read and the people that wrote them. But then there was some kind of trouble and Forbes left. I never did find out just exactly what happened. I was just a kid, then, you understand."

The corners of Hallam's mouth twitched, but he

didn't grin. "Reckon I do," he said. His expression immediately got more serious. "Was that about the same time that Emilie left?"

"It sure was. I never really thought about it like that. The school year was over, and Forbes left. Emilie left, too, but I didn't think about them being connected. I'm still not sure I understand."

"Maybe we're just about to get the answers," Hallam said, taking his foot off the gas and letting the jitney slow down on its own.

Up ahead, the Model T was turning right. It came to a stop, and then the taillights went off. Hallam let the jitney coast to a stop, and then he cut off the engine. He stepped out onto the running board and peered into the restless night.

There was another light up ahead, but the glow from this one was yellow. Hallam looked across the top of the bus, saw that Jimmy Daniels was standing on the other running board and looking in the same direction. "There a house or something up there?" Hallam asked.

"The old Barrett place," Jimmy said. "It's been deserted for over a year, though. Farm gave out on them."

"It's not deserted now."

Hallam dropped off onto the road. The farmhouse was only a couple of hundred yards away, but he felt reasonably sure that Ted Bondurant hadn't heard the jitney's motor when he got out of the Model T. Not with the sound of the wind on the rise.

"Reckon you best stay here," he told Jimmy.

"No, sir. You've made all these accusations about my friend, and I'm going with you."

Hallam reached under his coat and slid the Colt out

of the shoulder rig. The gun was really too big to be worn that way, but it was less obtrusive there than on his hip.

"Could be shootin'," he said. "I'd feel better if you were back here where it'll be safe."

He heard Jimmy's gulp at the sight of the big pistol. "I don't think—"

"Just stay put, boy," Hallam growled. "I'll see you get the straight of it when it's all over."

Jimmy sighed. "All right."

Hallam started down the road, Colt gripped ready in his fist. Wasn't the first time he'd walked down a road with a gun in his hand, and one thing never changed. Walks like this were always long ones.

A drop of rain hit his cheek, rolled down the creases and gullies of weathered skin like a tear. Hallam didn't even notice. .

The farmhouse bulked up out of the night. There was a fence around the front yard, but over half of it had collapsed and had never been repaired. Weeds had taken over the yard itself, growing tall, thick, and rank. There was definitely a light inside, though.

Hallam estimated that they had traveled about two miles from town. It wouldn't take Ted long every day, either before or after work, to run out here and drop off the lunch his mother had made. There were no other houses anywhere close, no lights to be seen anywhere around, in fact, so chances were that no one would know that someone was staying at the old Barrett place.

Hallam stepped over a section of fence that had fallen down, and catfooted it up to the house. He headed for the window where the light was showing and crouched beneath it. The glass was long gone.

Someone had tacked up a piece of feed sack for a curtain, and the light was shining, diffused, through the burlap. Hallam heard voices coming from inside, but thunder rumbled and drowned out the first part of the conversation.

"—didn't think it would cause any trouble, Ted," a female voice was saying as the thunder died away. "I just walked out to the end of the lane and back."

"I told you you've got to stay inside," Ted Bondurant snapped in reply. "I told you it's dangerous for you to be seen."

"But I don't see how it could be." The girl's voice was plaintive. "I'm getting tired of hiding here, Ted. It doesn't make any sense. Why should I have to hide?"

"Do you want those men to find you again and take you back to California? You want to see Forbes again, is that it?"

The boy sounded like he was on the edge, Hallam thought. Made sense that he was, having to hide what he had done.

"I still don't understand why you hate him so. I don't understand any of this, Ted, not any of it!"

The girl was well on the way to breaking, too. Hallam grimaced in the darkness outside and hefted the Colt.

Looked like it was time to push both of them over the edge, right out into the harsh glare of truth.

Hallam stepped to the porch, lifted his foot, drove his boot against the door. The door slammed open, and Hallam stepped in, Colt up and ready.

"Reckon it's time you understood everything, Emilie," he said.

TWENTY-THREE

THE STARTLED FACE peering at him was the same one he had seen on that wild night at Allan Wallace's house in the hills. Hallam saw the same soft, dark hair, the same deep blue eyes. And Emilie was staring at him with the same sort of shocked expression she had worn that night.

Ted Bondurant spun around and looked just as surprised. There was a tenseness about him that showed he was ready to bolt, but the muzzle of the big Colt was trained on him, and that was enough to keep him rooted to the spot.

"What the hell... ?" he said in a stunned voice.

Hallam glanced around the room. There was a cot tucked into one corner. A rough-hewn table and a straight chair were the only other pieces of furniture. Didn't look like much of a way to live.

"You just stand still, boy," he growled at Ted. Then he said to Emilie, "It's all right now, miss. You won't have to hide here any longer."

"You knew my name," she said. "But I don't... I don't know you."

"Name's Lucas Hallam. I saw you at Allan Wallace's house a few nights back." Hallam paused for a moment before saying, "I was the feller with Elton Forbes."

Emilie's hand went to her mouth. "My God, that's right! I knew you looked familiar. What is this, Mr. Hallam? What's going on?"

"Come to take you back. There's no need for you to hide."

She shook her head. "No. I won't go back to Professor Forbes." She turned to Ted. "You were worried that I wanted to see him again, Ted, but you never let me explain. I don't want to see him." There was fervent, unmistakable sincerity in her voice.

"He was always more important to you than I was," Ted said shakily. He hadn't moved since Hallam burst in, but Hallam could look at his eyes and know it was only a matter of time.

"Did Forbes hurt you, Emilie?" Hallam asked.

Again she shook her head. "I don't know if either of you can understand. It would be too... too embarrassing."

Hallam hadn't expected that answer.

"He knows about me," Emilie went on. "He knows that I'm... I'm a harlot, a fallen woman."

It sounded to Hallam like, a title card from an overly dramatic DeMille picture. DeMille was big on harlots and fallen women. But Emilie was sincere. To a young girl from a small town in Kansas, melodrama could be just as real as anything else, Hallam supposed.

"Damn it, don't talk like that!" Ted exclaimed. "We

never did anything to be ashamed of. If Forbes hadn't been such a fanatic—" He took a deep gulping breath as he tried to control himself. "He had no right to say those awful things to you, to call you those names. He drove you away from me, just because I was getting what he wanted!"

"That's not true! He didn't think of me that way. He said I was like... like a daughter to him." Emilie put her hands to her face and sobbed into them, a small wracking sound that still managed to fill the room.

The sound tugged at Hallam's own emotions, but there were still things he had to find out, things that had to be completely clear before he could take the next step.

"Forbes walked in on the two of you while you were—"

"That's right," Ted snapped. "Coming in there and screaming and acting like the wrath of God. He had no right to do that, no right to hurt us like that." He was trembling now, caught in the grip of emotion. "He drove Emilie away from me. I can't ever forgive him for that!"

"You went a long way toward payin' him back, though, didn't you?"

Ted took a step back and shook his head. "I don't know what you're talking about."

Hallam ignored him except for keeping the gun trained on him. He said to Emilie, "You left Holloway after Forbes caught you and Ted, is that right?"

"I couldn't stay here anymore," she said. "I couldn't face Professor Forbes day after day. He was so disappointed in me." She glanced at Ted. "He's a good man, though, no matter what Ted says. He forgave me. He found out where I was, and he sent money to help me get along."

"And then Claude found out that Forbes was sending money to you," Hallam mused. "He told Wallace, and Wallace figured things were different between the two of you than they really were. He thought Forbes was hidin' an old girlfriend."

"Don't talk about Claude," Emilie said with a shudder. "He's a horrible man. When those other men kidnapped me, they took me to him out in Los Angeles. I didn't want to go there. I certainly didn't want to see Professor Forbes again. I was grateful for the money, but I couldn't face the... the shame."

She was one mixed-up little lady, Hallam thought, and most of her problems seemed to be stemming from the influence of Elton Forbes. That didn't change what Ted had done, though.

"Wallace hired men to find you and bring you to Hollywood," Hallam said. "They must have come through here looking for your trail." He swung his gaze to Ted Bondurant. "They came to the boardin' house askin' questions, didn't they?"

"I didn't tell them anything, Emilie," Ted said quickly. "I promise you I didn't. But I knew they'd find you sooner or later, you could see that in their eyes. Since I couldn't find you..." His voice trailed off.

"You let them do the findin' for you," Hallam finished for him. "You never caught up to Emilie till that night at Wallace's house, though."

"I don't know what was a bigger surprise," Emilie said as she regained a little control, "to see Professor Forbes there or to run into Ted's arms after I got away from Claude. I... I was so very glad to see you, Ted."

"What happened then?" Hallam asked. He thought he knew, but he wanted to hear them say it.

"Ted put me in a car he had hired, and told me to get out of there. He said he'd make sure I wasn't followed."

"He made sure, all right," Hallam said bleakly.

Ted shook his head slowly. "Don't do it, damn it. Don't do this, Hallam."

Hallam looked at the two young people. A lot of this situation hadn't been of their own making. They must have felt trapped, both of them, torn by guilt and shame, love and hate.

But that didn't change the most important thing.

"He made sure that you weren't followed, all right," Hallam said. "While Forbes and I were chasin' you, he went back to the study, picked up a gun that was lyin' there, and filled Wallace and Claude with lead, all in the hope that Forbes would be blamed for the killin'. You got your wish, boy. Forbes is in jail back in California right now, waitin' to stand trial for murder."

Emilie was shaking her head, horror creeping onto her face. Ted just stared stonily at Hallam. His trembling had stopped, and something about him seemed as dead as his own victims.

"Then he met up with you and brought you back here," Hallam went on inexorably. "He hid you here and convinced you that you had to stay out of sight, else you'd be kidnapped again. Reckon it was pretty confusin' to you, but Ted had what he wanted. He had you back, obeyin' his every word, livin' like he said. He must've figured he'd finally beaten Forbes."

"I did beat him," Ted said softly. "He deserved it, the self-righteous bastard. All he ever did was cause trouble for people. He went crazy when he saw Emilie and me making love. He'd always been a moralistic old son of a bitch, but that pushed him over the edge. He became a full-fledged religious fanatic." Ted nodded jerkily. "Oh, I kept track of him, knew he went to California and became some hellfire and damnation preacher. My mother loved him, but he didn't care about that. He just up and left because he couldn't stand the thought of his little Emilie not being pure!"

"And revenge has been eatin' you up ever since, ain't it?" Hallam said. He sighed. "Maybe if you hadn't killed those men, I might've been able to summon up a little sympathy for you, boy. But not now. Now you're goin' back with me to face up to what you done."

"You're... you're a policeman?" Emilie asked.

"Private detective," Hallam grunted.

"I'm not going back with you," Ted said. "I'm going to stay right here. Emilie and I are going to be married."

She was staring at him now. Belief had obviously soaked in on her, and she was seeing him now for what he was—obsessed, out of control, a killer. No matter that once he had been her lover. Whatever had been between them, Hallam had killed it tonight.

A sudden gust of wind pushed against the feed sack curtain and one of the tacks pulled loose. The fabric fluttered in, and rain spattered on the floor underneath the window.

"No," Emilie said. "No, Ted. It can't be that way."

His lips drew back from his teeth in a grimace. "But it has to be," he almost groaned. "After all I did for us..."

She backed away, shaking her head. "No. Oh, no..."

From the open doorway, Jimmy Daniels said, "Damn you, Mr. Hallam."

Hallam's head jerked in that direction. The boy must have snuck up on the house and heard everything, or at least enough to realize that his pal, his hero Ted, was nothing but a cold-blooded murderer. Jimmy's face was pale, his eyes wide and staring, hair plastered down by the steadily increasing rain.

"Told you to wait at the car," Hallam said.

"How could you do that to my friend?" Jimmy wailed.

Hallam opened his mouth to say... something, he didn't know what. There was no explanation that Jimmy would understand.

He saw the flicker of movement from the corner of his eye.

Ted's hand was behind his back as he grabbed at something tucked under his shirt. Hallam saw the little gun gripped tightly in the boy's fingers as the hand came back into sight. Ted lifted it in what seemed like slow motion to Hallam.

But it wasn't slow motion. It was shavings of a second as the pistol came into line and Ted's finger began to jerk the trigger.

The barrel was pointed at Emilie, not Hallam.

After all he had done for her—the way he saw it— she wasn't going to turn him down now.

Her scream joined the howl of the wind outside in a wild melody.

Hallam fired the Colt without aiming, without thinking. The bullet slammed into the cylinder of Ted's pistol, smashing it, sending it spinning out of suddenly numb fingers.

Ted cried out, grabbed his hand, and fell to his knees.

Hallam heard what sounded just like a train rumbling by outside. Again acting instinctively, he reached out with one long arm and wrapped the fingers of his left hand in Jimmy's collar. He threw the boy forward and down, onto the rough planks of the floor, then spun to Emilie. He dropped the gun as he enfolded her in his arms and dove down, ramming into Ted Bondurant as he fell. All four of them sprawled out, Hallam shielding Emilie and Jimmy as best he could with his body.

The roof of the old Barrett place came off with a great ripping sound. Hallam felt the pull of the wind. Debris pelted his back. The roar grew louder and louder until it seemed to fill the whole world. The walls didn't last long, and then they were shredding and spinning off into the night just as the roof had.

Hallam kept his head down as the wreckage piled up around them. The chaos couldn't have lasted more than a few seconds, but it seemed to go on forever.

Finally, though, the tornado passed on over the farmhouse—or what was left of it—and went on to tear up a half mile of the field before lifting back up into the clouds.

Hallam lifted himself from the rubble and shook himself like a great bear. He was battered, bruised, and cut from the flying debris, but he'd been hurt worse lots of times and walked away from it. Emilie and Jimmy were both crying in fear, probably unaware that the storm had passed, but as Hallam knelt beside them, he saw that they were all right otherwise. His body had taken the beating for them and kept them from being pulled up into the funnel.

Ted Bondurant hadn't gotten off so easy. There was

a long bloody gash on his head where something had hit him, and Hallam felt his own heart pounding as he searched for a pulse in Ted's throat. He needed Ted to be alive; the boy had a date with the police.

Hallam broke into a grin as his blunt fingers found an erratic but strong pulse. Ted would be all right. He would live to pay for his own crimes and clear Elton Forbes.

Solving two murders and living through a tornado all in one night, Hallam thought. These wild nights took their toll. Damned if he wasn't getting too old for this!

Well, maybe not just yet...

TWENTY-FOUR

THE MORNING DAWNED bright and clear and considerably cooler than the previous day. The storm the night before had washed away some of the heat and humidity. It had washed away some other things, too, Hallam thought as he stood on the platform of the Holloway depot and waited for the westbound train that would take him home.

Standing beside him in handcuffs was Ted Bondurant, a white bandage on his head wound. On the other side of Ted was Holloway's constable and a deputy from the county sheriff's office. Both men were clearly excited about being assigned to help guard a prisoner who was being taken to California to answer to a murder charge.

The night hadn't been over when the tornado passed. Hallam had still had to get the three young people back into town and get Ted's injuries attended to, as well as his own. He was carrying a few bandages himself this morning.

Then he had rousted out the constable, told him the

whole story, and sent the first in a long series of telegraph messages to Ben Dunnemore. Jimmy Daniels had insisted on operating the telegraph key himself, despite being shaken up, and he had been kept busy by the constant flow of messages as Hallam attempted to sort everything out. Dunnemore hadn't been too happy to find out that Hallam was in Kansas, but his attitude eased somewhat when Hallam wired that he was bringing in the real killer of Allan Wallace and Claude Berlund. When the county sheriff himself arrived, he had taken statements from everyone involved. Faced with the stories of Hallam, Emilie, and Jimmy, Ted Bondurant hadn't attempted to deny his guilt. He had made a full confession.

All in all, Hallam thought now, it looked like a pretty decent morning.

Emilie came out of the depot wearing a new dress and a hat that obscured most of her face. Hallam could understand her not wanting to draw any more attention than she had to. She was fighting a losing battle, though. The whole town had already heard what had happened; the story had been passed around with all the details intact. When the proceedings in California were over, Emilie wouldn't be coming back here, Hallam thought. Once again, she would go somewhere else, somewhere she was a stranger, and she would attempt to start her life over again.

He hoped she had better luck this time.

Ted shifted his feet and sighed. "Won't that train ever get here?" he asked. He glanced at the crowd around the front of the depot. "I want to get out of here."

"It'll be here," Hallam promised him.

Jimmy Daniels came out of the depot and looked at

the little group standing on the platform. Hallam met his eyes for a second, and then Jimmy looked away. The boy didn't know what to say. Hallam didn't either.

Nothing ever worked out where everybody was happy. Hallam had learned that lesson a long time ago. But he still didn't like it.

He heard the faint wail of a whistle and looked down the track. A small black dot was moving across the fields toward them, a dot that grew bigger and finally resolved itself into the engine of a train. The whistle came floating to them again, louder this time.

Hallam was going to be glad to get home.

The train pulled in a few minutes later. Hallam, Emilie, and Ted boarded quickly. Jimmy Daniels would be staying behind; he could be brought out to California if need be for the trial, but Hallam didn't think it would come to that.

They were on their way in a matter of minutes, Hallam and Ted sitting together, Hallam on the aisle and Ted by the window. Emilie took a seat away from them, and Hallam didn't blame her.

He hoped they made as good time on the return trip as he had coming out here. He was ready to turn Ted over to the authorities in Los Angeles and be done with this case.

And yet it wasn't done, he knew. There was one question that hadn't been answered, because the answer wasn't to be found in Kansas. From the first moment he had known that Ted was the killer, he had also known that this particular question would go unanswered, at least until he got back to Hollywood. So he had put it out of his mind and concentrated on wrapping up affairs in Holloway. Now that was done, and he could think about that one nagging problem.

He thought about it all the way across the country.

———

ON THE SECOND morning after Hallam left Kansas, Elton Forbes left the Los Angeles County Jail a free man.

There were reporters and photographers everywhere as Forbes walked out onto the sidewalk flanked by Willard Riley and Mark Etchison, the attorney. Forbes's face was wreathed in a broad smile, his usual dour look discarded for this occasion. Quite a few of the flock from the Holiness Temple were there, and the first one to reach Forbes was Alice Grey.

Hallam saw the brilliant smile of her face from his vantage point on the edge of the crowd, half a block away. He saw the way she threw herself into Forbes's arms and hugged him tightly. Embarrassed, Forbes thrust her away and lost his smile for a moment. Then the reporters surrounded him, and Hallam couldn't see him anymore.

He wished that Alice Grey would show a little more sense. She was a nice girl, and he had liked her. She was too damn good for Forbes, that was for sure.

But, Hallam reminded himself, that was none of his business.

"I'm very glad to have had my name cleared," Forbes said in reply to a shouted question from one of the newspapermen. "I maintained my innocence all along, and I never lost faith that I would be exonerated. Now my prayers have been answered, and I thank the Good Lord for my deliverance from the Philistines."

"What's next, Reverend?"

"I'm happy to announce that we will be conducting a special service of praise and thanksgiving tonight at the temple. Everyone is invited to come worship with us!"

A short, rotund figure detached itself from the crowd and came toward Hallam. "Quite the spectacle, eh?" J. Emerson Drake asked as he walked up to the big detective.

"Reckon it's a big deal, all right. Funny thing, though. Riley's smilin', but he don't look too happy to me."

Drake chuckled. "I imagine he was rather disappointed when he found out he'd be going back to playing second fiddle. Maybe *he* can frame Forbes for a killing next time and do a better job of it." Drake became more serious as he studied Hallam's craggy face. "You know, when you were giving me the story last night, I got the feeling you weren't too happy with the way it turned out, either."

"I don't hold with murder, and Ted Bondurant shot those two fellers in cold blood. He's got to pay for that." Hallam looked at the crowd swarming around Forbes and grimaced. "But right there's the man who carries the blame for startin' the whole thing. If he hadn't driven Emilie away from Ted..." Hallam shrugged.

"I just wish that part of the story was coming out," Drake said. "It might put a dent in his following."

Hallam glanced sharply at the reporter. "What do you mean by that? Ain't the whole story bein' told?"

Drake shook his head and said, "My editor killed

most of it. So did the other papers. Forbes has clout in this town, my cowboy friend, and in this case, he's using it. He's calling in markers all over town, so to speak. The real story may never be officially told."

"But what about at the trial?"

"The way I hear it, the D.A. has already struck a deal with Bondurant. The charges are going to be reduced to second-degree murder, and Bondurant won't get the death penalty. He'll spend a lot of years in prison, but at least he'll be alive and might even get out on parole someday. And all he has to do is plead guilty, keep his mouth shut, and take his sentence."

Hallam felt a wave of contempt and disgust welling up deep within him. "Dammit, that's not right," he rumbled. He started toward the crowd on the sidewalk.

Drake plucked at his arm. "Wait a minute, Hallam. You can't do anything."

"The hell I can't!" Hallam threw back over his shoulder. He shrugged away from Drake like the man's grip was nothing.

Hallam bulled his way through the gang of reporters, shoving them aside until he was facing Forbes. Forbes looked up, breaking off his smooth oratory, to see Hallam glaring at him. The reporters fell silent as the two men faced each other.

"You ain't my client anymore, Forbes," Hallam said, "so I can speak my mind now. You may not be a killer, but as far as I'm concerned you're a hypocritical bastard who does more harm than good. There's two youngsters with ruined lives because of you."

Tight-lipped, Forbes said, "I don't know what you're talking about, Hallam, but you'd best watch your tongue. I appreciate what you did to help me, but I'm warning you: keep talking like that and you're leaving yourself wide open for a lawsuit, not to mention the loss of your license."

"I know you've got powerful friends. Don't give a damn. You didn't pull the trigger, but you're responsible for those killin's, sure as sin."

Forbes smiled thinly. "An apt choice of words. Sin is at the root of it, Hallam, the sins of the past that have finally caught up to the sinners. Vengeance is mine, saith the Lord. God has exercised His judgment on the sinners and meted out His punishment." His voice was rising now, just as if he were in the temple.

Hallam looked around at the reporters, who were watching in silence. "You boys want the truth about this, you talk to me."

They stared at him, said nothing.

Hallam knew then that Drake had been right. The real story would be buried, no matter what he did. Forbes had the influence to kill it.

"You see, Hallam," Forbes said softly, "you can't win." He smiled. "The Lord is on my side."

Anger surged through Hallam, and without thinking he lashed out and grabbed Forbes by the lapels. He jerked the evangelist toward him, right off his feet, and shook him like a terrier shakes a rat. "Next time I see you," Hallam said between clenched teeth, "reckon we'll both be tryin' to explain to ol' Satan that there's been some mistake made." He flung Forbes away from him, watching him bounce off Willard Riley and go to one knee. Hallam grinned savagely. "Be seein' you."

He stalked away, totally ignoring the threats that Forbes was screaming after him.

THE MINISTER at the mission looked down unbelievingly at the wad of money in his hand, then raised his eyes to meet Hallam's. "I... I don't know what to say, Mr. Hallam. Are you sure about this?"

Hallam nodded his shaggy head. "I took my expenses out of Forbes's fee," he said. "That's what's left. I don't want it. Reckon you could put it to better use than I could."

The minister glanced over his shoulder at the crowded dining room behind him. It was lunch-time, and the mission was full of men, Jeremiah among them, who had no place else to go, nothing to eat except what the mission provided.

"I can assure you," the minister said, "we *will* put it to good use. It's a wonderful gesture."

Hallam thought about the way he had left Elton Forbes frothing at the mouth. There was no rule that said you had to like your clients or that the truth had to be the best way for things to work out.

"Seemed fittin'," Hallam said.

HALLAM WAS SITTING in the Waterhole a few hours later when Neal Hart appeared beside the table, turned one of the chairs around, and straddled it. Neal grinned and said, "Howdy, Lucas. Hear you solved your case."

Hallam was staring down into the mug of beer on the table in front of him. "Yep," he grunted. "Turned out not to have one damn thing to do with Nola McGuire or Marty Cowling or anybody here in Hollywood, for that matter."

"Well, I guess a killer can come from anywhere." Neal signaled to the bartender for a drink, then said, "You do get into some of the damnedest ruckuses, ol' hoss. Heard about you tearin' into that preacher you were workin' for." His voice got serious. "That man could cause you some trouble, Lucas."

Hallam still didn't look up. "Don't rightly give a damn."

"Soon's I heard about it, I said, yep, that's Lucas. Just like when Frank Sheldon told me about you gettin' shot at outside that temple, I said to myself, nobody but Lucas Hallam could get himself into these scrapes."

"Reckon you're right." Hallam looked up from his beer now, and, surprisingly, there was a broad grin on his face. Leaving the mug more than half full, he pushed to his feet. "'Scuse me, Neal. Got some things to do."

Neal Hart frowned up at him. "Damn it, Lucas, I know that look. What kind of trouble are you fixin' to get into now?"

"No trouble," Hallam said. "I'm just goin' to visit a lady."

Neal Hart watched Hallam stride over to the bar, and the actor shook his head. He knew that look, all right. Damned if sometimes Hallam wasn't still a wild man.

There was a telephone on the wall at the end of the bar. Hallam turned the crank to get the operator and gave her a number. He listened to it ring on the other end for a few moments, then a woman's voice came on the line. "This's Lucas Hallam," he said. "Reckon I could talk to Frank Sheldon?"

Not many of the riding extras could call up a studio executive and get right through to him, but Sheldon came on the line a moment later and said, "Well, hello, Lucas. I heard you were back in town. With quite a splash, I might add."

"You know how it is, Frank. I'm a peaceable man, but trouble seems to sort of foller me around. Just thought I'd let you know that Nola McGuire didn't have anything to do with that case I was workin' on. I know you was fond of the gal. You were right about her." He didn't say anything about what he had found going on in Bentley's office out in Glendale. No need to bring that up now.

"I appreciate you letting me know, Lucas. What's on the agenda for you now? Going back to picture work?"

"Not just yet. Feel like I need to get off by myself for a while." Hallam paused. "Thought I might go back out to the ghost town. You remember Chuckwalla? A good place for an old-timer like me."

"I keep telling you you're not old, Lucas," Sheldon laughed. "Anyway, it sounds like a good idea. When are you leaving?"

Hallam thought about Forbes and his special service that evening. "The sooner the better," he said. "Thought I'd drive out this afternoon."

"Well, take care of yourself, as if I had to tell *you* that, and have a good trip."

Hallam said his good-byes and hung up, then waved to Neal Hart and left the Waterhole. As always, the bright sun outside hurt his eyes as he stepped out from the dim interior.

He was looking forward to seeing Liz Fletcher again. What he had told Frank Sheldon was the truth—Chuckwalla was a good place for an old cowboy like him. Maybe it was time he retired.

He had something to do first, though, and Chuckwalla was where it would happen.

It would be finished where it had all begun.

TWENTY-FIVE

HALLAM BROUGHT the flivver to a stop in front of the Silver Horseshoe Saloon and stepped out onto Chuckwalla's dusty main street. It was early afternoon, and the heat was really starting to build. A day a lot like that other one, Hallam thought. That seemed like a long time ago....

He had expected Liz Fletcher to meet him on the porch of the run-down old saloon. Surely she had heard the spluttering and popping of the flivver as he drove up. But she didn't appear in the batwings as Hallam had expected.

In fact, there was a real deserted feeling to the whole town.

Was it possible that Liz had left Chuckwalla? Hallam didn't think that was likely, but if it was true, that might be better for what he had in mind. At least that way he wouldn't have to worry about her when the shooting started.

He had stopped by his apartment and changed clothes, and now he wore the buckskins and wide-brimmed felt hat that he usually wore for picture work. The big Colt was belted and holstered on his hip, and the Bowie rode in its sheath on his other hip.

The flivver was the only thing to show that the man and the town were part of the twentieth century.

Hallam stepped up onto the porch and pushed through the batwings into the shadowy interior of the saloon. Dust motes danced in the shaft of sunlight that came from the window. The place was quiet, absolutely quiet. There was something eerie about it; the player piano should have been tinkling, there should have been the clink of bottle against glass, the shuffling of cards from the poker tables, the laughter of cowhands and of pretty women in bright-colored dresses.

The Silver Horseshoe would never know those sounds again, though.

Hallam called out, "Liz! Liz Fletcher! This here's Lucas Hallam. You anywhere hereabouts?"

There was no answer, nothing but dead silence.

Hallam was starting to get a bad feeling. He didn't think that anybody could have beaten him out here from town, but he supposed it was possible.

He was starting to turn back toward the door to the street when he heard a floorboard creak behind him.

Hallam turned slowly, not wanting to startle whoever was behind him. The door to the back room was open now, and two people stood there. Liz Fletcher was one, her face as pretty as ever but strained now by tension. She stood stock-still, the pistol barrel pressed against her neck rooting her to the spot.

Behind her, one arm looped around her waist and the gun in his other hand, was Frank Sheldon.

"Hello, Lucas," Sheldon said pleasantly enough. "I'm afraid I got here first."

Hallam heaved a long sigh of relief at the sight of Liz. She was all right, at least for the moment. He said, "Reckon I shouldn't have stopped to change clothes."

"I would have beaten you out here anyway," Sheldon assured him. "My Bugatti can outdistance that flivver of yours any day."

"Reckon you're right. Didn't figure you'd cut and run right away, though. Didn't think you could get away from the studio that fast."

Sheldon nodded. "For this, Lucas, I'd drop anything. You knew I'd come. You knew I couldn't resist the chance."

"Figured you were as tired o' beatin' around the bush as I am."

Liz swallowed nervously and said, "Lucas? Wh-who is this man? What's going on here?"

Grim-faced, Hallam replied, "This here's Frank Sheldon, the movie producer, Liz. He's the feller sent me out here to Chuckwalla in the first place. He's also the feller who's been tryin' to kill me for a couple of weeks."

"I waited a long time, Lucas," Sheldon said. "I tried to get to know you first. I thought maybe if I did that I wouldn't be able to go through with it. But the pressure just kept building over the years. I couldn't forget, couldn't forgive. My father wouldn't let me."

Hallam shook his head. "Don't reckon I know what you're talkin' about, Frank. Knew you had to be behind it, but I'm damned if I know why."

"I told you about my father, Lucas. I told you that

morning at Union Station. He was a good man, he did his best for me. Until you killed him."

Sheldon's sleek, handsome features were still perfectly composed. He looked calm enough, and his voice was controlled. But Hallam could see the fires of madness burning in his eyes now, fires that had been there all along, just carefully banked so that no one noticed the glowing embers of hatred and rage.

"I'm sorry, Frank," Hallam said slowly. "Don't recollect what you're talkin' about."

"It was a little town in Arizona, with a little bank. My father wasn't a real criminal. He just needed a little extra money to help us get along. He didn't hurt anybody. He could have killed the people in the bank, you know, but he didn't. Nobody would have gotten hurt if you hadn't come along."

Hallam remembered now, remembered walking down the street of a town much like Chuckwalla must have been, a town that had paid him eighty dollars a month to keep the peace. He remembered seeing a man back out of the bank, a pistol in his hand. Hallam had called out to him and warned him to drop it. His own gun was still in its holster. But the man had spun around and lifted the gun, pointing it at Hallam. Still Hallam had waited, telling him again to give it up, but the man had fired, the bullet whipping close by Hallam's ear.

There had been no choice then. Hallam had drawn and fired.

Until now, the man's name—indeed the whole incident—had been buried in Hallam's memory. Emory Sheldon, that was the name. No one had claimed the body, so the county had buried him. Hallam drifted on not long after that, so he would have had no knowledge of a boy coming into town and looking for his father....

"I'm sorry, Frank," Hallam said now. "But your daddy threw down on me, didn't give me no choice. It was my job to keep the peace."

"I don't want an apology, Lucas. It's much too late for that. The only way to make things right is for you to die."

"That why you sent me out here in the first place and set up that ambush?"

Sheldon nodded. "I thought I didn't care how you died, as long as you were dead. But then when you came into my office later that day, you gave me quite a shock. I realized I was glad that you were alive. I wanted to *see* you die." He chuckled. "You ran right past me that night in the alley beside the temple. I was watching from a doorway of one of the other buildings. You've got the Devil's own luck, though. My man would have had you if something hadn't tipped you off."

"Ate at you, didn't it? So you came right out in the open down at Union Station. Thought you'd stand right beside me while that feller shot me."

"I would have enjoyed that," Sheldon said wistfully.

"Always thought we was friends, Frank." Hallam's voice was sad.

"We are friends, Lucas. But there's a debt to be paid, no matter how much I've grown to like you."

He was crazy, all right, Hallam thought. And he was good at it, as good an actor as any who worked at his studio.

Hallam had already guessed most of what Sheldon had told him, but as long as he kept the man talking, Liz was safe. All he needed was some kind of opening, something that would distract Sheldon and get that gun away from Liz's throat.

"I knew as soon as you called me and told me you were coming out here that you had figured it out," Sheldon went on. "But I'm not sure how."

"Neal Hart told me," Hallam said, glad that Sheldon had given him a chance to stall some more. "You see, Frank, I never told the cops about that shootin' at the temple. When you said something about it the next day, and then Neal did, too, I just figured that word had gotten around some way. But then Neal said you told him. You could've heard about it some other way, too, but that got me to thinkin'. You knew I was comin' out here that day I got ambushed; you *sent* me out here. And you were there at Union Station. The way I saw it, it was just possible you had something to do with what was goin' on." Hallam sighed. "So I called you and told you I was comin' out here again. Figured we'd just see what happened."

"Well, now you know." Sheldon shook his head. "It seemed so perfect, like it was meant to be. You were involved in that other case, so even if you survived the attempt at the temple, you'd just think it was tied in with Forbes."

"And that's just what I thought," Hallam told him. "Once I knew that that boy from Kansas was the real killer, though, I knew them attempts on my life didn't have no connection. Ted and Emilie were already on their way back to Kansas when the shootin' started. Took me a while to connect up that first bushwhackin' out here. Liz and me thought it was somebody after her supply of whiskey."

"What happened to those two men, Lucas? They were supposed to be really good at their job."

"No matter how good you are, Frank, there's always somebody better."

Sheldon grinned savagely. "We'll see." He nodded toward the batwings. "Take a look out in the street."

Hallam hesitated. He didn't want to turn his back on Sheldon, though instinct told him that the man wouldn't shoot him in the back. This stalemate had to be broken, though; he couldn't stand there facing down Sheldon all day, especially not when the producer had Liz as a hostage. Moving carefully, Hallam went to the door, never taking his attention away from Sheldon until he reached the opening and could glance at the street.

Three men waited for him there.

They wore city clothes and carried funny-looking weapons like short-barreled carbines, only there were large drums of ammunition attached to them. Tommy guns, Hallam had heard them called in the past. Seemed like the owlhoots back in Chicago and places like that used them in their gang wars.

"Walk out into the street and face them down, Hallam. Face them down just like you did with my father."

For the first time, Hallam could hear the control slipping away from Sheldon. He glanced back, saw that the pistol was lodged just as firmly against Liz's neck. The strain was more evident on Liz's face, and Hallam had a feeling that if Sheldon was to let her go, she'd faint dead away. She was a strong-willed old girl, Hallam knew that for a fact, but this was a crazy man they were dealing with.

The men in the street outside weren't crazy, though. Just professionals. Good at their job. Deadly.

But then so was Hallam.

"All right," he nodded. "If that's what you want, Frank."

"No!" Liz cried. "You can't, Lucas! I saw those men, they're killers!"

Sheldon tightened his grip on her and dug the gun barrel harder into the soft flesh of her throat. A rumble of anger came from deep within Hallam as Sheldon snapped, "Shut up! Just shut up and stay out of it, you bitch!" Sheldon grinned widely at Hallam. "You've got to answer to the past, Lucas. Go out into the street."

"We've all got to answer to the past," Hallam said softly, thinking not only of Sheldon but of Elton Forbes and Ted Bondurant and the girl called Emilie. You might think you had put things behind you, but then they snuck up and got hold of you again, and things changed. Sometimes for the better, most of the time for the worse. But there was no escaping who you were or where you had been.

Hallam took a deep breath and stepped through the batwings onto the rough planks of the sidewalk, out into the heat and dust of the street. He turned to face the three men who were waiting for him.

Out of the corner of his eye, Hallam saw Sheldon forcing Liz out of the saloon and onto the sidewalk. He wanted to see the whole thing. He had waited long enough for it, and paid these hired killers enough.

The hour was early enough that the sun was no problem. The fight would be a fair one, as fair as three to one odds could be. One Colt against three Tommy Guns...

Hallam knew he might die here. Except for the fact that Liz would have to die as well, the thought didn't really disturb him. For years he had figured that when his time came he would have the big pistol in his hand and would be taking as many of his killers with him as possible. Lately, though, he had started to think that it might not be that way. It was a disturbing thought.

Something about him didn't want to die in bed.

"Start it!" Sheldon screamed, his control totally deserting him now. "Kill him!"

The Tommy Guns, held down at their owners' sides, snapped up in unison. The wait was over.

Lucas Hallam slapped leather.

He saw the first spurt of fire from one of the Tommy Guns as the barrel of the Colt cleared the holster. The tip of the barrel tilted up, and he had fired twice from the hip almost before he was aware of squeezing the trigger. Both shots slammed into the chest of the man on the right end of the line, driving him back in a staggering fall. The gun poured lead into the street in a chattering stream that lasted only seconds until the dead fist unclenched from the trigger.

By that time, Hallam was moving, throwing himself to the left, triggering off two more shots as he fell. Dust flew up around him, and he felt something yank at his right leg, not much but enough to throw him off-balance and make him land heavily in the street. But as he thudded to the ground, he saw one of the remaining killers drop his weapon and go into a crazy spin, his hands covering his face but not stopping the sudden flood of red there.

Hallam was breathless from the hard fall, and a numbness was spreading in his leg, so maybe the wound wasn't as minor as he had thought. But he stayed calm as he lifted the Colt. There was only one shot left in it, since he had never been in the habit of carrying the hammer on a live cartridge.

The last of the killers had stopped firing in surprise as his two companions fell. He glanced at the bodies. The second man had collapsed by now, and both of the men were still.

There was no way one old coot with a relic for a gun could take care of three experienced men armed with machine guns. There was just no way. The last man's lip curled in a snarl, and he bore down on the trigger, sending a burst at the big man lying in the street.

Hallam shot the man in the head with his last bullet.

None of them would be getting back up, Hallam knew. The three paid killers were down for good.

That left Sheldon to deal with.

Hallam climbed to his feet, his wounded leg sagging under him. He turned toward the saloon, forcing the leg to work even though he couldn't feel it. The pain would come later.

Sheldon took a step back as Hallam faced him. He still had his arm clamped around Liz, the gun at her throat. His eyes were wide and staring.

"You couldn't have," he said hollowly. "You couldn't have killed them. You're supposed to be dead."

"Not hardly," Hallam rasped. His hat had come off when he dove to the street, so the sun was beating down heavily on his shaggy gray head. He wasn't sweating, though; in fact, he felt a sort of chill go through him. Loss of blood, he knew. "Let her go, Frank."

Sheldon shook his head. "It's all going wrong. It can't be like this."

"You ain't got a chance, Frank. Let her go. Let it end now."

Sheldon pressed the barrel into Liz's throat until she gave a strangled, involuntary little cry. "No! You drop your gun, Lucas!"

It was Hallam's turn to shake his head. "Can't. This's between you and me, Frank. She's got no part in it."

Sheldon stayed where he was, breathing heavily and clutching Liz.

Ever so slowly, Hallam raised the Colt. Arm extended full length, he squinted down the barrel.. . right into Frank Sheldon's eyes.

"I'll kill you where you stand, Frank," Hallam promised.

Holding an empty gun.

The longest ten seconds of Hallam's life passed.

And then the pistol slipped from Frank Sheldon's hand and clattered harmlessly to the sidewalk. Liz Fletcher bolted out of his grasp as he slid to his knees. His shoulders heaved as he began to sob.

Hallam started breathing again. He holstered the Colt, went to Liz's side.

Sheldon buried his face in his hands and continued to cry.

Hallam drew Liz to him, crushing her against his battered old body with an intensity that surprised him. "You all right?" he murmured into her ear, breathing in the fresh scent of her hair.

"I'm fine," she said, "now. But you're hurt. Your leg—"

"It'll keep," he said. "Reckon we can use one of your petticoats to tie it up?"

Her quick grin was answer enough.

Hallam left an arm around her shoulders as he turned to look at Frank Sheldon. The man had gone over the edge, Hallam knew. The powerful movie producer was gone, and in his place was a vengeance-consumed husk of a man.

"I think this time we'll have to bring in the law," Hallam said softly.

"I think you're right." Liz glanced sharply up at him. "But those first two men—they'll find out we buried them across the creek..."

"That ain't important," Hallam told her. "Reckon it'll all work out one way or another. I'll take Frank back to the county seat; the sheriff can send out some men to finish the cleanin' up."

Sheldon slipped down onto his face, feebly pounding the boards in sheer frustration.

"That's an ugly sight," Liz said.

"Revenge makes a man that way."

"Lucas, even after all the two of you said, I'm still not sure what it was all about."

"The past. Reckon it's all about the past." His arm tightened around her. "I'll be back when it's taken care of. Then, you reckon a man could get a drink around here?"

Liz grinned up at him. "Sure thing, cowboy. Drinks are on the house."

A LOOK AT: DEAD STICK
A LUCAS HALLAM MYSTERY BOOK TWO

A HIGH-FLYING MYSTERY SET IN OLD HOLLYWOOD—A PRIVATE INVESTIGATOR NOVEL WITH INTRIGUE.

Given Lucas Hallam's background, it's not surprising that he's easily able to find work as an extra on the sets of various Hollywood westerns. This retired Texas Ranger gets a lot of work as stuntman and other work—work that isn't as much fun—as a private detective. It is in this role that Lucas finds himself hired to work on the set of *Death to The Kaiser!*

This is the first time Hallam has had the opportunity to be around an aviation picture. He's worked on a couple of war films, but—like most of his breed—Hallam regards a job he can do from horseback as a job worth doing.

His first day on set, one of the biplanes battling in the sky has engine failure and starts falling, and Hallam is tasked with stopping the sabotage on set. But since Count Wolfram von Ottenhausen—one of Germany's leading aces during WWI—was hired for the movie, the KKK has been ruffling feathers …

"Set in the 1920s, this intriguing mystery marks the return of likable Lucas Hallam … True-to-life characters with a dash of 1920s seasoning contribute to a satisfying read." —Publishers Weekly

AVAILABLE MARCH 2022

ABOUT THE AUTHOR

L.J. WASHBURN has been writing award-winning, critically acclaimed mystery, western, and historical novels for more than forty years. L.J. received the Private Eye Writers of America paperback original award and the American Mystery award for book one of the Lucas Hallam Mystery series, WILD NIGHT, and was nominated for a Spur by the Western Writers of America for a novel written with James Reasoner. Washburn also won the Western Fictioneers Peacemaker Award for the story "Charlie's Pie" and was nominated for two more stories.

Made in the USA
Las Vegas, NV
19 July 2023

74986413R00166